Thomas W. Hodgkinson is a book reviewer and travel writer, the author of the screenplays *Memoirs of a Stalker* (with Daisy Aitkens) and *The Magnificent Kate Morgan*, and the co-author with Hubert van den Bergh of *How To Sound Cultured: Master the 250 Names that Intellectuals Love to Drop into Conversation.* He is based in London, which means that that is where he lives. www.thomaswhodgkinson.com
@twhodgkinson

GW00566806

MEMOIRS OF A STALKER

Thomas W. Hodgkinson

SILVERTAIL BOOKS • *London*

First published in Great Britain by Silvertail Books in 2015
www.silvertailbooks.com

Copyright © Thomas W. Hodgkinson 2015

1

The right of Thomas W. Hodgkinson to be identified as the author
of this work has been asserted in accordance
with the Copyright, Design and Patents Act 1988
A catalogue record of this book is available from the British Library

Typeset by Elaine Sharples

ISBN 978-1-909269-35-4

For Mills

PART ONE

I

'WHAT DO YOU think? Shall we order a bottle of something?'

'Umm. Gosh. I don't know. What do *you* think, Mrs Howard?'

'But do you think we'll drink a whole bottle?'

'It's hard to say, isn't it. But I expect we'll manage.'

Mills's mother. Another posh piece from the top drawer. The drawback being her seeing me like this. A shipwreck. Some shell of a man, cast out upon the shore by some swell woman, a girl whose eyes were pearls.

A chance meeting. A surprise greeting. And now the two of us having lunch like this. Carluccio's. Bright lights, big windows. Just like old times, eh, Mills? Except it's not, because you're not here. You're nowhere near. It's just me and your mum: a dumb no-show of show-and-tell.

'We seem to have finished the bottle.'

'Would you like to order another?'

'That might be… pleasant.'

'You're so bad, Jack. *Leading me astray.*'

Show, don't tell. That's what they say, and that's what I've been doing. I've told her nothing, nothing true. I've shown her everything.

'How's the book coming along?'

She must be able to see (even she) the trembling in my gut. My D.T. hands. My dirty, matt-black hair. The sweat around my stare.

'It's coming along fine.'

'Is it still the same one you were writing before?'

'No, no. This is a different one. A new one.'

Mills must have told her of those texts I sent. Her mother must now know, be thinking now, about those late-night phone calls. Oh, she can see in my broken eyes some token of the truth, see proof in my unwashed clothes. She can trace in my unshaven face my memories of Mills.

'You look well, Jack.'

'Thanks.' Is she serious?

'I'm serious. You look… what's the word?'

Dead? Dying. 'Blooming?'

'That's it.' She smiles behind her wine. 'You writers…'

As if she knows some others. 'You don't mind the beard?'

'I've never been a big fan of facial hair on men.'

'How about on women?'

She laughs like an ambulance. Then sighs and makes eyes.

'There was that dreadful moment in the Seventies when everyone had those ghastly moustaches. On you, somehow, it doesn't look so bad. But then you always were a rather handsome fellow…'

And that's when the idea begins to form. Revenge.

I always knew she had a crush on me. And now, the opportunity.

Mills's mother. Nothing, of course, on Mills. No, nothing. (Incredible the one produced the other.) But with nothing on? You wouldn't say no. No, even now. I wouldn't, anyhow. Not now, with so much owed me.

'Oh, come along, Jack. You're very attractive. You know you are.'

Revenge. For everything. For all the horror and indignity. That time I called her up (could barely breathe) to say the thing I'd never said before.

She said: *it's nice to hear you say it.*

4

'Well, so are you, Mrs Howard, if it comes to that.'

That time at work when dark water seeped into my heart. I wrote the same sentence over and over again. The same sentence. I wrote it over and over again. That time at work when dark water...

'Oh no. Once, perhaps.' She sighs (the size of her eyes). 'When I was Camilla's age, there were quite a few men who were after me. But it doesn't last, that *thing*. What was that word you used?'

'I can still see lots of bloom.'

This is going to be easy. 1) She's drunk. 2) She lives just round the corner.

Revenge. Back to her place, her on her back, legs round my waist, legless. Oh, Jack! Jacking off on my relative youth. It's all relative.

'Oh, Jack! You're flattering me.'

Rain slides down windowpanes like women's tears.

My clothes smell rained-on. My body smells. Can she smell it? She can certainly see it, my body in the mirror at our side. Can see our table (iced bottle almost dead). Can see the room behind. Walls hung with kitchen implements (a cheese grater, a sieve). The staff in white-washed uniforms. The fit young mothers with their bawling brats.

No. She can't see anything. She's drunk (blind-drunk) and so am I. Too drunk to do it? Imagine that. Fumbling with her bra hook in the hall. Mrs Howard bent over the table where the post gets put, spreading her ancient legs. And there's me, shit-faced with a floppy cock. No!

Can't do it; couldn't. It isn't done. You don't fuck mothers (you know what that would make you). Anyhow, any second now, she's going to notice (as the old lush reaches for that second empty wineskin) my sickly blush, the blood-rush to my face, my skin.

5

'You're clever too. I love what you do for *The Londoner*.'

It's called the *London Review* and they sacked me.

'I read it religiously every week.'

Surrounded by candles?

'In the bath.'

Saucy.

'It's absolutely my favourite magazine.'

Strange she hasn't noticed my absence from the masthead.

'It's so clever and… what's the word?'

'Articulate?'

Sacked. That's why I'm here. At *LR*'s offices in Westbourne Grove, I turned up at twelve, my collar turned-up, two months after being turned out, to collect my humiliated belongings. No one said a thing but 'Hi, Jack' in passing. My hijacked life a source of momentary discomfort to others. To me? Well, let that be. There's time enough for that.

So I packed my haversack. I strapped it to my back, and went, without another word. And then, on the wine-dark pavement: 'Hi, Jack.'

Mrs Howard. Struggling with bags and a big pink umbrella.

And now her moat of shopping obstructs the waiter (he has to *lean* to slide a third fresh bottle into the sopping bucket). White paper bags with strings. A calendar, a colander. Gifts for herself, but not for Mills, who always seemed to bore her. Her inconvenient daughter, as clear as sparkling mineral water. And what a bore to have so beautiful a daughter, when you yourself were never much more than alright-looking, and all you ever really wanted was to be wined and dined and done by someone with an appetite for mutton.

'It's such a shame things didn't work out between you and Camilla.'

'Yes. It was sad.'

'You,' (she points at me) 'were always my favourite of her

boyfriends. Not that she's had that many. Rather few, in fact, over the years. But then Camilla was always so sort of *backward* when it came to things like that. There was that fellow at university. What was his name?'

'Bug.'

'That's right. Bug. Awful name for a man, as if he was an insect or something. I always thought he seemed rather creepy.'

'Crawley.'

'Crawly?'

'That was his surname. Which may explain the…'

'Oh, I see.'

'I never met him.'

'No, you wouldn't have done, but you can take it from me, he wasn't remotely suitable. There was his background, for one thing. I know one isn't supposed to care about things like that anymore, but I'm sorry – no! What his parents must have been like, I dread to think.'

'Is she seeing anyone at the moment?' I ask casually.

'Well, she's oddly secretive with me when it comes to the details of her romantic life. But no. Or not as far as I know… And as for a job, you can forget it. Of course, she still temps, but she's been doing that for ages and it doesn't lead to anything. Where are you going? Oh.'

In what Mills and I used to call 'the Lou Reed' (and others call the lavatory) I rock, teeth gritted, wringing moisture from the fabric of my eyes. *Not as far as I know*. So she might be. *Secretive*. The bitch!

Scratching her rich itch with all the thick Sebastians of London. The Damians and the Henries. Perhaps the Jacks.

The creepy-crawlies.

I'm cubicled. I'm compartmentalised.

I've got log cabin fever.

Outside, in the restaurant, my bag lies under my chair. Like

7

me, it looks normal, relatively speaking. You wouldn't want to open it.

'Camilla was terribly upset when you two broke up.'

I sit back down. I smile.

'Would you like another glass of wine, Mrs Howard?'

I'm going to do it. I'm sorry, but if you knew, if you only knew it, the things that Mills has put me through, you wouldn't be so shocked (another glass of wine knocked back): it wasn't the knock-back of getting dropped, no, getting ditched, getting dumped, no longer getting humped, fucked up by no longer getting fucked (her mother's getting fucked and later she'll get fucked, you see). It was the fact that though Mills knew the effect, the impact, although she knew it shipwrecked me, and knew that I was going down, SHE DID ABSOLUTELY NOTHING TO HELP.

And there's no meaning, none – oh no, no, no, there's none – and I've known that for years, but walked quite willingly beside those putrid waters: prided myself perhaps on knowing they were there, not averting my gaze like all those other bums who shuffle crablike, their bums and backs to the total absence of a wall. Then quite unexpectedly I find myself grabbed by the scruff of the neck, my face thrust into the mire, the bog, the ungodliness – can't speak, can't breathe, pulled out (one gasp of air), vomit, then forced back down into my own acid. See?

And she was there. And she did nothing.

'I know you probably have to…'

'What?'

'Be making your way back to the office, but…'

'What?'

'I was wondering if there was any chance you might be able to…'

'What?'

'Help me with these.'

8

Her bags. Brilliant. The bill comes; goes; returns (paid).

And we step out from Carluccio's into a black-and-white city. London. A city of rains. A city of overflowing drains, drained of all colour but Mrs Howard's pink umbrella. I've got her bags and she's got me. Picture it. A brolly blooms in slate-grey streets. A shuffling, four-legged flower.

No! My wrecked body. My racked back. Can a man in pain perform?

And that's not even to mention my clicking joints, my whistling ear, my teeth that grind in the night. I'm like a fucking one-man band.

Fuck that. A kiss is all it takes. And then: a text to Mills. 'YOUR MOTHER TASTES DELICIOUS.'

I need this. A kiss. I. Need. This.

The shadows of the past. The shadows of other people, their walking shadows hurry past. And the city darkens, turns aside. It doesn't want to know. We go. We pass. We seem to slow as we go past my office. There's the glow of lights above; below, Tesco Metro, closed for refurbishment. A bedraggled tree, bark dark with rain, which now has turned to drizzle. A public bin, from which protrudes a copy of the *Big Issue*.

Her arm. My waist. Significant pressure.

'It's so nice having a man around.'

No! She's human too. What underwater caverns must she know, what canyons since her husband's death? His absence from the mast, to which he once so willingly was lashed. The sea change. Oh, you who turn the wheel and look to windward, consider Mrs Howard, who has been human as you. For I have known them all already, the sunless places, the caves and chasms, the fishes goggling in the gloom; the footfall from the farther room, and women's faces. And now there's Mrs Howard's, under our brolly's water-shade. Her profile: a pencil sketch of Mills in middle age, but with none of the cherubic sensuality, lacking her daughter's lush, inadvertent sexiness. (Who me? Fine then: screw me.) Screw that. I can't kiss someone who's missing another man. I'm human too. No!

We're at the corner. Soon we'll reach the porch. And then?

She expects it. I mustn't disappoint. Besides, I'm dying for a piss. I'll just drop in and do this; and then, if there's a kiss, it happened. I didn't push for it. The yellow false acacia tree that guards the Howards' house, it looms. It's neat and black. No blooms as yet in this weeping winter street.

We're there. We're at the gate. Mrs Howard goes first, penetrating the familiar threshold gap. I hang back. And then, when I glance up (as I might easily not have done), I glimpse, at an upper window, her.

'Are you coming in?'

She didn't see me. Her back was to the pane.

'Jack?'

It hadn't occurred to me that she might be home.

'Jack?'

I'm standing with white bags, being rained on.

'Are you coming in? You must come in for a few minutes at least. Camilla will be so upset if she finds out you were here, and didn't say hello.'

I saw her back, her hair. She was brushing her long brown hair.

The silence grows. And slowly my machinery groans, grinds into life. I step into the porch, put down those bags, and say, 'I'm sorry. I can't.'

'Not even for five minutes?' I shake my head. 'Okay. Well, it was lovely to see you, Jack. Even if we did both have a bit too much to drink.' I smile. I nod. 'Good luck with the new book.' I smile and nod again.

'Have a nice time in India, Mrs Howard.'

'Golly, yes! I haven't packed, and the driver's here in an hour.'

10

I know I should say something about Mills, some casual message, but I don't want to risk it. Who knows, if I opened my mouth, what might come out? In any case, what would I say? *Give Mills my love?* She already has it. *Please give her my best?* She's got that too. Or else, alternatively: *Would you just tell her that when she went out of my life she took with her all the colour, that it's as if all the things in the world have been turned inside out and I've seen the underside of every stone?*

That might not sound sufficiently casual.

Retreat into the street. Return into the rain, head bowed.

(Mills might be watching.) But at the gate, I pause. I turn. I look.

Look. The closed front door. The blank face of the house. Lips sealed. A scar runs down one cheek (a fissure in the paint) unhealed; above, eyes closed (first-floor curtains drawn); then, slap-bang in the middle of the forehead (floor three), like painted extra eyes, Mills's bedroom. The room in which she's bedded, slapped and banged. I stand. I look. Look.

You know what they say to children with hands over their eyes: just because you can't see someone, it doesn't mean they can't see you. With me, you see, it's the opposite. Just because I *can* see her, it doesn't mean she can see me. You see? (I'm behind the tree.) In fact, I can't see her just at present, because she's moved away from the window. But I know she's there. I saw the back of her head. I saw her hair. And I can still see in my mind's eye (in my painted extra eye) her brown hair blown back by the wind as we walked in the harbour, the old Roman port, during our island time. And she looked at me and blushed, because she was embarrassed (she was always embarrassed), because she supposed the wind was whipping up her hair and making her look stupid, not knowing it made her look lovely, of course, as I looked at her, and that made her lovelier.

11

Or then, when we lay and baked on the low flat rocks, before slipping into the wine-cold sea, and instead of tea we sipped cold white wine, which was as cold as the sea. It made our teeth ache. And in the port that night, we saw a cat, a little kitten. And I like cats and Mills likes dogs, but she was the one who got down on one knee and oddly mewed. But the little thing fled. And Mills looked up and lamented, 'It went away.'

And I laughed, and thought: *See? She can be funny too.*

Christ, I need a piss!

And I'm cold. Don't want to leave, though. First need a glimpse, a taste of her. And is that all? I want to swallow. To follow, then: some kind of conversation. I'll speak to her. Yes. We'll chat. That's why I'm here, you see? That's why I'm getting wetter, under this false acacia tree. (Its leafless branches make a bad umbrella.) Her drunken mother didn't see my scalped soul, so why should she? I must be getting better.

Still no sign of her at that top-drawer window.

Lately, I must confess, I haven't done much talking. Lunch was the first time in days I quenched more than my thirst. Forget food. Sometimes I feel the appetite for words. And even Mrs Howard soothed my stomach with her stale patter, her pale and static chatter. But I'm still not sure, if I broached the door, if I rang the bell and stood well back, I'd cope. What if Mummy answers? Nope. Two hours and she's gone.

The Jaipur Festival. (Fuck knows what she does there.)

That's ample time for me to drop into the Cock & Bottle and knock back a bottle or two, so I'm more cocksure and don't bottle out. Maybe I'll even indulge in a bit of banter with my neighbour at the bar, just to get the words flowing. And then, when I'm ready, when I'm feeling more secure, I'll schlep back over to Milton Road, and ring the bell.

And say what? *I just happened to be passing…* Or *Hi, Mills. I chanced to be in the area and I thought…* Or else, safer, *I saw your mum for lunch, but then I had to…* Something simple. The key's to see how she reacts.

Because, back then, her mother let slip a piece of information that interested me. 'Camilla was devastated when the two of you broke up.'

Devastated, eh? If that's true, maybe she's been pining.

I have no bad intent. You see? I'm leaving this leafless tree. The rain in London mainly falls on me. I'm just going down the road to have a drink, as I have every right to do. And if, then, when we talk, she gives me some hint of her real feelings, or implies with her eyes that she knows she made a dreadful error, I guess I'll take this as my cue to confess, bless her for seeing the truth that I've felt, which is that we're somehow meant to be together. And I know that any mention of fate usually has people running for the door, so let's not use that word. Let's call it luck. Luck it was, that two young people so well suited met. Because – and this is the miracle you must try to comprehend – I was clever and she was beautiful.

But she thought I was beautiful and I thought she was clever.

II

THE BLACK TAXI purrs, its engine ticking over, as the Ukip-supporting driver, biting his tongue to prevent the conventional outpouring of filth, helps Mrs Howard with her bags. She climbs aboard. The windscreen wipers wag. Slips out of neutral (purr rises to a whistle) and then the thing moves forward, a slick black cat bound for Gatwick. I turn aside as they slide by, and examine with interest a brick wall: the entrance to Kildare Gardens, if you're interested, which I imagine you're not (but then again, who is?). It's darker now, don't you find? I find it gets darker after the sun goes down. Some things remain the same even when your life has been turned inside-out so that colour and form have changed places, and dark is light and light is dark, and your personalities, your fear-riddled guts, have been dragged out and wound round your face and torso till you're swathed like a mummy and everyone can see the blood-caked failure of you as you walk down the street. I may be a little drunk.

It's possible, because I feel quite strange. And any minute now, I know, I'm going to speak to Mills. So let's linger awhile to consider this feeling. It's not depression (my old comrade-in-arms). No, it's not so heavy. It's a high, tight feeling, like the stretched-silk note of a violin, and it's just above my eyes (not squatting like a frog in the bottom of my brain).

And I'll tell you why it scares me, this lightness in the head. When I had it before, it was accompanied by the desire to kill myself.

Right. No more lingering. Life: happens now.

I'm going to do it. I'm going to ring that blasted bell. Going to squeeze the universe into an image of my white thumbnail letting out a yell.

> What is this life if, full of care,
> We have no time to stand and stare?

The stalker's anthem.

The house stares back in nocturnal negative: face dark, windows lit.

And then, just as I'm on the point of stepping out of the shadows, the mouth gapes. Front door opens to reveal a tongue-coloured umbrella.

It must be Mills. Christ! I can hardly breathe.

Nor can I see her face, but I know it's her. I can hear her voice, talking on her phone as she descends the steps. My mouth opens and closes.

It reminds me of those times when I would call her in the small hours, knowing she wouldn't answer, but just wanting to listen to the recorded message. Her infamous infant voice, with its apologetic tone.

'Hi. This is Camilla. Please leave a message after the bleep.'

Instant music to my ears. But let's hang up. Rewind.

The front door. An open umbrella. Which now rises, but not so I see more than Camilla's skirted legs and waist. It tilts as she glides forward, still singing on her phone (she is near), my enemy, my nemesis (she's nearly here), my hopes and fear, my thrills and spills, my laughter and my tears. My shadow. My reflection. (She is here!) My dark, satanic Mills.

She is gone.

She didn't see me, though I was just standing by this false acacia tree, rooted to the spot, tongue torn out by the roots. It all happened so fast and now – look there – she walks on down the street. I'll follow her.

But at a distance, no? It's no damn good if she can just turn and spot my retro spotted jumper, which we bought together from some rusting rack on Portobello. I do up my Army surplus greatcoat another button. (Is there no end to this infernal rain? I feel like some foot soldier on Caesar's first campaign.) Because this is the trouble with 'stalking' someone who already knows you. They know what you look like. Which makes it so much harder. But let's be clear on this: I'm not a stalker. I'm a talker. I want to talk to her. So why don't I just run up behind her and tap her on the shoulder? She's having a natter. I'll wait until she's done.

O clouds – there is no end to this internal rain – unfold!

Hello. Would you like to accompany me on a trip to Portobello?

That's not where she's headed. She's going south in the winter. She has the spring in her step. I still haven't seen her face, but it somehow fits that she flits like a down-trodden flower through the backstreets of this town, this sodden, this pitiful city. Flits? No. Shimmies or sashays. Her butt, her backside, her smooth round peach of an arse, it makes an S motion as she goes, bringing back such barbs, such shards of memory. She's my Promised Land. Do you see? Do you begin to understand? I feel her fire. She knows my broken arrows of desire. And once we're reunited, my sword shall not sleep in my hand – no, not till I've made her beg, not till she has wept and prayed for mercy, mercy, mercy from me.

Mercy? Me? I wouldn't say so, no. But. (B.U.T.)

She must be made to see. Actions have consequences.

There are more people now, milling round Camilla, belched from the hell of Notting Hill Gate tube station. But only one of them has got a pink umbrella. She's closing it. Quick, hide! I enter a second-hand bookshop. Comics. (Where's the erotic comics section?) I should be sectioned: that's the look I'm getting from the guy behind the desk, some pale-faced geek in untidy, tie-dye T-shirt, looking like he's never seen the sun.

'Can I help you at all?' he asks.

'I don't think so. No. But thanks for the thought.'

I step back out into the night. No sign of her. Is it possible? I can't even keep her in my sights for more than five minutes. Think! She was furling her umbrella, but the rain still falls. She must have been about to go into some shop. Not for second-hand books (that's not her style) but for something else. A newsagents. That's where she'll be. In *there*.

I'm sidling, sliding forward. Reach the door. Look. And see her.

And see in that moment that all my fears (that I was getting things out of proportion, somehow building her up in my head into something she wasn't) were unjustified. In the glimpse I have of her, she's receiving a packet of Marlboro Lights from the dark hand of some man (and it's nice to see she still smokes) at the same time as blushing and smiling, and noticing, as she often does after she smiles, one tooth has snagged slightly on her lower lip, and then lowering her head and pressing tight her lips, while blushing all the more, and smiling at the corners of her mouth.

That's all I see. Because then I have to flinch away, and pretend to join this bus-queue of people. Number 27. The door slides open. They get on. I don't.

And she's off. Pauses at lights; waits for the green man; goes.

And I go. And I know what she's thinking. To me, you see, as I follow Mills (at a suitable distance), she's the only real person, the one true human mixing with actors. She and I, we're real. The others are extras, relaxing off-set during breaks between filming. But this is not a plot, and I am no great actor. But say, for the sake of argument, it were a film, what kind would it be? A thriller, of course. A thriller. Then, I suppose, I'd have to kill her. How? Macabre inquiry! I've no bad intent. Just want to talk to her, to chat. Which I could do now, since she's no longer on her phone.

But somehow, I don't. I follow her. I'm her follower.

At school I had this friend who used to hide in other boys' bedrooms, crouched on top of their cupboards. If anyone saw him, he just laughed. He did it to me once. I picked my nose for a bit. Then rehearsed a speech I had to learn for a competition, adopting silly accents. And then this guy leapt down off my cupboard with such a yell. It gave me quite a turn.

But I begin to understand, as I watch Mills wander, his interest.

We're never ourselves in company. To know what someone's like, you require surveillance. It's the only way to get that special insight.

As Mills proceeds down Holland Park Road, she loiters or lingers, as if she might be early, or just taking a stroll. Absent-mindedly strokes some railings with her fingers; then frowns to see the tips dirty. Searches for somewhere to wipe them. There being nowhere, she slips her hand slyly, and with a sideways guilty glance, into her jacket pocket.

My lovely clown. My lonely cloud. My…

Fuck! I've got too close. She only has to turn.

But she doesn't. Mills doesn't turn. She doesn't see me.

And this must be one of the advantages stalkers have. Unless you know you're being followed, you're unlikely to notice it. People don't, as a rule, stop in their tracks, spin round and stare. They don't wrench aside curtains and glare into the street. They don't scan tubes and buses, just to see who's there. Perhaps we all have stalkers. It's just that we don't know it.

I stop in my tracks. I spin round. I stare. There's no one there.

Either that, or they're very good at what they do. And there are people who do it for a living. Of course there are, and they get well paid. They're called detectives. Tecs or dicks. They know how to stalk. They know the tricks. And you can just imagine the dinner party conversation.

'What do you do?'
  'I'm a dick.'
Or alternatively (from another angle):
  'I'm a stalker, since you ask. I stalk people.'
'Is that a fact? How interesting. Where are your offices?'

She's getting away.

I was so blindfolded in thought, I barely noticed as she swung a right. The rain has increased. The street's a stream. To summarise: I'm splashing through the backwash of London, swimming in the slip-stream of a slip of a girl, who is dressed in a slip.

And for the first time, now, it occurs to me to wonder why she's so dolled-up. Tonight Camilla Howard is wearing a strapless dress with a gold-traced hem. And now I come to think of it, when I saw her mouth, it was glossy. It was bright. Is it a date?

My heart rate quickens. She stops. Lights a cigarette. Her umbrella fills with smoke.

Is it a date? She checks her mobile phone.

And just as I'm telling myself that it's extremely unlikely, because, for all her beauty, she never went on dates (shyness was her chaperone), no, she must be waiting outside that restaurant for a friend, a female friend… a fat black cab pulls up beside her, and a man steps out.

A beige overcoat. A mane of same-colour curls. He stoops for a kiss on the cheek. Takes her umbrella. Furls it. And leads her inside.

Leaving the world to darkness and to me.

He was tall. Oh Christ! He was tall. Made Mills look even smaller. And he was broad. Filled out the shoulders of his camel-hair coat. Who is he? No friend, or none that I once knew. And she, *she*, proffered her cheek to be kissed. Her cheek, note: he could just be a friend.

I should leave, I know, but I don't. I approach the restaurant. Broach the door, breath held, heart pumping, almost bumping into the woman at the desk. She tries to take my bag, but I won't let her. My coat? No thanks. She murmurs, 'I see you got caught in the rain.'

Give the girl a Cuban. Now where are the others?

That's what shocks, you see. Another other.

I had thought this was going to be a two-hander, just Mills and me. But then suddenly, as if from behind a screen, steps this third. This man. And he *is* a man. That's what I don't like. Not some boy, like most of her male friends. He looked, fuck, forty. Thirty-five…

They can't have gone far. I enter the bar. Nothing but extras. Reverse. The rest is restaurant. I need the restroom.

The broad at the desk holds her pen like a cigar.

'Can you tell me the way to the Lou?'

My voice sounds reedy. Hers is velvet.

'It's down the stairs.'

Underground.

The décor: lush. Black-wood tables. Screens. A Moroccan theme. Even the lavatory is beautiful, painted with pheasants and peacocks. I get out my cock and have a pee: Christ, that's pleasant! Oh man! And as I'm standing at the urinal, the man with the mane emerges from the closet (the sit-down place), walks past me – my dick in my hand – and returns into the restaurant. And I want to scream: 'He didn't wash his hands!'

Nor, I realise, did he flush. I peer in, to see what he left behind. The bowl is empty. What on earth was he doing in there?

I wash my hands carefully, taking care to wash between the fingers, prodding with a finger from the other hand. Then I go in search of them. I need to know, you see, if it's a date. That's all. Once I know that, I'll go. I scan the place. There's no sign of them. I can hear nearby some corporate group, despoiling a private room. But this central space, this 'exceptional reception area with divine divans', is empty. I feel a little ill.

I enter the next room. Tables. Couples. Is this restaurant reserved for romance? They're gazing into one another's eyes. I feel, if anything, iller.

And there's Camilla, up a few steps, in a kind of raised conservatory.

I take a step back – she has her back to me – and find a free table with a reasonable view. She and her man, they're bathed in light, the scenery like a colonial terrace or veranda, metalwork splashed in white, wedding-cake white, a white spiral staircase rising into the light, with one or two lime-coloured cushions, but otherwise everything white and gleaming there in the limelight. As for me, I'm in the shadows. I'm in the dark. But I can still see them. I can see him. The man with a mane. Mane man.

And he can see me. But fortunately for him, he doesn't know me. He doesn't know the number of times I've had sex with the girl he's buying food for, how often she rocked on top of me and let me know that she was coming. We had sex every time we saw each other during our two-year stint. It became a point of pride. Just think about that. There wasn't a night we saw each other when we didn't have sex. We went out for two years. We saw each other, say, three times a week. You do the maths.

He doesn't know that. She does. And she knows me. All she has to do is turn. So I turn. I reach for my damp bag, take hold of the zip, and draw it down to reveal: my notebooks and my newspapers, my tatty copies of *The Times*. Pull one out, and as I do, uncover packets, each printed with the word ZALEPLON. Sleeping pills. I take them with me everywhere, because you never know. I pick a paper and pretend to read it.

21

In fact, I'm watching them. He's watching her. Her, she's talking. And that's one of the things that strikes me as odd. Because when we went out, Mills didn't say much. I was the one who usually held forth, inspired (by her) to flights of fancy, to graceful silliness. Or else I'd tell her things she didn't know.

But now, for some reason, she talks, while he listens.

I can't hear what she's saying, but I can watch the reactions on his leonine features. He's not handsome. His face is heavy. (A dumb or ugly lion, a lion made of lead.) And, in fact, he doesn't react. He seems almost comatose. And just as I'm thinking this, Mills falls silent. There's a pause. Does she require a response? And then he tilts back his leaden, heavy head, and roars with laughter, his eyes watching her all the time.

'Sir?' A waitress. I wave her away.

She climbs the few stairs to the conservatory, steps into the light, and stands by Mills and her big stuffed cat. Takes their orders. Goes. And then I see Mills twist and turn aside. Her face is screwed up. Has she seen me? She looks like she might be sick. And then she sneezes.

I feel dizzy, a little faint. It takes a moment to recognise this feeling, to identify it, and remember its name. It's called Love.

I love Mills. It breaks over me like a wave.

I feel ill, spun upside-down. I can't breathe. I love her.

I love her like I hate the rain, like a sugar rush, like the lack of pain. I love her in the way people love people when they love them. And that's when I realise that this – what I can see – must be a date. Dumb of me to doubt it. Wishful thinking, I suppose. And although it's possible this man is no more than a friend, some work colleague perhaps, some muddy-mettled rascal who's mad about her, but whom she finds a little dull – if that were really the case, then why would they be dining?

'Sir? Are you ready to order?' I pick the first thing on the menu.

Then it occurs to me that I should make a note of the price: of my main, and also of the wine. Because, if they should leave suddenly, I may wish to follow. I mustn't be left behind, waiting for my bill.

It's a date. You only have to look at him.

He's wearing a shirt of a pale-pink colour, open at the collar by two buttons, enough to reveal a hint of golden hair glazing the full pectorals.

Is he foreign? Only a foreigner would dress so formally.

Mills is talking. And turning. I raise my copy of *The Times*.

But my ears are tilted, for a cry or sudden silence. And Mills keeps talking. I've never known her so verbose. While golden boy, he says nothing. Perhaps it's because he's foreign. Perhaps he can't understand a word she's saying. Perhaps when he laughed earlier, he just judged it was the moment by the expression on her face and the fact that she'd shut up. Or perhaps the reason why he isn't saying anything is because, secretly, all he can think about is having sex with her.

That must be it. He's a sex addict. You only have to look at him.

Any man who takes so much care over his appearance (there's not a chest hair out of place) must be seriously perverse. And do I detect the sheen of sweat over his plastic, playboy features? That must be what he was doing earlier in the lavatory, knocking out a quick one before dinner, crouched forward to one side, his fist gripping the hard flesh of his...

Mills is rising. The scrape of a metal chair pushed back.

I raise my paper high. But by cruel chance, here comes the waitress with my wine. There has never been such a now. She splashes blood over the bottom of my glass, and I mutter, 'I'm sure that will be fine' (aware at the same time of the footfall from the farther room, the demented sound it makes as Mills descends the steps, then pauses) keeping my copy of *The Times* at forehead height. My glass is brimmed. The waitress goes.

'Jack? Is that you?'

There's such a roaring in my ears as I slowly lower the paper and look at Mills, at her face that steals my breath, and her form that, in that dress, stabs my eyes, and her proximity, which sounds so loud that I can barely hear her voice, as she hesitantly asks, 'What are you doing here?'

And I can hardly hear my own, as I reply, 'I'm stalking you.'

She blushes. I clutch my glass of wine.

'Seriously. Are you having dinner on your own?'

It wildly enters my head to invent a date. Someone famous perhaps. But then I realise this won't wash. The other place-setting has already been removed. And now (a slow voice in my head is telling me) too much time has passed since she asked the question.

'No,' I slowly say. Then, 'I mean, Yes.'

'Why?' She blushes again.

'I was working late.' Pause. 'At work.'

'But I thought that they…'

'They did. But then they found they couldn't do without me.'

And nor can you, Mills. Nor can you.

'They invited you back? That's great.'

For a moment we look at one another. And in my head I'm saying so many things, but no words reach my mouth. I think maybe if I open my mouth, I'll say something. Not a chance. I close it again. And Mills, she glances over her shoulder at the conservatory, where her companion isn't paying attention. He's talking on his iPhone, turned away.

She looks at me again and smiles.

'Well, I guess I'd better…'

'Where are you going?'

Another of her blushes.

'Ah. The Lou Reed.'

'What do you mean?'

'The Lou Reed. Remember?'

24

Don't play these games, Mills, please.

Eventually she nods. '*Perfect Day.*'

Our song. Or one of them.

'It was nice to see you.'

'Mills, wait.'

She looks at me and knows. She always knew. That's why she didn't ask me how I was. She doesn't want to know, because she knows. She knows about my half-life, my dark-life, my life half-lived between the living and the dead. She knows, too, that this is my one bright chance to tell her straight, in this half-light, to put things right, by force of words.

But can I so presume? And how should I begin? And slowly she notes, with something like relief, that the moment is passing.

She smiles. 'I like the beard, by the way.'

All I can say is (with a pained look): 'Thanks.'

And she goes.

That's it.

She's gone.

Listen. There's a drum roll.

I'm serious. Some dumb drummer up above is beating a tattoo, as if to say, *you're a bum, you're a bum.* Then I realise: it's the rain. Fumbling, bumbling, floundering down on the glass ceiling of the conservatory, and every note is bum. For think of all the things I could have said. The painful things: the way, each morning when she woke, she used to say: 'I love you.' It was the way she greeted the day.

I could have reminded her of that. Or…

- The toothbrush holder in the bathroom, on which, to make her laugh, I'd written HIS and HERMAN'S.
- Breakfast (she in my second dressing gown, which I'd worn while writing essays at university, and which I later ditched because it reminded me of her). Orange juice. Eggs.

25

- On the bus to work, we used to play a game of my invention. *Man With A Bag.* You got points (obviously) for seeing a Man carrying a Bag, but also if you were the first to spot (and say the words) Purple Garment, Manly Woman, Facial Hair, Lycra, or Hat – and a massive bonus (it goes without saying) if you chanced to spot a bearded, rucksacked transsexual, dressed in purple Lycra and a cap.

I could have mentioned that, or that, or that. I didn't.

And I don't, as she hurries back through, avoiding my eye.

In the white operating theatre of the conservatory, he greets her; sheaths his iPhone. She murmurs something. And then, though she tries to stop him, he leans, squinting past her into the gloom. I meet his gaze. So for a moment, I'm looking at him and he's looking at me. There was a time I could have faced him down. But now my pale heart quails before his stare. There's nothing there. I hide behind my paper.

When I look again, he's still looking. And as our eyeballs clash, he reaches for Camilla (eyes crashing or smashing against mine) and hides her hands with his. Then, turning, he leans towards her, and…

I rise clumsily. Knock over my glass of water, which spills across the table. Moisture subsides, fizzing, into the embroidered cloth. And I glance once more at their table. And once more, he's looking at me, attracted by the noise. But now his face is mad, expressionless. A mannequin.

I turn my back on him. I'm shaking.

I move cutlery, napkin, place mat, glass of wine, water glass, place mat, cutlery, napkin, bottle of wine, vase of flowers, cutlery, condiments, vase of flowers, water glass, so I'm sitting facing away from them.

After that, everything goes a bit strange.

26

* * *

I remember having a conversation once with a girl who was studying for a PhD in psychology and she told me (the notion wasn't new) that there was no clear dividing line between sanity and insanity; more specifically, you could say, therefore, that everyone was a little bit schizophrenic, or bipolar, or whatever; or more interestingly still, she told me that most of what gets diagnosed as psychological disorder is merely an anxious response to perfectly normal brain functioning. The most obvious example of this is when a line from a song gets stuck in the head. This happens to most of us at one time or another, but we don't go rushing off to our doctors to complain of auditory hallucinations. The anxious type, however, driven to distraction by emotional strain, he or she, hearing the sound of Lou Reed, thinks it's some kind of message. Something similar happens now to me.

* * *

Here comes the night. It comes. And it's upon us.

Stepping out into the rain, which falls like hammer blows (it's monsoon rain), I see, beneath the umbrella of that leafy tree, him – holding up her umbrella, while she climbs into his taxi. I follow as it draws away, rain weeping on my face, thinking: that's why he chose that place. It's close, but not too close, to where she lives. Expensive, but not suspiciously so. Perfect, in other words, for the three-course lunge. (Starter; main; and here's my tongue.) The business lunge. (I have a proposition.) The boozy lunge. (If you've got the bottle.) The brunge. (A morning move.) But him, he's opted for the posh lunge. The plunge. Allow me to buy you dinner, no really, I insist. Allow me to listen to your stories, and laugh when you pause. And now, allow me to escort you home. No, really. I insist.

I realise that I'm running. I must, to keep them in sight. It's steep, this street, but I continue running. Harder. They're turning right. Farther. I'm sprinting. Arrive at the top at Ladbroke Grove (the street streams) just in time to see them cross, and I cross (the traffic screams) and take the road they took. Each time I reach a street, they're leaving. But now the road is downhill, and I'm clattering down it, down-hilling, eyes rolling, arms wind-milling, while all around, people step back, lowering their umbrellas, and raindrops explode like light bulbs.

I realise that I'm shouting. I don't care.

It's a long straight street, studded with mini-roundabouts. At each of these, their taxi slows. I don't. And at the second one, I'm struck. I'm hit.

Roll over a bonnet. Get back on my feet. A window is lowered: 'You wanker!' I turn. Approach the driver – who takes one look at me and then raises his window again. I'm running. Fuck. Some muscle's gone in my leg. Fuck. And where are they? I slow. I'm walking. Pain.

There. Roadworks. Temporary traffic lights. Red.

I'm running. Green. I'm running.

Carluccio's. No breath. Tesco. Little death.

I'm coming, Jack. Oh my god, I'm coming. And I'm spent…

Milton Road. Hunched forward, gasping, soaked in rain and my own sweat, my hands gripping my knees. Look up: to see a taxi door opening. The lunge lizard climbs out. He helps her out. He even takes her fucking hand. Then he slips his other arm around her waist, and together they waltz up to the porch of the house, and plunge inside.

The street's empty. I limp towards the gate. See curtains being drawn by female hands. They're in the drawing room. But as I watch, light rises through the house. Hall. Staircase. Master bedroom. Higher landings, leading up, upping the ante, to antechambers, until: the light ignites in Mills's room. And her hand lowers the blind.

Leaving me blind. Losing my mind. Losing.

Loving. 'It's better to have loved and lost,' they say.

To which I say: 'Show me someone who's done both, and agrees.'

* * *

I'm in the back garden, head thrown back, with rain, endless rain, nothing but the wild rain falling on the stony ground around my mouth, which is open, though no sound comes out, open, filling with rain, like my eyes, which are wide, open and filling with rain, which falls, pirouettes down, like snowflakes, lit by light from all the windows of this many-floored mansion, which are leading my sight up, to the dizzying, the dazzling light of that not-empty bedroom.

* * *

In the back garden. On my knees. Grass. Mud. Rain. It's very cold. What time is it? I'm on my front. It's darker now, don't you find? No light falls from the windows of the house. I'm very cold. And something crawls like a reptile from the cracks inside my soul.

* * *

Shivering. Shaking. Crawling. On my belly. Rain. Mud. Stone. Steps.

Down. A window. There's an open window.

And I'm in.

PART TWO

NOTES

Everything that has happened has made some sense at the time. It's only now, as I look back, that it seems unreal, like something remembered in a dream. For example, when I woke up that first morning, I knew where I was, despite the fact that it was a room I'd never been in before. It was a store-room in the Howards' basement, filled with junk and bric-a-brac. The kind that might once have been called a lumber room.

Mills's father had been quite a traveller in his day. And wherever he had gone, he had brought back souvenirs, most of which seemed to have ended up down here. There were Incan masks, Indian fabrics, Melanesian figurines. Precious stones and tumble stones. A range of national costumes on a rail beside the wall.

I don't suppose I took all this in immediately. The first thing I would have registered, as likely as not, was how much my leg ached. And my mind must then have gone back to the night before, and picked its way through the grim debris of the evening. The exchange with Mills in the restaurant. And then the ignominious ending.

Man, my leg was sore. I tugged down my trousers, which were caked in mud, and examined the spread of a bruise. When I rose to my feet, I found that I could stand, which suggested the damage wasn't more serious. But that wasn't to say it didn't hurt. It hurt like hell. I limped painstakingly to the door of the room and pressed my ear to it.

I knew that Mills didn't have a full-time job. Her mother had said, with all the disdain of one who had never had a regular job herself, that she was 'temping'. Which meant that she might be at home or, alternatively, she might not. I should have left by the way I had come in. I know, I know. It was what I meant to do. But first I listened. The house seemed silent. Carefully, I tried the handle of the door. It was locked.

I should have climbed back out and reversed my steps of the previous night, returning into the street. Then? Just got on with my life, I suppose, if 'life' is the right word to describe the sequence of non-days and non-nights that had characterised my recent past. Instead, I peered through the keyhole. It was blocked by a key, which had been inserted from the other side. I found a sheet of paper and slid most of it under the door. Then I took a wire coat hanger and unwound its head until the two ends sprang apart. I prodded one of the ends into the keyhole and jiggled it around a bit until the key dropped on the other side.

I waited for a moment, to see if anyone would come. Then I drew back the piece of paper under the foot of the door, bringing with it its burden of the key.

As I climbed the stairs from the basement, I proceeded slowly, ready to retreat at the slightest noise. The house was silent, but my head was loud with the echoes of remembered conversations. For every room held memories for me. It was as if each stick of furniture had been tagged with a label. 'This was where you kissed her for the first time.' Or: 'It was here that you learnt her father had passed away.'

As I entered the drawing room, the clamour grew even louder. So much had happened here between the two of us. I sat on the sofa for a time, losing myself in reminiscences. It was a nice feeling while it lasted, like being pleasantly drunk. But it left an emptiness.

At a certain point, a noise startled me. On the long low table, a phone had begun to vibrate. It was Mills's phone, which she must have left behind in her hurry to get to work. With each buzz, the handset rotated by 45 degrees on the glass that overlay the tabletop. Before it had completed a full turn, I had it in my hand.

I let it go to voicemail, and then listened to the message. It was the guy from the night before, the one she'd taken home with her. His name, it appeared, was Bernhardt. He was apologising. Apparently, he had come on too strong and they'd had some kind of row. At a certain point, he said, 'I should not have pressured you. Forgive me.' I listened to the message again, to make sure that I understood. Then I deleted it.

It was pretty clear that they hadn't slept together. And why hadn't they slept together? The most likely explanation, I realised, was that the sight of me in the restaurant had made her nostalgic. It had reminded her of all the good times we'd had together. Idly I browsed through the text messages on her phone, only to discover, to my amazement, that she had saved all the messages I'd sent her while we were going out. And what possible reason could she have had for saving them?

I paced the room excitedly as I thought about this, considering the implications from every angle. Then an idea occurred to me, something so bold that whenever I thought about it, I had difficulty breathing. Acting swiftly, so I wouldn't change to my mind, I grabbed up an umbrella from the hall, and ran outside into the rain.

If I remembered rightly, Mills usually got back from work at around 7.30. So to be on the safe side, I made sure that everything was ready by 6.30. The bottle of prosecco was keeping cool in the fridge. The dinner I had cooked for her was staying warm inside the oven. To pass the time, I watched a little TV. But it was hard to concentrate. At 6.45, I turned the TV off and moved to a chair facing the door into the hall. Once I was settled, I began to rehearse what I was going to say to her.

'Hello, Mills.'

'Mills, *hello*.'

'Surprised to see me?'

'Are you *really* surprised?'

'It's just like old times, wouldn't you say?'

I couldn't say nothing when she walked into the room. I knew that. It would seem strange if I just stared at her. And I knew she might be surprised to find me there. It was possible she would be a little taken aback. But I was sure I could put her at her ease. I just had to hit upon the right formula of words. I thought about it hard, my mind darting this way and that. I tried out different gambits, saying sentences aloud. But I still hadn't made a decision, when I heard steps arriving in the porch.

Involuntarily, I rose to my feet and retreated into the semi-darkness of the dining room. I was behaving rather surreptitiously, which hadn't been part of my plan. But before I could steel myself to step back out into the drawing room, something happened which stopped me in my tracks.

It was her name. That familiar single syllable.

The front door opened, and a voice called out, 'Mills?'

I retreated into the kitchen.

Peering through into the drawing room, I saw the owner of the voice enter from the hall. It was a girl in her twenties: small, wearing a long coat, a scarf knotted at her neck. She unwound it as she sat down in front of the television. Somehow, she didn't seem to be aware of my presence. She hadn't noticed the flames of the candles that were flickering on the dining table. She hadn't even smelt the food that I'd been cooking in the kitchen. But I knew it could only be a matter of time.

My mind raced as I tried to think what I would say to her when she spotted me. There was nothing that came to mind. My next thought was to try to creep through the dining room, and then make a bolt for it. I was about to do this, when I remembered that I'd left my backpack on the floor beside the sofa. It was in plain sight of this girl, but somehow she still hadn't seen it. After a moment, she rose to her feet and left the drawing room. I could hear her descending into the basement.

As quickly and as quietly as I could, I took the food from the oven and stashed it out of sight on top of one of the kitchen cupboards. I did the same to all the dirty pots and pans. Then I hurried into the dining room and, licking my fingers, extinguished the candle flames, before continuing into the drawing room. I grabbed my backpack and carried on into the hall, my hand reaching out for the handle of the door. But a key was turning in the lock on the other side.

At the same time, behind me, the other girl was returning up the stairs.

I ducked back into the drawing room, paused for a moment in indecision, and then moved quickly over towards the bay of the window. I slid behind the heavy gold brocade curtain, just as the two girls came in from the hall.

The other girl, whose name was Clare, was American. A new friend, I supposed.

They settled down to watch an episode of *Strictly Come Dancing*. After a while, I allowed my knees to bend, and carefully I leaned back against the window sill. It was only then that it occurred to me to look over my shoulder. Although I was screened from the sight of the girls in the drawing room, I was exposed to anyone who chanced to be passing in the street. And people did pass along it, from time to time. None of them, though, paid me much attention. None of them, that is, until a little old woman came tottering along with her dog. The dog was also little, and also old. When it reached a lamppost it barely had the strength to raise its leg. It wasn't short on lung power, though. I discovered this, because, a moment later, it spotted me, and began to yap furiously. The old woman raised her umbrella, which before had concealed her face, and stared at me with a look of wizened suspicion.

I attempted a smile, and made my hands into claws. My idea was to suggest that I was playing some kind of game with the occupants of the house. I put a finger to my lips mischievously. The dog's yapping increased in volume and urgency. The old woman looked unimpressed, even disgusted. She yanked at the leash with her bony hand, and dragged her mutt, still yapping, away down the street.

The girls didn't speak much during *Strictly Come Dancing*. Occasionally, I heard Mills's laugh, which was a sound I had always loved. A giggle, a gurgle even. It was like the laugh of a baby, the kind that might be used in an advertisement. Clare's laugh, by contrast, was short and dry. It was an unamused laugh.

After the programme had finished, I heard her do her short dry laugh, and then the sound of her leaving the room. When she came back in, she was carrying something from the fridge, which she hadn't expected to find. It was the bottle of prosecco, which I'd forgotten to hide. Fortunately, the two of them decided that it must have been put there by Mills's mother before she'd left for India.

I heard the pop as the cork came out of the bottle. And then the froth and the fizz as two tall glasses were filled. While they drank my prosecco, Clare interrogated Mills about her date of the previous evening. When Mills described how she had bumped into me in the restaurant, Clare did her sawdust laugh.

'Maybe he was stalking you,' she suggested wryly.

Apparently that thought had occurred to Mills. But since I had claimed that that was what I was doing, she'd decided that I couldn't be. Then Clare asked for more information. What else had been said? And what had happened afterwards? My ears pricked up when she asked Mills why she hadn't slept with Bernhardt.

Mills replied that it hadn't felt right. Yes, I wanted to say to her, but *why* hadn't it felt right? Fortunately, Clare asked the question for me. Going further, she asked if it had anything to do with the fact of having bumped into me. She even asked her straight if she was in love with me. Mills's response was brutal.

'Definitely not.'

How could she be so sure?

'I just am,' came the reply.

It was something I disliked in Mills. When she was fond of you, there was no one sweeter or more affectionate. But when she wasn't, she could be pretty cold.

'Maybe,' Clare suggested, 'you're in love with him subconsciously.'

'If so,' she countered, 'it must be very subconscious.'

By then, I had heard enough. But there was nothing I could do about it, as the two of them carried on talking. Mills began to sing the praises of Bernhardt. Above all, she said, what she liked about him was the fact that he was 'a grown-up'. She felt safe when she was with him. Apparently, his arms were very strong.

She talked at some length about Bernhardt and how wonderful he was. Then finally she announced that she was going to bed. Clare stayed up for a while longer, drinking alone, and channel-hopping. Then, eventually, she too turned in.

I stayed where I was, reasoning that there was a chance that one of them might come back in. While I waited behind the curtain, I looked out of the window at the street, at the shadows that were cast by the pale street lights, and the reflections on the rain-wet Tarmac. At a certain point, a fox appeared, padding silently, its back slightly arched, along the pavement. It kept close to the parked cars until it had passed the house. I watched as it crossed the street, and ducked under the railings into Kildare Gardens.

Then silently I raised my hand and moved aside the heavy material of the curtain. The drawing room was dark and empty. As I stepped forward, my leg gave way under me. It had been pressed for so long against the window sill that it had fallen asleep. I collapsed to the floor and, lying there, I believe I cried a little.

Most people, in my opinion, have a lie that they tell themselves, which makes it easier for them to get up in the morning. And if that lie is taken away, it can feel as if they have nothing. That was how I felt that evening.

Even after I'd stopped crying, I didn't get to my feet. I just lay there, where I was. And after a few minutes, I became aware that I wasn't alone in the room. There was a little creature, which had crept forward out of the shadows. I watched as the small dark shape moved silently, pausing beside the carpet. Then it moved forward again, and paused once more. It seemed to be looking at me.

'Hello,' I said aloud.

The mouse fled so fast, I didn't see where it went. I found myself wondering if I had really seen it, or if it had been a figment of my imagination.

* * *

The next morning, I waited until I had heard the front door slam a second time. Then I emerged from the lumber room. I had done a lot of thinking during the night. How was it, I asked myself, that mice could live in people's homes without being seen? The answer was they were unobtrusive. But this begged the question of whether a man could manage a similar trick. It would be harder, because he was so much bigger. But the principles were basically the same. Like a mouse, he would have to stay out of sight while people were there. Otherwise, he could

40

do what he wanted. The more I thought about it, the more it struck me as feasible.

Watching TV. Gossiping. Drinking. Sending emails and texts. Most of the things we spend our time doing are unnecessary. The only essential things are eating and drinking, sleeping and going to the loo. If I stuck to the essentials, I reasoned, all I would need would be to come up with some unobtrusive way of performing them. I resolved that I would stay in the house for a couple more days, to see if this were possible.

It was the challenge of the thing that appealed to me. There are some ideas that, once they've occurred to you, are impossible to avoid. It would have been shameful, in a sense, if I'd just left the house and gone home. Cowardly, in a way. Certainly at the time I wasn't aware of any ulterior motive for wanting to stay in the house. It's probably relevant too that I didn't have much else going on in my life at that time. I checked my diary and my week turned out to be pretty free.

When it came to food, I knew, I could just nip out to the local shop. But I didn't want to do that. For one thing, I didn't have any money. It had been weeks since I'd received any income and I had been leaning heavily on credit. For another thing, it struck me that this would be avoiding the challenge. The mouse didn't have the option of popping down to Tesco Metro whenever it felt like a piece of cheese.

RULE ONE: I wasn't ever allowed to leave the house.

The mouse, whom I had christened Matthew, got by on crumbs. And so could I, as long as I didn't take too much. This was based on what I called a Percentage Principle. The more of an item was in the kitchen, the more I could take. If there were six apples in the fruit bowl, I could get away with stealing one of them. If all that was left was a small morsel of cheddar, I had to restrict myself to a sliver.

RULE TWO: I would always observe the Percentage Principle.

When it came to drinking, there was plenty of water in the tap. I just had to wash up the glass after use, dry it, and return it to its previous place inside the cupboard. Going to the loo required similar precautions. I favoured Mills's mother's bathroom, which was the one that was least likely to be visited by either of the girls.

RULE THREE: I must always remember to clean the bowl after use.

Sleeping was the easiest of the three challenges. As long as I managed to get a few hours in the night, I could catch up with a nap during the day, while the girls were at work. I didn't mind the hardness of the floor of the lumber room. There's a passage in one of Byron's letters where he writes of his satisfaction at finding he's as capable of sleeping on hard ground as Albanian brigands. I must admit I was proud of my ability to do without a mattress. I found the best way to get a few hours was to lie on my back. If I turned on my side, the discomfort would wake me in the small hours.

RULE FOUR: I had to revise and improve my rules constantly.

* * *

I was pretty sure that, as long as I stuck to the four rules, the risk of being caught was almost non-existent. It just goes to show how wrong you can be.

On the second morning of my challenge, I put my clothes on to wash in the washing machine in the basement, and then went up to the master bedroom and ran myself a hot bath. I didn't luxuriate. I just soaped the parts that needed it and rinsed everywhere else. I drip-dried while standing in the bath. No need, that way, for a bathmat. Then I towelled my hair, dried the inside of the bath and around the sink, and patted dry the cake of soap. Naked apart from my towel, which I had draped around my neck, I walked out into the bedroom. At the same time, a woman walked in from the landing. She took one look at me and let out a scream.

I shouted back at her, and as I did so, covered my genitals with my hands.

It was the Howards' cleaner, Aisha. A Romanian. I'd never met her, but I had heard her name being mentioned. She was a short, dumpy woman, clad in a shawl and a head scarf. Her eyes bulged as she glanced down, involuntarily, at my hands. I tugged down the towel from my neck, and wrapped it around my waist. The movement seemed to disturb her. She grabbed a hairbrush, which was the first thing that came to hand, and pointed it at me like a knife. An image came to me of Aisha forcibly brushing my hair, and involuntarily I smiled. This didn't reassure her.

She sucked in a deep breath, as if she was going to scream again.

'Wait!' I cried. She caught the breath up, trapped in her lungs. 'Listen. Please. I'm a friend of Mills.' She tilted her head. 'I'm a friend of Mills. Please…'

The breath slowly released, like air escaping from a football.

Finally she spoke. 'You friend Miss Mills?'

'Yes. Yes, exactly. I friend Miss Mills.'

She hesitated. 'Miss Mills very nice.'

'She's lovely,' I agreed.

Hesitantly, Aisha replaced the hairbrush on the table.

'Me no like other girl,' she volunteered after a moment.

'Clare? No. Nasty girl.'

'She give me bad face.'

'Did she?' I said, wondering what on earth this could mean.

She waggled a finger. 'She give me very bad face.'

'What a bitch.'

43

A thought occurred to her. 'You boyfriend Miss Mills?'

I wanted to say yes, but I shook my head. 'No,' I said. 'I'm just a friend.'

I told Aisha I had come over for dinner the night before and ended up staying the night. Mills had said I could hang out in the house and get some work done, and given me permission to wash my clothes in the washing machine. Aisha seemed to accept my story. In the end, she even offered to iron my clothes for me, after they completed their cycle in the tumble drier, and it struck me that it would be rude to refuse.

While she ironed my T-shirt, I asked her casually about her work. I wanted to know the next time she was going to put in an appearance, so I could be prepared. After she had gone, I noted down her answers in my phone.

Then, dropping to the floor, I did a series of press-ups until my pectoral muscles ached. The encounter with Aisha had shaken me. I realised it had been a mistake to think the task I had set myself would be so easy.

* * *

When I look back now, it's pretty clear that for much of the time during those first days in the house, I was suffering from depression. I remember, for example, that on one occasion I lay for two hours on my back in the drawing room, watching a fly pursue strange trajectories in the space above my head. It repeatedly turned back on itself, as if it were drawing arbitrary triangles inside an invisible circle.

One of the symptoms of depression is that you're convinced you're always going to feel that way. After a few days, however, I became aware that a minimal amount of energy had accumulated in my soul. And once that happens, the rest is up to you. You have to make plans and carry them out. I began to jot down notes in my phone. And I formulated a new rule, Rule Five, which I added to my previous four.

RULE FIVE: After each setback, I would come back harder.

· What this meant was that, every time I screwed up or failed to meet my own expectations, I would punish myself. I would adjust the challenge, to make it even harder than before. At first, my only goal had been to pass unnoticed in the house. All I'd had to do was stay out of sight while the girls were around. But the encounter with Aisha had been a major miscalculation. Accordingly, I adjusted my challenge, making it harder. Now, I told myself, I would develop ways of being able to move around the house even when the girls were here. This was going to be tough to pull off. Indeed, it made me shiver when I thought about it. The onrush of adrenalin, triggered by fearfulness, helped to lift me out of my lethargy.

The house was big and old, which helped my cause. However, it was also tall and thin, with only one flight of stairs. It was here, on the staircase, that I was most likely to get caught, so I decided I would get to know the stairs as thoroughly as possible. I walked up and down each flight, moving from side to side, to find out which steps were creaky and which were safe to tread on. With the creaky steps, I tested to see exactly which parts creaked. I noted down the results in my mobile phone.

I practised, rehearsing the route that ran the least risk of my making a sound. It required me to pursue an odd zigzag path up and down the stairs, which I did repeatedly until I had fixed it into my muscle memory. It was a mistake, I found, to try to descend too fast. I maintained a medium pace. Even then, I became aware of a slight noise when I moved. It was the material of my trousers, which was brushing together between my thighs. I took my trousers off. Underneath, I had on a pair of cycling shorts. On the day when I'd bumped into Mrs Howard in the street, I hadn't had any clean boxer shorts, so had just pulled on this old pair of cycling shorts instead. When I'd originally bought them, they had been a bright pink, but they had since faded to the colour of dirty skin. I removed my T-shirt as well, and found that now, when I descended or ascended the stairs, I was completely silent.

It felt streamlined, to be wearing the shorts. Operating on a similar principle, I decided to shave off my beard. It had been starting to annoy me, having reached the length where the little bristles rub against each other and become itchy. I didn't have my trimmer with me, but I found a safety razor in the cupboard of Mrs Howard's bedroom and set about the task. Once I was done, I examined myself in the mirror.

I went down to the lavatory in the basement, and grabbed a pair of silver scissors. I hurried back up to the bathroom, following my new zigzag route. Again I hesitated in front of the mirror. I took between finger and thumb a lock of hair, to the side of my forehead, and snipped it off with the scissors. Then I did it again. And again and again. I began cutting faster and faster until my scalp was a harvested field. Then I made use of the razor, until I had cleared the hair down to the skin.

It felt strange, being shaven-headed. The skin revealed by the razor was pale. Over the days that followed, I involuntarily raised a hand to it from time to time.

* * *

I have a theory about heartbreak. It goes like this.

When we're born, we believe we're the centre of the universe. Life is a process of learning that this is the opposite of the truth. In infancy, our every need is catered for. We're hungry? *Here's food.* We're sleepy? *Try this cot. Comfortable, isn't it.* Yet as time goes by, the reality is revealed to be a bit more complicated. It turns out we're not, despite appearances, the last emperor of

China, but just a helpless scrap of humanity, being catered to by parents who can be tired, impatient or neglectful, and who will eventually expect us to fend for ourselves. But our first understanding of the world has been this sense of imperial significance. And it's hard to let it go. So what we do is adapt it into a secondary kind of egotism. We tell ourselves that we're special. We may not be imperial, but we're definitely special.

This develops into the life lie of our ultimate lovability. Like all good delusions, it contains a mechanism for dismissing evidence to the contrary. For if we ever meet anyone who doesn't love us, we can tell ourselves that they don't really know us. If they knew us, their love would be inevitable. It's a pretty watertight argument.

The problem comes when someone who does know us, who knows us well, nevertheless decides that they don't love us. This, you see, is why the experience of being rejected by a lover is one of the most painful ordeals you will ever face. For it destroys the Life Lie of your Ultimate Lovability.

* * *

I feel a temptation, in describing these events, to exaggerate the extent of the orderliness of my life, to emphasise patterns and stress self-control. I suspect this is inherent in the nature of writing. Sentences naturally lend themselves to describing processes with a beginning, a middle, and an end. They constantly imply a measured progress towards a definite conclusion. Life, of course, isn't like this, and if I'm honest, most of the time I was working things out as I went along. Some of my key breakthroughs came by chance, rather than by force of insight or intellect.

There was one time I had been doing sit-ups in the gloom of the drawing room. I had taken to closing the curtains after the girls left, so I wouldn't be seen by anyone in the street. As I say, I had been doing sit-ups, driving myself to the limit of my endurance. I let out a sigh, then, and relaxed back, relishing the burn in my abdominals. After I'd been lying there a while, I became aware of a scuffling sound. At first, I didn't move. When I slowly turned my head, I saw the mouse crouched by the edge of the carpet. 'Hello, Matthew,' I said. (Matthew, you'll remember, is the name I had given him.) He was in the same place where I had seen him on that first night. After a pause, during which we looked at each other, he scarpered. But this time, I saw where he went.

Behind the TV, in the corner of the room, was a place where the floorboards were exposed. One, the furthest in the corner, was missing a segment. It was small, but it was probably the place into which Matthew had disappeared. To test the theory, I took some chocolate from the fridge. I ate a bit, to check it wasn't stale. Then I ate another bit, just to be on the safe side. I was very hungry. Finally, I broke off a third bit and placed it on a chopping board. I sliced it into tiny morsels with a paring knife and placed the pieces beside the hole in the floorboard, to tempt Matthew. Then I moved away and sat in the farthest corner of the room, with my back to the wall.

I had to wait for almost an hour but eventually Matthew appeared. He approached the chocolate and began to nibble at it. It was a lot for him to eat. Nevertheless, he managed to finish it. Then he retreated again into his hole. That evening, I overheard the girls having an argument. Clare was accusing Mills of having eaten some chocolate from the fridge. Mills denied it and I happened to know she was telling the truth. How did I know? Because in my mood of triumph, after I had located Matthew's entrance hole, I had eaten the rest of the chocolate myself.

Clare was convinced that Mills had done it but there was little she could say in the face of her denial. Eventually she asked Mills if she'd heard from Bernhardt. The question was clearly intended to cause pain, and it had its effect, because Mills sounded upset when she admitted that she hadn't. I felt bad for Mills but the news also gave me a sense of satisfaction. A couple of days before, I had been up in her room, passing the time, when it had occurred to me to check if she had left her laptop logged into Facebook. As it turned out, she had. I tracked down Bernhardt among her friends, and blocked him, so he wouldn't be able to send her a message.

* * *

After Mills broke up with me, I went mad. I don't know how else to describe it. And funnily enough, I had used to joke about this when we were going out, despite the fact that I knew Mills hated it. *I'm a writer*, I used to tell her. *I'll probably end up going mad*. And then I did go mad, and it wasn't at all amusing. It's hard to give a sense of madness to someone who's never experienced it. There are feelings you can have, like happy, sad, angry and so on. Mad is a different one. It's like another colour.

The best approach I can think of is to write a list of things I can remember, which I know to be true. By this method, perhaps, I can convey a sense of what it was like:

I stopped sleeping for more than a couple of hours a night.

I threw away everything that reminded me of her.

I became afraid of social contact.

I sometimes said aloud, 'I love her.'

I sometimes said aloud, 'I'm going to kill myself.'

I kept checking my phone to see if she'd called.

I could only read books that I had read before.

I walked to and from work, because it took longer.

I thought about her all the time.

I watched a lot of costume dramas and slept on the sofa.

I became convinced that we were fated to be together.

I took pride in the fact that I hadn't cried or vomited.

I imagined getting her back and decided I wouldn't want her.

I took Night Nurse, which made me groggy during the day.

I ate lunch on my own, and did the *Times* crossword.

I realised I didn't have any friends.

I became convinced that I was going blind.

I bought new pairs of reading glasses.

I went to the doctor with what I thought were genital warts.

I was told that they were freckles.

I was given sleeping pills.

I masturbated a lot.

I drank hot milk at night with a spoonful of honey.

I got drunk during the day.

I suffered from circular thought processes.

I dwelt on painful memories.

I got a text from her: 'Hope you're writing is going well.'

I felt sickened by her illiteracy.

I invented the acronym FLAB for her (Fat, Lazy And Boring).

I murmured 'Flab' to myself as I walked down the street.

I wondered if I had some kind of degenerative disease.

I hated her for the way she'd treated me.

I struggled to convince people that she'd treated me badly.

I listed the good things in my life: my flat, my job.

I lost my job.

I sat on park benches.

I visited the Viewing Platform at Heathrow Airport.

I dreamed about her a lot.

I thought about writing her a letter.

I thought about sending her compilation CDs.

I was disproportionately moved by bad films.

I was horrified by the sight of her new Facebook profile picture.

I thought it made her look like a slut.
I deleted her from my list of Facebook friends.
I deleted her number from my mobile phone.
I tried to forget her phone number but I couldn't.
I kept on hearing it, repeating in my head.
I turned my phone off at night so I wouldn't be tempted to check it.
I turned it on again in the small hours, to see if she'd called.
I couldn't think of anything that gave me pleasure.
I thought about different ways of killing myself.
I composed texts to her which I didn't send.
I wrote: 'You've taken all the colour out of my life.'
I wrote: 'I miss you so much.'
I wondered if I would ever get better.

* * *

The playwright Edward Albee has said that the first moment he began to suspect he had been adopted was when he was criticised by the people he thought of as his parents for taking a book down off a shelf. It wasn't that the book was immoral or a rare edition. It was because they didn't like the gap it left on the bookshelf. That story had always reminded me of the Howards. They had a library in their house, on the first floor, but it was just for show, part of Mr Howard's pretensions to being a man of letters. I had never known Mills or either of her parents enter this room.

The shelves were stocked with leather-bound books, some of which had pages you had to cut. There were complete sets by authors such as Kipling, Waugh and Greene. The very ones, in other words, you might expect to find in a house like this. There was even a copy of the book I've always associated with the worst kind of upper-middle-class smugness: Nancy Mitford's biography of Louis XIV, *The Sun King*.

51

I hasten to add that I've no particular desire to knock Kipling, Waugh or Greene. In fact, I tend to think of Graham Greene as the greatest English novelist of the 20th century. Whenever I see one of his books on a shelf in somebody else's home, I feel an urge to take it down and leaf through it, in search of my favourite passages.

One evening, that was what I did. After the girls had gone to bed, I went into the library, and, using the flashlight on my iPhone, made my way to the bookshelves at the other end. I sought out *The Quiet American*, took it down and examined it. I ran a fingertip along the compressed edges of the pages, and saw the path it cleared in the dust. Squatting on the floor, with my back against the wall, I began to flick through it. I found the passage where the two main characters are trapped in a watchtower in the middle of the Vietnamese countryside. As I read, the library seemed to melt away and I was in the watchtower with them: isolated, waiting for the dawn. Then the door into the library opened and the lights blazed on.

Clare crossed the room and approached the farthest set of shelves. She went up to the set of Greenes and paused in front of them. She was looking at the gap that had been occupied by *The Quiet American*. I stayed where I was, trying not to move a muscle. All she had to do was glance down and to her right, and she would have seen me. My head was lowered. I looked up at her from under my eyelids. She was a small, plain girl, barely more than five foot tall. She had to stand on her tiptoes to examine the books. At length, she took one down and smelt it. She almost sneezed, but managed to control it. Then she left, forgetting to turn off the lights.

As soon as she was gone, I moved over to the other end of the room and hid behind a chair. I knew there was a chance she might come back in, to turn off the lights. After a while, I could hear her in the bathroom upstairs, and I emerged from my hiding place. I moved back across the room and scanned the shelves, interested to see which Greene novel she had taken. The one missing was *The End of the Affair*.

The episode had been strangely dreamlike. While she'd been in the room, Clare had been oblivious to my presence. I had felt I could have waved a hand in front of her, without eliciting a reaction. At the same time, I knew it had been an incredibly close call. I had been careless, and according to Rule 5, I had to be punished.

It was time to initiate the third phase of my challenge. The goal of the first had been to avoid detection. That of the second had been to move around, when the girls were home. But it wasn't enough, I decided, to hear Mills. I wanted to see her too.

In her bedroom, facing the bed, were two tall mahogany wardrobes, one of which contained her clothes. The other had always been locked and I knew for a fact that Mills had mislaid the key. I knew this not only because I remembered her telling me so, but also because I had recently stumbled on this key, stashed away at the bottom of an ornamental sewing box. When I opened the wardrobe the following day, I found it contained a collection of toys from her childhood. There were games of Mousetrap and Hungry Hippos. A My Little Pony, with most of its pink shiny synthetic hair missing.

I removed these contents and carried them down to the lumber room. Then I did the same to the shelves, after sliding them out of their grooves. Once the shelves and toys had been stored away, I hurried back upstairs with Mr Howard's toolbox. I drilled three small holes in the doors of the now empty wardrobe, each in places where there was already a natural knot in the wood. Then I swept up the fallen fragments of sawdust and stood back to inspect my handiwork.

The Howards' home was unusually badly lit. I had always assumed this was one of Mr Howard's affectations. He had wanted to create the musty air of a museum, all shadows and display cases. For example, in one corner of the dining room – which, lacking windows, was the gloomiest room in the house – he had stationed a full-size stuffed grizzly bear, rearing for the kill. It had freaked me out at first, this creature, and whenever I'd walked through the dining room, I had tended to avoid looking at it. Recently, though, I had found it didn't bother me as much as it had used to. And what was true of the bear was true of the general ambience. I had grown to appreciate the aspects that before had made me uneasy.

Mills's bedroom wasn't the gloomiest room in the house, but it wasn't especially well lit. If you sat on her bed, you could barely see the holes I had drilled in the wardrobe, especially in their darker settings within the wood-knots.

At five in the afternoon, after shaving my head, I dropped to the floor of the bathroom and did press-ups until my pectoral muscles cramped. Then I had a bath, before slipping back into my skin-coloured cycling shorts. I went up to Mills's bedroom and climbed into the wardrobe, locking the door on myself from the inside. Through one of the holes, I could see the entrance to her room. Through another, her bed. Through the third, her dressing table. When I was in the least inconvenient position, with my knees up by my chin, the easiest hole to look through was the one that afforded a view of her bed.

As chance would have it, though, the day I'd chosen for progressing to Phase Three turned out to be one of the rare occasions on which Mills had evening plans. After a few hours, when nothing had happened, I got bored and left the wardrobe. I crept down to the landing and listened. Clare was in the kitchen. I could hear her opening a bottle of wine. Over the previous days, my powers of hearing seemed to have grown more acute. As Clare poured the first glass of wine out of the bottle, the liquid sound was as clear as if I had been in the room with her. I retreated back up the stairs, and locked myself in the wardrobe.

It was quite boring, squatting in the darkness of that space. To pass the time, I hummed the Lou Reed song *Perfect Day*, hearing the words in my head.

In the end, I think I nodded off, because the next thing I knew, there was light coming through the three holes and I could hear a female voice. It was Mills's voice, singing softly to herself. And the song she was singing was *Perfect Day*.

She sang in a soft, babyish voice, with the tone you would use if you were singing to a baby. A lullaby, to lull the thing to sleep. Was I the baby? Was she singing it to me? In my confused state, it struck me she might somehow realise I was crouched in her wardrobe, and this might be her way of letting me know that she knew.

I forced the rational part of my brain to engage. There was no way that Mills could know I was there. And if she had become aware of it, she would have been unlikely to sing me a lullaby. She was singing that song for no more sinister reason than because she liked it. And she was singing it in that tone because she was drunk.

Careful not to make a noise, I moved my eye to the nearest of the holes. She was lying on her bed, singing to herself. But she didn't sing the words as they should have been. She sang instead of drinks and Graham in the park.

It was a joke we'd shared, one of a series of comic mishearings of song lyrics. Another we had liked, which had made a nice pair with the 'Graham' mishearing, was the opening of the Simon and Garfunkel song *The Sound of Silence*. We'd liked to imagine the first line was actually addressed to someone called Douglas. And for a while, because of this, Mills had entered me in her phone as Douglas, so that when I rang, Douglas was the name that came up on the screen. I had responded by saving her number in my address book under the name of Graham. That had been in the early days, when a sense of humour was almost all we had in common. Later we had replaced these nicknames with our real names. And when I look back now, I feel that this may have been one of the early stages in our long process of decline.

When I put my eye to the hole again, Mills was no longer on her bed. I moved to the next hole along, and saw her at her dressing table. She took off her coat and then, crossing her arms in front of her, attempted to raise her top. It caught for a moment on her face. When she managed to pull the thing off, she was smiling, as if amused by her own clumsiness. Sitting there in just her bra, she brushed her hair for a while. Then she put the hairbrush down on the table in front of her and reached behind her to take off her bra. She found the clasp and unhooked it. The bra loosened and she removed it. Bare to the waist, she examined herself in the mirror.

A phone began to ring in the pocket of her coat. She reached for it and looked to see who was calling. The discovery made her frown. She tossed the phone away from her onto the bed, pulled on a dressing gown, and left the room. The phone continued ringing. Eventually, it stopped. But then it started again. Mills came back into the room and in exasperation picked it up and answered. The way she sat, perched on the edge of her bed, I could only see the bottom half of her. But I could tell from the conversation that the person she was talking to was Bernhardt. Her tone was hard at first, but it gradually softened. She even became apologetic. He was accusing her of having blocked him on Facebook. I wanted to call out from my hiding place and warn her not to let him twist things round like this. If anything, he was the one who ought to be apologising, for the outrageous way he had treated her. There had been a time when I had benefited from Mills's gullibility. It had seemed like a blessing to me, then, but now I cursed her for that quality.

In the end, to my horror, she even invited him to a dinner party she was organising. As I listened to this part of their exchange, the darkness surrounding me in the wardrobe seemed to grow a little darker. It wasn't just that he was back on the scene. It was also how pleased Mills seemed to be about it. After hanging up, she moved out of sight, and when she reappeared, she had taken off the dressing gown and pulled on a pair of knickers and a T-shirt. She went to the bathroom to brush her teeth. Then she came back in and got into bed. The light went out and I could hear the tinny buzz of her headphones playing music.

I waited until her breathing was regular, and then I unlocked the wardrobe door and opened it silently. The room was dark, but there was a little light. I could make out her face in the gloom. I could see the shape of her hair, spread out upon the pillow. I stood at the end of the bed, and watched her for a while.

* * *

It wasn't my fault, strictly speaking, that Bernhardt had got back in touch with Mills. But I still interpreted it as a failing on my part. Rule 5 was invoked once more. I abandoned Phase Three and moved on to Phase Four. Remember the time I had taken some chocolate from the fridge to give to Matthew, and what had happened as a result? The girls had had an argument about who had eaten the chocolate. In other words, I had done something that had had a direct impact on their lives. This, I decided, would be the basis of Phase Four. I had listened. I had watched. Now I would develop a way to have an impact on proceedings.

It wasn't going to be easy. As always, when I embarked on a new phase, every time I thought about it, I became excited. And as often, I turned to Matthew for inspiration.

Why is it that mice are assumed to be so interested in cheese? It sounds like the kind of common perception that's unlikely to be true, like the idea that bulls are infuriated by the sight of a red rag. But if you're looking for proof, I am in a position to provide it. I found a piece of cheddar wrapped in cling film in the fridge. I took it out and unwrapped it, before cutting the thinnest slice from each of its six sides, so it was left in the same shape as before. Then I broke up these rectangular wafers into more manageable crumbs of cheese.

I laid these out in a trail, starting from the mouse hole and leading out in a curve to the edge of the carpet, upon which I was seated cross-legged, naked except for my skin-coloured cycling shorts. Finally, Matthew appeared. He made his way forward, pausing by each fragment of cheese, to nibble on it. He really did seem to enjoy it. He reached the last bit, which was a few inches from my feet. He swallowed. Then he sat upright on his haunches, with his little legs raised.

How, you may be wondering, did any of this provide me with inspiration? It was nothing in particular that Matthew did. It was his way. He had a silence. It was how long he had waited before he had appeared at all. This is how it works in the animal kingdom. Silence is all-important. If you're a predator or if you're preyed upon. Silence and stillness. The ability to become your surroundings. And knowing the ways, when movement is required, to minimise it.

* * *

On the morning of the dinner party, I went into the kitchen and let fall a droplet of washing-up liquid onto the centre of every pot and pan. In each case, I then added a splash of warm water. I tilted the water this way and that until it covered the base. Then I shook out the water. I went into the drawing room and selected a CD from the case that's in the low cupboard against the wall, under shelves of pristine books, beside the rows of African throwing spears that Mr Howard brought back from one of his many visits to South Africa. I put the CD in the CD tray and played it once through. Then I descended the stairs into the basement for the tool box, which I knew contained a tube of superglue. I tore off tiny pieces of paper from a sheet of A4 and chewed them until they tasted bitter in my mouth. I stuck up with blu-tac a fresh sheet of A4 on one wall of the dining room. Then from the other side, I practised blowing spitballs of paper at a target. I carried on until I was pretty accurate.

Then I dropped to the floor and did a series of sit-ups and press-ups.

THE DINNER PARTY

Written by
Jack Raphael

69 Milton Road
London W11
jack_raphael2015@outlook.com
0044 7985 ******

INT. STAIRCASE AND HALL. EVENING

In a grand, dimly lit hallway, a large gilt-edged oval
mirror hangs on the wall. MILLS, a beautiful girl in
her mid-twenties, comes running downstairs, dressed to
the nines. She quickly checks her reflection in the
mirror and then she answers the door.

Outside it's raining hard. Taking shelter in the
porch is an English couple. The boy, CHARLIE, has a
small body and a large head. The girl, BRIDIE, is
taller than him. She has a large mouth and small
breasts.

                    CHARLIE & BRIDIE
                   (in unison)
          Millsworth!

                    MILLS
                   (apologetically)
          No one's come—

She is blushing as they kiss hello.

                    MILLS (CONT'D)
          Three people cancelled. Which
          means we're only five.

                    CHARLIE
                   (walking in)
          Perfect. I can't stand other
          people.

He produces two bottles of wine, which he hands to
Mills, and a six-pack of lager, which he keeps.

                    MILLS
          Hello, Bridie.

                    BRIDIE
          Hello! Hello!

                    MILLS
          I'm sorry about the rain.

                    CHARLIE
          It's hardly your fault, old
          sausage.

                    BRIDIE
          But isn't it beastly, though?

As they dispense with coats and umbrellas, CLARE, a
diminutive, pointy-faced American in her late
twenties, descends the stairs. She hasn't bothered
to dress up, and doesn't greet Charlie or Bridie
with much enthusiasm. They aren't her friends.

INT. DRAWING ROOM.

It's a dimly-lit, eccentrically furnished room,
with a low lime-green coffee table, some African
throwing spears on stands against the wall, and at
one end, a large bay window veiled by a heavy gold-
thread brocade curtain. In front of it stands a
spacious rich-red Slovakian marriage chest.

                    CHARLIE
               (holding up a can)
          Mind if I tuck in?

                    BRIDIE
          You're looking gorgeous in that
          dress, Camilla. Who's the
          mysterious fifth guest?

On cue, the doorbell RINGS.

INT. HALL.

BERNHARDT is waiting in the porch. Six foot tall, broadly built, with long, luxuriant hair. He is wearing Chinos, brown suede shoes and a Barbour coat. In one hand, he carries an umbrella. In the other, he holds a plastic bag. Mills steps forward to kiss him. But he makes a formal bow, snapping his heels together, and bending at the neck.

> BERNHARDT
> (in a Teutonic accent)
> So sorry to be late.

> MILLS
> You aren't late.

> BERNHARDT
> I am ten minutes late.

> MILLS
> (dubiously)
> Okay. Well, you're forgiven.

> BERNHARDT
> (handing her the bag)
> I brought you these.

> MILLS
> That's so sweet of you.

Mills unwraps the first of two wrapped gifts, to discover that it contains a packet of rodent killer.

> MILLS (CONT'D)
> Gosh. That's really—

                    BERNHARDT
                (hanging up his Barbour)
            You said that you had mice.

                      MILLS
            I see. How practical.

The second gift is a box of Swiss chocolates.

                   MILLS (CONT' D)
                (genuinely pleased)
            Lindt! My favourite!

She kisses him delightedly on the cheek. After a
pause, they kiss properly. We view them from above,
as if we were spying on them. Finally Mills takes
Bernhardt' s hand and leads him into the drawing room.

INT. DRAWING ROOM.

                      CHARLIE
                 (offering a hand)
            I' m Charlie.

                    BERNHARDT
                  (taking it)
            Bernhardt.

                      CLARE
                (offering no hand)
            Clare.

                      BRIDIE
            Bridie.

                    BERNHARDT
                 (making sure)
            Bridie?

                    BRIDIE
          I know. Isn't it awful? When I
          was little, everyone used to
          call me 'Bridle' because I was
          so obsessed with horses.
          Bridie's a slight improvement,
          don't you think?

                    CHARLIE
          She also sounds like a horse.

He glances at his girlfriend, and then lets out an
extravagant neigh. Bridie glares at him at first,
but she finds it funny really. (When she laughs,
she actually does sound a bit like a horse.)

                    MILLS (O.S.)
                (calling from the kitchen)
          Where's the corkscrew?

Clare sighs. We follow her into the dining room.
But then we duck under the dining room table and
view the bottom halves of Mills and Clare, in the
kitchen.

                    CLARE
          That's really weird. It was
          definitely here yesterday.

INT. DRAWING ROOM.

Charlie, Bridie and Bernhardt smile at each other.
Charlie is the only one who has a drink. He sits on
the chest, which stands in front of the curtains.
The chest is big enough that it might conceivably
hold a person.

                    CHARLIE

                    (making conversation)
               Ghastly weather we've been
               having.

                         BERNHARDT
               This is London, after all.

                         BRIDIE
               What's that got to do with it?

                         BERNHARDT
               England is rather famous for its
               rain.

                         BRIDIE
               And I suppose it never rains in
               Germany.

                         BERNHARDT
               Austria.

                         BRIDIE
               What?

                         BERNHARDT
               I am from Austria.

Charlie finishes what's in his glass.

                         CHARLIE
               I'd better give the girls a
               hand. If we can't find the
               corkscrew, there's always the
               old thumb trick.

He waggles his thumbs as he goes out.

Bernhardt and Bridie are left in the room. She's seated in an armchair. He stands, pretending interest in the African throwing spears. There is an awkward silence between them, which Mills registers as she comes in.

> MILLS
> (brightly)
> Shall we have some music?

When she tries to eject the CD, she finds it's stuck. She tries again, with the same result. Charlie reappears, a beer in one hand, a bottle of wine in the other. Clare accompanies him, with four glasses.

> MILLS (CONT'D)
> The tray won't come out.

> CLARE
> Just play whatever's in there.

Mills presses play and a song starts. It is the BBC charity cover version of Lou Reed's *Perfect Day*.

> MILLS
> (sniffing)
> I always loved this song.

> CLARE
> But not this version, right?

> MILLS
> Isn't it strange, the way—

> CLARE
> (gleefully)
> Mills? Are you crying?

                    MILLS
              (turning away)
          Of course not.

                    CHARLIE
          Do you want me to turn it off?

                    MILLS
          No. Leave it on.
              (distracted)
          Leave it on. I like it—

The CAMERA moves around the room, as if searching
for someone. Behind a chair. Under a table. Then it
moves out into the hall and rests on the first
flight of stairs. Two bare feet are visible on the
top step.

INT. KITCHEN. LATER

Perfect Day still plays in the background. Mills is
at the stove, stirring a pot. Behind her the
unfocused figure of a man, who appears to be naked,
moves swiftly into the dining room from the hall,
and is then lost from view. Oblivious, Mills tastes
the soup and frowns. Something's not right. She
adds a pinch of salt.

INT. DINING ROOM. LATER

The dining room is dark apart the flickering light
from candles in the centre of the rectangular
dining table. In one corner, shrouded in darkness,
is a full-size stuffed grizzly bear. *Perfect Day*
continues to play.

                                        CUT TO:

Bernhardt looking down at his soup.

                                        CUT TO:

Bridie looking up at the ceiling.

                                        CUT TO:

Clare forcing herself to take a sip, without
pleasure.

                                        CUT TO:

Mills looking from one to the other of them in
dismay.

                                        CUT TO:

Charlie devouring his soup with relish.

                    CHARLIE
               (glancing up)
          What?

                    MILLS
          It tastes of soap, doesn't it?

                    CLARE
          Maybe a teensy bit.

Bridie snorts. Bernhardt smiles, but not
convincingly.

                    CHARLIE
          Is there any more?

                    BRIDIE
          I don't know how you can eat it.

                    MILLS
          It's so awful! I'm so sorry!

                    CHARLIE
               (taking a slurp of beer)
          You're all talking rubbish. I
          think the soap's delicious. The
          soup, I mean.

Bridie and Clare laugh. Mills smiles nervously, and
looks at Bernhardt for support. He doesn't offer
it.

                    CHARLIE (CONT' D)
               (rising to his feet)
          Mind if I help myself?

                    CLARE
          Don't forget to use your soap
          spoon.

                    CHARLIE
          In my opinion, it's the soap of
          the day.

                    CLARE
          The *soap du jour*, you mean.

Mills reaches across and squeezes Bernhardt's hand.

                    MILLS
          Are you okay?

                    BERNHARDT
          Of course.

Mills attempts to force a smile from him. It
doesn't come at first. But at last he smiles and

squeezes her hand in return. The song comes to an end in the drawing room. There's a pause. Then *Perfect Day* starts again.

>   BERNHARDT (CONT'D)
>   (rising abruptly)
>   Forgive me. May I?

>   MILLS
>   I think it's stuck.

>   BERNHARDT
>   We can listen to the radio.

He strides out. Clare and Bridie exchange looks.

>   CUT TO:

A burst of laughter.

>   MILLS
>   I've got a good one. Can I tell
>   you mine?

The music playing is classical, more cheerful. They have nearly finished their main course. The only sign that there was anything wrong with it is the way they have all left their onions on one side of the plate.

>   MILLS (CONT'D)
>   What do you get if you put a
>   baby in a blender?
>   (beat)
>   An erection.

Charlie laughs. Clare smiles. Bridie doesn't get it. Bernhardt gets it, but winces. He doesn't like it.

Later. They have moved on to cheese. Charlie's head droops a little. Four empty cans stand by his plate. There follows a medium-length silence, of the kind you don't get if a dinner party is going really well.

                    CHARLIE
              (rising clumsily)
         Think I might move on to wine,
         if it's all the same with you.

Bernhardt takes out his iPhone. He checks the screen.

                    BRIDIE
         Can I ask you something?

                    BERNHARDT
         Of course.

                    BRIDIE
         What do you do?

                    BERNHARDT
              (pocketing his phone)
         I'm a banker.

                    BRIDIE
         Yes, I know, but what do you do?

                    CHARLIE
              (with a new bottle of wine)
         Ta-dah!

Charlie attempts to push the cork of the bottle in.

                    BERNHARDT
        It's a little hard to explain.

                    BRIDIE
        Give it a go.

                    BERNHARDT
                (looking at Mills)
        I try to make money for people
        who already have a lot of money.

Charlie succeeds in forcing the cork into the
bottle.

                    BRIDIE
        Yes. Thank you. I know what it
        means to be a banker. But what
        do you, personally, do?

POV CHANGE. We are looking up at the table from a
level below it, and from further away. We can hear
suppressed breathing. We seem to be viewing events
through the eyes of someone hidden behind the
stuffed bear.

                    BERNHARDT
        As I said, it's difficult to
        explain.

                    CHARLIE
                (topping up Clare's glass)
        Give the guy a poor— I mean,
        give the poor guy a break.

                    BRIDIE
        I'm only asking him what he
        does.

                    CHARLIE
          (topping up Mills's glass)
     That really is one of the most
     boring questions you can ask
     someone.

                    BRIDIE
     It's only boring if the answer's
     boring.

From our POV, we can see a straw being raised, and
pointed at the dining table. Specifically, it is
aimed in the direction of Bernhardt.

                    CHARLIE
          (topping up Bridie's glass)
     Do you know what Dai Llewellyn
     used to say, when people asked
     him what he did?

                    CLARE
     No. What did Dai used to say?

                    CHARLIE
     When people asked him what he
     did, Dai Llewellyn used to say,
     'I fuck Alsatians in lifts.'

Charlie and Bridie burst out laughing. Clare
smiles, shaking her head. Mills glances at
Bernhardt, who is wincing. Still laughing, Charlie
reaches forward with the bottle of red wine to fill
Bernhardt's glass.

We hear a sharp exhalation.

                    BERNHARDT
              (pushing back his chair)
          God in heaven!

He rises to his feet, legs apart, arms held out,
gazing down at the front of his white shirt, which
is now speckled with red wine. Charlie stares in
dismay at what he thinks he has done. Bernhardt,
who also assumes the wine must have splashed as
Charlie poured it, glares at him, furious.

                    CHARLIE
          Lord. Sorry.

                    BERNHARDT
          You fool.

He looks down again at his wine-marked shirt, his
mouth twitching. Then he leaves the room.

Bridie lets out a loud raspberry.

                    MILLS
          It's not funny, Bridie.

                    BRIDIE
          It's quite funny.

                    CHARLIE
          I don't know what happened. I
          was just pouring the wine—

                    BRIDIE
          You're just a fool.

A paper pellet, soaked in wine, lies under the
table near Bernhardt's chair. No one suspects
anything is amiss, except Clare, who has noticed a

line of red specks crossing the table at an angle.
She turns and looks at the grizzly bear, as if she
thinks it might be responsible. She approaches,
then peers behind it, squinting into the shadows.

There's no one there.

INT. BASEMENT LAVATORY.

Bernhardt is sprinkling water on his shirt front
and wiping at the red wine stains. He mutters his
annoyance in German. A noise makes him turn and
look at the door.

The glass is frosted, so he can't see what's on the
other side. But there's no shadow or silhouette.

INT. DRAWING ROOM

The classical music on the radio is growing louder.
Bridie has the remote control in her hand.

                    CHARLIE
          A waltz!

He grabs Clare and starts to waltz her round the
room. Mills is on the sofa, smoking, casting
glances at the door, through which she expects
Bernhardt to come in.

INT. BASEMENT LAVATORY

Bernhardt is still examining his shirt front,
tutting to himself. Again, a noise makes him turn
and look at the door. Again, there's nothing to
see.

He moves to the door to leave, but the door won't

open. He tries the handle firmly. It's definitely
locked.

>   BERNHARDT
>   Hello? Is anyone there?

There's no response.

>   BERNHARDT (CONT'D)
>   Charlie?
>   (beat)
>   I am sorry I lost my temper—

He tries the door more forcefully. It still won't
open. He bangs on the glass with his palm.

>   BERNHARDT (CONT'D)
>   Let me out. This isn't funny.

INT. DRAWING ROOM

The music is loud enough now that no one would be
able to hear if someone were calling for help
downstairs. Bridie has grabbed one of the African
spears from the wall and is dancing around with it,
warrior-style.

INT. BASEMENT LAVATORY

>   BERNHARDT
>   (shouting)
>   Camilla? Hello?

He hits the door with his fist and turns away,
sitting on the lavatory, his head in his hands.

INT. BASEMENT

The only light in the basement comes from the
lavatory door. In the darkest corner of the
basement, we can make out a pair of feet. They
approach the lavatory door. A hand reaches out. It
holds a key.

INT. DRAWING ROOM

The music is now even louder. Bridie is whooping,
her hand to her mouth, like a Red Indian brave. As
Charlie waltzes Clare, he reaches out and grabs
hold of Mills's hand. She tries to resist, but has
no choice but to be drawn into the dancing.

INT. BASEMENT LAVATORY

Bernhardt reads a book of cartoons by Giles.

INT. BASEMENT

The shadowy hand moves silently to the lock of the
door. It turns the key, unlocking the door. But it
doesn't open it. The hand retreats.

INT. BASEMENT LAVATORY

Bernhardt suddenly puts the book down and runs to
the door, grabbing the handle. His surprise on
finding that it opens is surpassed by his even
greater surprise at the sight revealed by the
opened door.

Just a few feet away is a semi-naked figure, caught
in the act of creeping away. The figure is very
thin and very pale. He has a shaved head. It is
JACK.

                         BERNHARDT
                    (astonished)
              Who are you?

                         JACK
              Please—

                         BERNHARDT
              Who the fuck are you?

                         JACK
                    (approaching)
              Please— Don' t tell her.

                         BERNHARDT
                    (pushing past him)
              This place is a madhouse.

                         JACK
                    (grabbing his arm)
              No!

Bernhardt, who is bigger than Jack, easily shakes
him off. Then he starts to climb the stairs. Jack
lunges after him, managing to grab his ankle.
Bernhardt falls hard, and slides down the stairs.

INT. DRAWING ROOM.

The music is wilder than ever. Mills and Clare have
seized spears like Bridie. The girls are dancing
round Charlie, who is pretending to plead for
mercy.

INT. BASEMENT.

Bernhardt is on his feet again. He pushes Jack away
and turns to climb the stairs. But Jack is after

him. This time, when Bernhardt falls, he hits his
face on a step. He touches his cheek and finds
blood on his hand.

He advances on Jack and grips him round the throat.
Jack's eyes widen. His hands are round Bernhardt's
wrists, trying to prise him off. Then one of his
hands moves behind his back, reaching on the side
table that holds, in addition to a set of smart
ivory-backed hairbrushes, a pair of silver
scissors.

A moment later, it is Bernhardt's turn to widen his
eyes. He releases Jack and steps back. The light
from the lavatory reveals a new stain spreading
across his shirt. A brighter red. Jack is coughing,
one hand at his neck, where he was being throttled.
In the other, the scissors gleam wetly.

Bernhardt bends forward, his hands on his stomach,
and turns to climb the stairs. He doesn't get far.
Jack is on his feet, the scissors gripped in his
hand. He slams them into Bernhardt's back.
Bernhardt falls again. Jack straddles him, and with
difficulty, he pulls the scissors out. Then,
gripping in both hands, thrusts them down again.

INT. DRAWING ROOM

The music is reaching its climax. The girls are
pretending to sacrifice Charlie with their spears.
Charlie clutches his stomach, and falls
theatrically across the coffee table. As he does
so, he knocks over a glass of red wine, which he
tries unsuccessfully to prevent from spilling.

                    MILLS
          Charlie!

                    CHARLIE
        Oh Christ. Sorry.

                    CLARE
        I knew that was going to happen.

                    BRIDIE
        Quick. Someone get some salt.

                    CLARE
        No. Salt's no use.

                    BRIDIE
        What are you talking about?

Mills comes back into the room with table salt.

                    CLARE
        You got any white wine?

                    BRIDIE
            (taking the salt)
        Here. I'll do it.

                    MILLS
        Will someone turn that music
        off?

Charlie picks up the remote and silences the radio.

                    CLARE
            (to Charlie)
        Not your lucky night.

                    CHARLIE
        Well, if you will insist on
        stabbing me to death, what do
        you expect?

They watch Bridie pour salt over the wine stain.

                    MILLS
          I hope Bernhardt's alright.

                    CLARE
          Where did he go?

                    MILLS
          Downstairs, I think.

                    CHARLIE
          To check his hair.

Mills gives him a look.

                    CHARLIE (CONT'D)
          I mean, to clean up.

                    MILLS
          But he's been gone for ages.

                    CHARLIE
          He's got a lot of hair.

                    MILLS
          I'd better go see if he's okay.

                    BRIDIE
          No. Let him sulk for a while.
          He'll come back up when he's
          ready.

Mills hesitates.

                    BRIDIE (CONT'D)
          Right. I think that's all I can
          do.

The wine stain is now completely covered with salt.

                    BRIDIE (CONT' D)
                 (getting to her feet)
          Would anyone else like coffee?

                    MILLS
          Would you make it, Clare? I
          really think I should check on
          Bernhardt.

INT. BASEMENT

Mills descends into the dark basement. When she
tries to turn on a light, she finds it doesn' t
work.

There' s no sign of Bernhardt. Nor, in the gloom, is
there any indication that a struggle has taken
place.

                    MILLS
          Bernhardt?

There' s no answer from the shadows.

INT. DRAWING ROOM

Mills appears in the doorway.

                    MILLS
          He' s gone.

                    CHARLIE
          What do you mean, gone?

                    MILLS
          Well, he' s not downstairs.

                    BRIDIE
          You mean he just buggered off?

                    MILLS
          It looks like it.

                    BRIDIE
          How unbelievably rude.

                    CHARLIE
                (blaming himself)
          Millsworth, I'm so sorry.

                    MILLS
          I can't believe he just went.

                    CHARLIE
          You're sure he's not upstairs?

                    MILLS
          His coat's gone.

After a pause, a phone VIBRATES, making them all
jump. It's Mills's, on a shelf beside the music
system.

                    MILLS (CONT'D)
                (picking it up)
          It's from him.

                    CHARLIE
          What does it say?

                    MILLS
                (reading aloud)
          'I'm so sorry I left. I just
          felt that you would all have a
          more enjoyable evening if I was
          not there.'

                    CHARLIE
          How very peculiar.

                    BRIDIE
          It's still jolly rude. I hope
          you're not going to reply.

                    MILLS
               (dejected)
          No, you're right. It's really
          rude.

                    CLARE
               (appearing with a tray)
          Coffee.

INT. STORE ROOM. LATER

In the centre of the room is a wooden rocking
horse, its face concealed by a Barbour coat, which
has been thrown over it. On the floor lies the body
of Bernhardt, face-down, the shirt soaked in blood.
Jack is crouched in a corner, as far away from the
body as possible. He is hugging his knees. There is
blood on his hands and also smeared across his bare
torso.

He tosses an iPhone away from him and it lands on
the blood-stained shirt. It pauses there a moment,
before sliding off on to the floor.

                                        FADE OUT.

INT. STORE ROOM. FANTASY - NIGHT

Jack's face grimaces in pain. When he opens his
eyes, the body of Bernhardt has disappeared.

There is a KNOCKING, to which he doesn't respond.

When he blinks, the body is there again. When he
blinks again, it has vanished. Then Jack sees DEAD
BERNHARDT astride the rocking horse. There is the
sound of MOCKING LAUGHTER. Grim-faced, Dead
Bernhardt holds the reins of the rocking horse with
one hand. With the other, he holds out a plastic
bottle, filled with urine. Voices echo in Jack's
head.

                    VOICE 1
          She give me bad face.

                    VOICE 2
          Leave it on. I like it.

There's a knocking at the door, which he ignores.

                    VOICE 3
          Do you think you're still in
          love with him?

                    VOICE 2
          Leave it on. I like it.

Dead Bernhardt shakes the urine bottle at Jack.

                    DEAD BERNHARDT
          Prost! Prost!

Again there's a knocking at the door, which he
ignores. Reluctantly, Jack takes the bottle from
Dead Bernhardt and unscrews the cap. He takes a sip
of urine followed by a series of gulps. Dead
Bernhardt wrests the bottle from him and pours it
over his head.

INT. MILLS'S BEDROOM. FANTASY

Mills and Jack are in bed, making love.

> MILLS
> (smiling up at him)
> You're so fucking fit.

There's a KNOCKING. Jack turns to look at the door.
When he turns back, it's not Mills he's in bed
with, but Dead Bernhardt.

> DEAD BERNHARDT
> (smiling up at him)
> You are so fucking fit.

INT. STORE ROOM. FANTASY

Jack cowers in the corner of the store room, one
hand to his mouth. He vomits through his fingers,
trying to catch the spilling vomit in his other
hand.

There is APPLAUSE. Turning, Jack sees not faces but
hands at the window: hands clapping, applauding his
performance. He looks for Dead Bernhardt, in order
to conceal him, but he is nowhere to be seen.

There's a KNOCKING at the door.

INT. MILLS'S BEDROOM. FANTASY

Jack is in the darkness of Mills's wardrobe,
looking through one of the peepholes. On the other
side of the peephole, another eye appears, staring
back at him.

INT. STORE ROOM. FANTASY

Roaring like a monster, Jack trashes the store room, pulling over the rail of national costumes, breaking up furniture. He stops when he notices the mouse creeping in through a crack at the foot of the door.

Overcome with pity, he picks the mouse up. He holds it in his hand like a jewel. He starts to sob.

PART THREE

III

AN INTRODUCTION TO PARKOUR

To the uninitiated, parkour involves jumping around on rooftops. To devotees, it's a way of life. It's a philosophy, emotional as well as physical, a means of achieving freedom through movement, closing the gap that man has created between himself and his environment, returning to harmony with our surroundings and also mastering them. Unsurprisingly for a movement (or, as it has been called, a *movement movement*) which sprang up here and there, and accumulated influences from a range of sources, it isn't easy to give an authoritative account of the origins of parkour. But it's generally agreed that a key figure in its early history was the French naval officer Georges Hébert. In 1902, Hébert was stationed on the Caribbean island of Martinique, when the volcano erupted. In the ensuing crisis, during which he personally facilitated the evacuation of some 700 people, he was frustrated by the clumsiness of the evacuees, and by what he saw as his own inefficiency in trying to help them. From this single seed grew two shoots that would become central to the spirit of parkour: the first being the speed and efficiency of movement, the second being the duty and ability to help others. Or as Hébert himself put it, encapsulating the movement's philosophy in a phrase: *être fort pour être utile*. He went on to write *Methode naturelle*, a manual summing up his theories on movement. In due course, this book was studied by a French soldier named Raymond Belle, who fought in Indochina during the 1950s. He developed many of its ideas and combined them with techniques that had already been used by the Army in tackling assault courses, which in French are known as *parcours du combatant*. Hence the name *parkour*. Raymond's son David (b. 1973) has popularised the sport (although many parkour practitioners regard sport as too trivial a term to describe what they do) by his appearances in commercials and in the Luc Besson movie *District 13*. Its influence is also clear in the opening of the James Bond film *Casino Royale* and in certain scenes in the Jason Bourne franchise. Traceurs, as parkourians call themselves, have defended this exposure, pointing out that these films show parkour used in emergency situations, as a way of moving from one place to another as quickly and efficiently as possible. They are less forgiving of freerunning, a rival sport that encourages competition, favours flashy tricks, and which, many traceurs say, is in direct conflict with the spirit of parkour.

The following terms are commonly used in parkour:

Atterissage réception: landing
Équilibre: moving along the crest of something
Équilibre de chat: moving on all fours
Franchissement: moving through a gap between obstacles
Laché: swinging and dropping
Passe muraille: scaling a wall
Passement: vaulting
Planche: pulling yourself onto something with your arms
Roulade: forward roll
Saut de bras: jumping and catching onto something
Saut de précision: jumping from one stationary position to another
Saut de mur: jumping onto a wall

IN THE BEGINNING WAS THE WORD
And how fucking boring must that have been,
when there was just one fucking word? Whoever
heard of such a thing? When there was just one
word to sing, what kind of song was that?
A dirge. A monotonous moan.
What was the word? I'll tell you. It was ME.
And ME was man. And man made God contented
for a time. But ME was lonely. So God created
a second word. The second word was WE.
WE was woman, the opposite of ME.
And God created poetry.

* * *

Harder to write a poem than a novel.
That's why no one does it anymore.
Harder to read a poem than a novel.
That's why no one does it anymore.

* * *

I spend a great deal of my time on the lavatory,
coaxing my sphincter with an exploratory finger.
You see, since recent events, I haven't been able
to go. No, not once. It's a burden, I can tell you.
It's shitter's block, if I may coin a phrase.
I've been sitting not shitting on this lavatory
for days. What can the matter be?
When it comes, it's splatterpunk.
It's grand guignol. Jackson Pollock

would envy my blacks and reds.
At the same time I let out a sound,
half roar, half strangled shriek,
the rawest noise I've made all week.
I stand and spin. I spatter ivory-backed
hairbrushes, Victorian photographs,
dark-eyed boys with centre partings,
a group of gamekeepers staring,
glaring at posterity. At me.

I'm red in tooth and claw.
I'm natural. I dip my paw
in blood-black shit and give myself a stripe
on either cheek. It's camouflage, you see?

Now you see me, now you don't.
I explode up the stairs like blood-shit,
streaking through the empty house,
this way, that way, I'm a ballerina.
Into Mills's room and fuck the bed.
This is easier said than done, but
somehow I manage it.

You reach a point,
you too will reach a point,
where the past is more
real than the present
and the only future you have
is the hope of getting her back.

The hope of getting her back,
the hope of getting on with her,
the hope of getting on to her,

the hope of getting her on her back:
that's what keeps me going,
that's what gets me going,
when I think of it,
and I think of it
all the time.

I can make it happen,
I'm going to make it happen,
I'm going to make it with Mills.
I'm going to use my superpowers,
my powers of invisibility,
my powers of movement,
my insight into the female mind.

IV

TODAY I'M HANGING out in the American's space. And the contrast is stark. Camilla's room, you'd think had never seen a cleaner. Clare's? Oh, see the OCD! When she makes her bed, she folds back the sheet-corner, like some mad maid in a hotel. Her concise collection of books shows a marked preference for short novels with the word 'sea' in the title.

The Old Man and the Sea. The Sea, The Sea. The Sea.

The OCD's a given. Do we now add ADD? Indeed we do.

Or maybe those sliver-books, designed to deliver their shiver in a single sitting, suggest a controlling temperament. Clare folds, like bedsheets, the corners of her pages. Makes notes in their slender margins. Read, for an example, what she has written on page 22 of *The End of the Affair*.

The invisible style. Greene writes so well, he ceases to exist.

That's beautiful, don't you find? The idea that a writer, if he writes well enough, literally disappears. Every good book, then, is ghost-written.

For another sample, at the top of page 90, there's this:

Pride in the poison. The more hate, the greater is God's love, for forgiving him. The sinner sanctified. The damned divine.

I'm less impressed. I know where that thought came from.

I snap shut the book and glance at the snapshot on my phone, to ensure it's back in the right position. Then I snap into an *équilibre de chat*. Laché. Franchement. *Forward roll.*

Clogged with clothes, I'm silent still. Still silent but not still. As I move or groove downstairs, I dance. I'm a dancer. I glance into the drawing room, see Clare and carry on down. Into the basement, where I dance on Bernhardt's grave.

Atterissage réception. Passement.

I've never rated the rain. Like the lack of Mills. Like a sugar low. Like pain. The only way to avoid it is to stay indoors, which is what I've been doing. Forty days and forty nights. Fasting. Lasting. Listening in the dark. The time has come to fast-forward into the present. I'm a time traveller, me. Here is my coat, these are my shoes, this is my travelling bag. I'm a visitor from her past. I *am* her past. I'm starting to catch up with her.

It will be good to catch up, I think. It'll be a blast.

I lumber into the lumber room. I raise the rained-on pane.

And I'm out.

As I skirt the house, I keep a hand against the wall. I pause at the corner, to let some passers-by pass by. A gang of girly gigglers. To get from here to the porch, I shall have to break my contact with the house. I take a deep breath. Release it. Then I plunge forward into the black air of the night, blade-nicks of rain cutting my lips and eyelids like a shower of razor blades, as I scuttle from my shuttle in a V-shaped trajectory. Reach the steps, plant a hand on the bollard, and wrench myself up. Into the blessed porch.

I touch two fingers to the side of my throat. My pulse throbs. I wait half a minute, to regain some sangfroid. Then compress the ball of the bell.

The door opens. Clare says, 'Yes?'

'Is Mills in?' I ask, knowing the answer well.

'No. She's out. She should be back soon, though.'

She looks me up and down. Trainers. Trousers. Hat.

'Do you want to come in and wait for her?'

'Yeah. That'd be ace. Thanks for that.'

(*Ace?* What was that about, you prat?)

It's so long since I spoke to anyone, I have to plan each sentence, as if I'm speaking French. How, for instance, should I introduce myself? *I'm Jack.* Sounds a bit curt. *My name is Jack.* Semi-autistic. *I'm Jack, by the way.* That's nearer. *I'm Jack, by the way. I used to go out with Mills.* Don't be a volunteerer.

'I'm Jack, by the way.'

Clare double-takes. Mills's ex (she must be thinking).

Her mouth purses into an interested, an almost wily smile.

'I'm Clare.' A hand appears in mine. 'Pleased to meet you.'

In the withdrawing room, she offers me a G&T. I see spread-eagled on the coffee table her blotted copy of *The End of the Affair.* My interest's on the dangerous edge of things. So while she's faffing in the kitchen, I seize a moment, and send Mills the next text from Bernhardt's iPhone.

I am on my way. Apologies. B.

I have an hour, but probably not more.

I wander through to where Clare is slicing a lemon. Like her, the knife is small and sharp. It sinks through zest and pith, and pith and zest, down to the solid chopping board. She squeezes the quartered slice, sluicing its juice. Then drops in two fat ice cubes, which fracture and fizz.

'It's better if you put the ice in first, and more.'

She contracts her narrow brow. 'Why's that?'

Froth rises, almost overspilling the brim.

'The point of ice is that it makes the drink colder. So you may as well put in a lot, and make it really cold. If it's cold, the ice melts less, meaning the drink stays stronger for longer. It's not so diluted. If you can, you should always use a tall glass and fill it to the brim with ice cubes.'

Her expression alternates. Confused then amused.

'And why should I put them in first?'

'Because then you can fill the glass to the right level.'

'Do you work in the drinks industry by any chance?'

I chuckle strangely. 'No, I'm a writer.'

'Oh yeah. Mills told me, actually.'

That's an admission: she knows who I am.

I take a sip and shrug. 'Delicious.' And it really is.

The medicinal taste caresses my gums, soothes them against the ache of the coldness. It's been weeks since I had a proper drink.

In my pocket, Bernhardt's phone vibrates. I ignore it.

Round 2. We've withdrawn into the drawing room.

'Mills says you're writing a novel.'

'That's one word for it.'

'A novel?'

'Writing.'

'What are you doing, if not writing it?'

'I'm bleeding it. I'm breeding it. I'm feeding it with my soul.' I offer an apologetic smile. 'It can actually feel that way. What?'

Then I realise. Without thinking, I'd removed my woolly hat, to reveal my damp tonsure. My tight, Tibetan head. She's staring at that.

'That's quite a statement.'

'I save money on shampoo.'

'I actually kind of like it.'

'Really? I mean, you do?'

'It's quite intense.'

I let her stare. And then I carry on.

'Since you mention it, I'm not sure "novel" is the right word to describe the book I'm working on. It's broader than that. Sort of multi-media.'

'You know I'm a literary agent?'

'I didn't. Who for?'

'Peters, Cooper, Digby & Graham.'

'PCDG? Impressive.'

'I have a few clients.'

'Then I should probably rehearse my pitch. The idea of the book is that, through history, the dominant narrative form has kept changing. To start with, it was poetry. Thousands of years ago. That's how stories were told. In verse, because it was the only way anyone could remember them. Then you got the printing press, which made novels possible. They started out poetical, to be as much like the older form as possible. But then gradually, they got less poetic. They got prosier. Which meant that they got quieter. And the quieter they got, the closer they came to being like films. Because that was the next form to take over and rule the roost. Hollywood. Which is cock of the walk. No one gives a damn about novels anymore.'

'Sounds like I'm in the wrong job.'

'There's nothing wrong with novels. They're just out of date. But there are things you can do with them, which you can't do with films. There are things you can do with each of the forms, which you can't do with any of the others. You see what I'm saying? I want to write a book that combines all three: poetry, prose and filmscript. And which at the same time will be a rough cut, or a kind of demo, as it were, of their respective potencies.'

'A demo?' She's thinking: *is he for real?*

'Yup. Or a memo.' I'm thinking: *I am.*

She eyeballs me over our highballs.

'This is the strongest G&T ever. It's the shit.'

'I prefer to call it the cock.'

'I don't think that's an expression.'

'I'm hoping it'll catch on.'

The ice cubes wince and cackle. Clare's smile is growing

sloppy. She's sliding down the side of the sofa, like an errant five-pence piece.

'So what's next, Jack? What comes after Hollywood?'

Now there's a thought that hadn't crossed my mind.

'Box office figures are in melt-down,' I ruminate. 'We're obviously set for the next big thing. Immersive cinema? 4DX?'

'You might be onto something.'

'One thing you can bet, it'll be technology-driven. I can foresee a time when, to get their narrative hit, people will stay at home. They'll strap themselves into dream machines, and let the imagination roll.'

Round 3. And the devil is bartending. So I plunge on in.

'Would you be up for having a drink some time?'

She frowns. 'Isn't that what we're doing now?'

'Yes, but I mean, *go out*. You see? '

'Why would I want to do that?'

'No, you're right. It was just… '

'I'm fucking with you. Sure.'

'Okay. I see what you did there.'

'As long as Mills wouldn't mind.'

'Why should she? She's got a boyfriend.'

'So you know about him.'

'We met in a restaurant.'

'And what did you think?'

'I thought I'd like to kill him.'

'So you're definitely over her, then.'

'Oh, yes, definitely. A hundred per cent.'

'You wouldn't say you were still in love with her at all?'

'No. Why? Is that what she thinks?'

'I was just wondering. Because…'

'You've been hurt before?'

'No! Are you mocking me?'

'I was actually being serious.'

She looks away, then seriously says:

'I don't think I can tell when you're being serious.'

'I'm always serious. Everything I say is a hundred per cent serious.'

'So when you met Bernhardt, you really did want to kill him?'

'I wanted to rip his fucking head off.'

'Are you serious?'

'Of course not. I'm happy for Mills. I'm happy she's found somebody who's properly equipped to look after her.'

'You mean financially?'

I don't respond to that one.

'There's that moment in *Annie Hall* when Woody Allen goes up to this couple and says, "You look happy. How do you manage it?" And the girl replies, "I'm really shallow and empty, and I have no ideas and nothing interesting to say." And the guy says, "And I'm exactly the same way."'

'That's harsh. That's very harsh.'

'But you know what I mean.'

'Oh, completely. She can be quite…'

'One time, I remember, I mentioned Rimbaud, as in the poet. And she thought I was talking about a Sylvester Stallone movie.'

'Get out of here.'

'When I told her I was a fan of Titian, she said *bless you*.'

'Bullshit. You made that up.'

'Okay. That never happened. But this next one is true, I swear to god. She thought that Schiele was a woman.'

'As in Egon Schiele?'

'Yup. She thought he was Australian.'

'She thought his name was Sheila?'

'Exactly. As in, *G'day, Schiele!*'

'*Brace yourself, Schiele!*'

'Fair dinkum, Schiele!'

'Hey, Schiele! Let's put another shrimp on the barbie!'

We're both laughing so hard, we don't hear the front door. We don't hear it when it opens, and we don't hear it when it closes. The first we know of Mills's presence is when we see her, in the doorway.

She's looking at me. 'What happened to your hair?'

V

SHE CLOCKS CLARE'S starry gaze, my glassy stare.

'Would you like a G&T?' Clare asks innocently.

Then (who knows why?) she smirks.

'Jack's been giving me cocktail lessons.'

She excuses herself from the scene. Leaving the room to Camilla and me. Actually that's not quite true. There's a third presence in the room. There's Mills, there's me, and there's our mutual history.

'Hello, Graham,' I say at length.

'What are you doing here?' she asks.

'I was in the neighbourhood.'

She undoes her duffel coat.

'You work two streets away.'

'I happened to be passing.'

'Don't give me that.'

'Okay. I wanted to apologise.'

'For what?' She frowns as she sits down.

'For that time in the restaurant.'

'In Julie's? That was ages ago.'

'It's been on my mind. I behaved badly. It was just, I was taken off-guard. I hope I wasn't rude to that guy you were with. I was really out of it that night. Been having a nightmare at work. I won't bore you with the details. But I hope I didn't seem at all psychotic.'

'You always seem a little bit psychotic.'

Can you credit it? She says this with affection.

106

'But you don't like this.' I stroke my scalp.

'I was actually quite a fan of the beard.'

'It's for swimming. It makes me streamlined.'

She smiles. 'Like a permanent swimming cap.'

'I'm serious. They have to cordon off a special lane.'

'You were always a wonderful swimmer.'

She smiles, then recollects herself.

'I still don't know why you're here.'

'I thought I'd see how you were.'

'That's so nice of you.'

She doesn't sound convinced.

'Where have you been,' I ask, 'on a night like this?'

'Oh, nowhere,' she replies

She doesn't sound convincing.

'Sounds wonderful. Who else was there?'

The pressure builds, until at length she blurts it out.

'What would you think, if someone arranged to meet you for a drink, and then just failed to show, and didn't bother calling to explain?'

'There must be a good explanation for it. I mean, I'm sure he would have turned up, if he could. He must have been unavoidably delayed.'

'You're just saying that to be nice.'

'I promise that's not my motive.'

'You think he was delayed?'

'He might have been held up.'

'By what, for example?'

'I don't know. A pile-up.'

'Oh, brilliant. Thanks for that.'

'Or maybe he was knifed by a lunatic.'

'Okay, Jack. That's enough. This isn't helping.'

'I'm just saying. Things like that have happened.'

'The truth is,' she blushes, 'he must be going off me.'

And what a blush it is. Plush. Purplish. The busted flush of her cheeks, it beats my pallid pair. The opposite of a poker face.

'If that's the truth, he must be a bloody fool.'

Her ruddy blush. Her rush of blood to the head.

'Let's not rush to judgement. But if it becomes a pattern, if he repeatedly lets you down, then yes. You shouldn't stand for it.'

'It's the first time it's happened.'

'Then it's not a big deal.'

'But if it becomes a pattern.'

'That's all I'm saying, Mills.'

She sighs and smiles. And I smile back.

'You're probably right,' she says. 'He must have been... what was that phrase you used? *Unavoidably delayed*. I'm sorry. Do you mind?'

She steps into the hall to call him again. My pocket starts to buzz. I slide a hand in and reject it with a finger. She comes back in, dejected.

'He's still not picking up. I hope nothing's happened.'

Her housemate appears with a tray of G&Ts.

'Mills has been stood up,' I tell her.

'It's so humiliating.' She's such a blusher.

'Someone doesn't appreciate her.'

'You said he was *unavoidably delayed*.'

'You told me he was going off you.'

'Oh god, you're right. He probably is.'

I rise as Clare tries to hand me a drink.

'I won't, actually. I've got to hit the road.'

'Oh.' She seems disappointed. 'I was hoping you might stay for supper. We've got loads of food. Mills, help me persuade him.'

'I'd have loved that. But I've got to go to this gig.'

The truth is, it's cost me enough, to maintain this contact, to sustain this human act. Since Mills got back, it's really taken it out of me. And any minute now, my mask might slip.

'I would suggest you both came too. But the girl I'm going with, I think she has a thing for me. She might, you know, take it amiss.'

I do a little giggle. (I should make myself scarce.)

As I kiss Mills on the cheek, I look at Clare.

'But we're still on for that drink? I'll drop you a line.'

As I kiss Clare on the cheek, I look at Mills.

'I really hope Bernhardt resurfaces.'

She's looking at me, frowning.

'He's just preoccupied,' I say.

She nods. She even attempts a smile.

'I'm sorry for just dropping by like that, completely unannounced. Although Clare and I did end up having quite a hilarious chat.'

'It certainly sounded like it.'

Clare smirks. 'It was the cock.'

I echo the phrase. It's our private joke.

Oh, ha ha ha. Ho ho.

The street's a scene of starry light and snow. No, not snow. But the pale light of the streetlight shines winter white on the cold wet paving-stones. I'm in a Merry Christmas kind of mood, as I snowboard down the steps and hook a left, drop off the ledge into the alley at the house's edge.

My lingering fingertip traces its trail along the crumbling brickwork, and I'm back in the back garden. So hard, some tasks. Others so un-hard it gives me a hard-on. It gives me wood. I reach to weigh up my options.

When it comes to Mills, there's just one thing to say.

I would.

I slide back into the lumber room like smoke. I lock and load. Unlock the door and lean. I'm a mean machine. My head is growing clearer. And I'm moving ever nearer, as I tiptoe up those tried-and-tested stairs.

109

To where I hear a pair of petulant tones.

'He's my boyfriend!'

'Bernhardt's your boyfriend.'

'Okay, then. He *was* my boyfriend.'

'Then he's not anymore. So what's the problem?'

'I just don't want you to start seeing my ex.'

'That's pretty fucking selfish of you.'

'In what way is that selfish?'

'I don't have your support network, angel. I can't dip, whenever I want, into some communal pit of Henrys and Hugos. I'm a little more specific.'

'What are you even talking about?'

'This is your country. You can't walk down the street without bumping into someone you were in the pony club with.'

'That's nonsense. I was never in the pony club.'

'Anyway, you said you didn't care about Jack.'

'I never said that. When did I say that?'

'You almost spat out your lollipop.'

'I did what? What lollipop?'

'I'm speaking figuratively.'

'I don't know what that means.'

'Well, try reading something.'

There's a pause, then. An almost visible silence.

Then Mills asks, 'Why are you being like this?'

I hear her move into the dining room. I shift into the space behind the door. She carries on past me, making for the stairs, and I smell her scent as she goes. The scent of Spanish oranges. It's Tommy Girl, if I recall aright.

It's all gone like a clockwork orange. I should be pleased or proud, but I must confess I'm neither. I can't bear the thought of Mills being upset. So why did Clare have to be so damn aggressive? Sometimes I could kill that girl, I swear.

I swear. And type a text on Bernhardt's iPhone.

110

I will call you tomorrow to explain. B.

Something to console her, since I'm not allowed to hold her. I could or should have told her she shouldn't trust Clare. Her second-rate best mate. Unlike mine, who's first. Who's that? Matthew, of course. My best first-mate. My house-mate. My mouse-mate. My rodent Sancho Panza.

But wait a second. What's this, nudging my toe?

Hidden behind the door, a plastic tray. My midnight eyes draw focus. Some lurid-coloured crumbs of death. A tray containing rodent killer. The chemicals Bernhardt left, his lethal legacy.

So that's the plot. To murder Matthew.

Roulade. Lâché. *Planche*.

NOTES

What happened with Bernhardt wasn't planned. I thought he was an idiot, but I didn't hate him. And in any case, even if I'd hated him, that wouldn't have meant that I wanted to kill him. It was an accident. It wasn't planned. It didn't even seem real, when I found myself thinking about it afterwards. I knew I'd done it, but it sometimes seemed as if I hadn't, as if I'd dreamed it, or it was something I had merely witnessed. An unfortunate glimpse: the start of a genre movie, in which the good guy will be chased down by the baddies because he saw something he shouldn't have. I knew it had happened, but I couldn't help reflecting on how easily it might not have done, which seemed to make it even more unreal.

Bernhardt's violence had taken me by surprise. That's right. I said Bernhardt's violence. What sort of person tries to strangle someone, just because they bump into them unexpectedly at a party? Bernhardt had no idea who I was when he attacked me. For all he knew, I might have had a right to be there. I might have been a late arrival, or an eccentric relative, whom Mills had been embarrassed to mention. Just bear with me for a moment and consider Bernhardt's strange personality, the bizarre blend of old-fashioned clothes (the Barbour and umbrella) with that powerful, gym-built body. The latter alone is pretty telling, because if anyone spends that much time in the gym, it usually stems from some kind of inadequacy. The main reason, anthropologically, for having a powerful musculature is in order to carry out acts of aggression. Think of his hair. What the hell was that about?

Remember the reason he and Mills hadn't slept together. It was because he had pressured her. And there was more, if you're interested. I knew that he'd been cheating on her. The reason I knew this was because I had access, through his iPhone, to his Facebook account, and I could read his messages. The day before the dinner party, he had spent the night with a French chick called Nicole. I'm not saying that he deserved what happened to him. All I'm saying is that, objectively speaking, Mills was better off without him.

One last thing. Because what happened was an accident, it deserves to be judged differently than if it had been planned. In the 1950s, the author William S. Burroughs killed his wife by shooting her in the head. He didn't mean to shoot her, in the head or in any other part of her body. They were both blind drunk at the time and had decided to play a game in which he would try to shoot a glass of gin off the top of her head, like a pissed-up William Tell. Trouble was, whether because of the booze he'd drunk, or because that was just the way it was, he turned out to be a lousy shot. He got her between the eyes.

What would Freud have to say about that? Freud would say that William S. Burroughs had really wanted to kill his wife, that though he liked and valued her as a companion, as his wife she represented the last vestige of the conventional, from which he had to free himself if he was to penetrate the hitherto unexplored corners of the human condition that interested him as a writer. Freud would also inevitably point out that his wife had clearly wanted to be killed. Why else would she have agreed to have pot-shots taken at her by her paralytically drunk husband? The point I'm trying to make is that, a lot of the time, Freud didn't have the faintest idea what he was talking about.

113

But consider this. Burroughs also said that, although what had happened was so awful that he couldn't bear to think about it, he was convinced it had made him a writer. As Aeschylus remarked, suffering leads to knowledge. And, as he might have added, knowledge leads to art. Which leaves me wondering what Aeschylus must have been through, to write *The Oresteia*. But we're getting off-topic. If killing his wife had made William S. Burroughs a writer, then what had killing Bernhardt made me? That was the question that occupied me. And for now, I'll leave it hanging in the air.

* * *

Bernhardt was dead. There was nothing I could do about it. All I could do was consider how to proceed. Honesty wasn't an option, clearly. If I had told Mills the truth, she would have been horrified. On top of which, I would have had to explain that I'd been secretly living in her house for weeks without her permission. No, it was out of the question. The best thing, I decided, would be to maintain the illusion that Bernhardt was still alive, while contriving to reduce the level of intimacy between them by natural degrees.

My key advantage here was his iPhone. This gave me access to his Facebook and emails, as well as the opportunity for sending texts, as if from him, whenever it seemed appropriate. Keeping Mills in the dark turned out to be the easy bit. It emerged that Bernhardt had never been a very enthusiastic talker on the telephone. He was one of those people who don't pick up when you call them, but allow their phone to go to voicemail. Then they listen to the message later, and respond eventually, if at all, with the briefest of texts. This trait proved rather helpful in keeping at bay the curiosity of acquaintances. Bernhardt didn't seem to have close friends. He had business contacts and relatives: that was all.

As chance would have it, he had recently quit his job working for a bank and set up his own company, along with a colleague of his named Philippe, providing boutique stockbroking services to a handful of private clients. Pretending to be Bernhardt, I emailed Philippe, and told him there had been a death in the family. I asked him if he would take over my clients for a few weeks while I headed to Austria. I have to say, he seemed happy to help. I had the sense that he relished the edge this lent him in our relationship. It gave him a chance to get to know my clients better on a one-to-one basis, while also meaning that I would owe him one: an emotional chip that could be cashed in at some future time of Philippe's choosing.

This was practically the only arrangement that was needed. Bernhardt wasn't close to his parents. He didn't have a dog. I told his cleaner her services would no longer be required.

* * *

When I was at school, if the teacher was ever late, we used to play a game that involved trying to do a circuit of the classroom without touching the floor. You would climb from a windowsill to a radiator, say, then jump to a cupboard, clinging with your fingertips. Not long after the Bernhardt incident, I began to play this game in the house, moving from one room to the next, applying the lessons I was learning from the parkour instruction videos I had found on YouTube. I reached the point where I could move, without touching the floor, from the bottom to the top of the house. The hardest part, I found, was passing through doorways. It was tricky but not impossible. As the days went by, I was growing fitter and stronger. I had no desire, it goes without saying, for the kind of show-off *Men's Health* muscles in which Bernhardt had invested so much energy. It was wiriness and stamina I was after. And balance, it's true. And grace. And perhaps a certain degree of style.

Playing this game gave me a new perspective on space. Most people, when they look at a room, see only a room. I would see a network of routes. I would see terrain. I learnt to navigate the nooks and crannies of the house, the parts that often get neglected or ignored. The space behind the washing machine. The dusty vacancy underneath the bed.

I remember a story I heard as a child. There was an old woman who lived in a cottage in the middle of nowhere. Her only companion was a little dog, who slept under her bed, and when she woke up in the night, she would reach down, and the little dog would lick her hand to comfort her. One night, she was woken by a strange noise. She didn't know what it was, but it had sounded like an odd sort of whimper in the corridor. She reached down, and felt the little lick that reassured her that she wasn't alone. Then finally, after listening for a bit longer, and hearing nothing else, she got up and left the room to go the bathroom. On the landing, she found her dog nailed to the wall. There was a note attached, which read: 'Maniacs can lick too.'

I didn't have a dog, but I had my equivalent. Is it strange to regard a mouse with as much warmth as some people would feel towards a dog? It's another mammal, warm-blooded and furry, and as capable, arguably, of affection and loyalty. If a stray dog turned up at your home, you might try to drive it away. But would you poison it? Of course you wouldn't. Then why would you do that to a mouse? Is it just because it's smaller? Is it a matter of size? And if so, does that mean it's less of a crime to kill a small man than a big man? Is it better to kill a child? Or is there some kind of hierarchy among species? You can poison a mouse, but not a dog. It's fine to roast a pig, but if you were to do the same to a cat, it would raise eyebrows. Okay. Last question: is it definitely worse to kill a man in the heat of the moment than deliberately to kill a mouse by leaving out poison for it?

I searched the house and found three trays of mouse poison. There was the one behind the door into the dining room, another behind the sofa, and a third underneath a wardrobe in Mills's bedroom. I emptied their contents into a small plastic bag I took from under the kitchen sink. I tied a knot in it and then buried the noxious substances in the bottom of the bin. After that, I took a few cornflakes from the girls' cereal packet. Having washed the trays, to make sure they bore no traces of poison, I sprinkled them with crushed-up fragments of cornflakes. Then I splashed these with some food dye I had found. The shade of green wasn't exactly right, but it was close enough.

* * *

My life may seem unconventional, but that doesn't worry me. I don't have automatic respect for conventionality, not when it hasn't been properly thought through. Let me give you an example. London is the richest city in the world. This means the people who live in it are the richest. They are, as a result, unusually likely either to have second homes, or else to do jobs that require them to be away a lot. The consequence is that London, more than any other city, consists of houses and apartments that, for long periods at a stretch, are empty. Couple this with the fact that it's the homeless capital of the world and what do you have?

Take a stroll around Knightsbridge or Pimlico on a Sunday afternoon, and it's clear that you're surrounded by empty real estate. Beds keeping no one warm. Roofs that shelter no one from the rain. Look closer and you'll see bundles of bedding in doorways. Descend into an underpass. There'll be someone lying on a square of cardboard, or strumming on an out-of-tune guitar. It makes me fucking furious, I can tell you. What I'm trying to say is that if you have nowhere to go, and if there's a house that's empty, you have a moral right to be there. Call me unconventional. No, really. Go ahead. I'll take it as a compliment.

My mode of living wasn't conventional, but it was natural. There was a rightness to it, a conformity to a deeper morality. I had the sense that, although previously I had been living in a way that was out of synch with the rhythms of the universe, now, by this adjustment of my directedness, I was proceeding forward at a terrific pace. Who knew where it would take me? For example, that evening when I'd dropped by to get to know Clare (having first made sure that Mills was out of the way) I had made so much progress, it made me dizzy to think about it. I had learnt that although Mills might not have still been in love with me, she could be made to feel jealousy. That was a breakthrough in itself.

I had learnt too that she was insecure about her relationship with Bernhardt. These two facts, taken together, were going to make my job so much easier.

* * *

It is time to write about Mills. But what should I say? First this, perhaps. Before I met her, I had never previously come across anyone with such an incredible degree of humility.

That may not sound like the most glamorous of compliments, but consider it in the context of her other remarkable qualities, and you'll have to admit it's extraordinary. Then remember her background. She was from a class associated with arrogance. She was preternaturally beautiful, which you might have thought would be likely to make her even more arrogant. So why did she blush, whenever she entered a room? Was it that she didn't realise she was beautiful? Or was it that she knew she was, but found it embarrassing, as if there was something a little crass in being so blatant about it? I liked the idea of the latter explanation but I always suspected it was the former. She didn't like the way she looked. It's really amazing, how often this seems to be the case with beautiful women. If you did a survey, I'd bet that half of hot women don't think of themselves as hot. Get inside the head of a supermodel, and you'd learn that she thinks of herself as a lumbering beast, with clunky hips, and stupidly large, plumped-up lips. Men don't tend to suffer from such doubts.

When I thought about Mills, what I most wanted was to try to persuade her that she was wrong about herself. She shouldn't be so timid and embarrassed. She shouldn't be arrogant either, but there was no need for this note of apology in her every action. 'You're beautiful, darling.' That's what I would have liked to say to her. 'And that's okay. It's okay to be beautiful. You don't have to apologise for it. You don't have to persuade yourself that it isn't really true. It's just a thing, a fact, like being short, or clever, or born in France. You're beautiful. Welcome to the truth.'

The other thing I wanted to say to her was that I was sorry. She had met me during an awkward chapter in my emotional development. It can't have been much fun.

In the days when we'd got together, I had had a suspicion of commitment that was unusual even for a man in his twenties. At one point, I'd even planned to write a book on the subject. It was going to be called *Against Love*, and its main aim would be to prove that Love didn't exist. I had actually gone so far as to write a proposal to send to publishers. It may sound crazy but I had done all the necessary research, devouring the works of sociologists and comparative litterateurs. My aim was merely to point out that there were a few ideas commonly associated with Love – the notion of love at first sight, for example, or the belief in a love that was unconditional – that were obviously drivel.

* * *

What distressed me the most was the idea that by the time we'd broken up, Mills had been less self-confident than she was when I'd first met her. This was the wrong that I wanted to right. If I could only persuade her to get back together with me, I could set about repairing the psychic damage. Unfortunately, in the short term, I needed to deliver another blow to her self-esteem, and convince her that Bernhardt was losing interest in her.

The venue I had chosen for their first non-meeting had been the Rivoli Bar at the Ritz. The venue I chose for the second was a bistro in East London. This provided variety after the Ritz, and was also annoying for Mills, as she had to spend an hour on public transport, only to find herself stood up. I didn't call her to explain. It was tempting to try, but I didn't think I could get away with faking Bernhardt's voice. Instead I texted through some apologies from his iPhone, and vague references to the pressure of work. Then I undermined those claims by going onto Facebook and re-posting some old pictures of him partying in glamorous settings, as if they showed events he had only just attended.

I've mentioned already that on the evening when I had 'dropped in' on the girls, I had learnt two things. The first was that Mills was insecure about Bernhardt. The second was that she was jealous, when it came to me. I suspected, in retrospect, that these two feelings were directly connected. The more insecure she felt about Bernhardt, the less she liked the idea of me and Clare going on a date together. I had overheard the girls talking about it again one evening, and Mills had sounded on the point of tears.

Afterwards, Clare texted me: 'I've been forbidden from seeing you.' I didn't reply, and five minutes later, she sent a follow-up: 'So when d'you wanna meet?'

This was the start of a long exchange of texts and Facebook messages between myself and Clare, which I won't bother to summarise. Suffice to say, I was shocked by the bitchiness of her tone whenever she mentioned Mills. Not as shocked, however, as I was by a revelation Clare came out with towards the end of a long exchange of texts one morning. We had been discussing property in London when, as if it somehow proved her point, Clare gave out that she had started to suspect there might be someone living secretly in her basement.

Her suspicions had first been aroused by an unpleasant smell when she'd gone down there to wash some clothes. It had been a weird sickly-sweet smell, she said, like the smell of a tramp. On another occasion, she had listened at the door of a store room (the key to which had mysteriously gone missing) and she could have sworn she had heard breathing.

I asked if it had occurred to her to wander round to the back garden and have a peek in through the window, to see if she could spot anyone. She replied that it had occurred to her, and she planned to do it, but she hadn't got around to it. From this I concluded that either she was scared, or else she didn't believe her own theory. In any case, two things were clear. The first was that Clare didn't yet have any evidence, nothing she could have presented to the police. The second was that I couldn't, on any account, remain in the lumber room.

* * *

It was time for a new level of intimacy. It was time to initiate what I thought of as Phase 5 in proceedings. I went online and made my first ever order from Ocado.

I hadn't previously made use of the online shopping service, taking pride instead in salvaging all my dietary requirements from the scraps left by Mills and Clare. And if this meant I'd been losing weight, so much the better. The thinner I was, I reasoned, the less likely I was to make a noise as I moved around

121

the house. I entertained the fantasy that if I lost enough weight, I might disappear altogether. I might become a ghost and be free to roam without fear of being perceived. There was a poem by W.B. Yeats which made the point that ghosts don't drink wine, they merely 'drink from the wine breath', meaning they 'drink in' the aroma of wine that sits above a glass of wine on the table. This was the way I liked to think of myself. I drank from the wine breath. Which was why my order from Ocado didn't include any food. It was restricted, if you must know, to six rolls of cling film. I wasn't sure that I would need so many, but Ocado were doing a special offer. If you bought two rolls, you got one free. It seemed a shame not to make the most of it, especially since there was a chance I might have need of more cling film in the future.

Having completed the order, I ran to the top of the house. The landing there gives onto two rooms: Mills's and Clare's. There is a balustrade at the top, which joins with the banister, to prevent anyone falling. I climbed on to the corner, where the banister meets the balustrade, and reaching up with my hands, slowly straightened my legs. I could just reach the trapdoor that was in the ceiling above my head.

I gave it a little push and it came down again on the points of my waiting fingertips. So I gave it further pushes, harder each time, until it went banging down on the other side. I managed to grip with my fingers and jump up, getting one forearm flat, which took my weight. The rest was painful but not impossible. I raised myself into the dark and dusty space of the attic.

These, I had decided, were to be my new quarters. The space was huge, restricted in terms of head space by the sloping roof on either side, and by the ancient wooden rafters that divided the length at intervals. Nevertheless, the floor space had the dimensions of the house. And how typical of the Howards, I thought to myself, that they hadn't taken the trouble to convert. The only light came from a meagre window, so filthy and veiled by cobwebs that the little light it permitted had a sepia quality. In this restricted glow, I was able to see that there were no proper floorboards. The floor was divided up into sections by wooden stanchion supports, with the space in between occupied by yellow insulation foam. Under it were boards that looked to be no more substantial than plywood. In any case, I didn't trust them to take my weight, and resolved that when I was moving around I would always tread on the stanchions, and never on the spaces in between.

Carefully, in the gloom, I explored the rest of the attic, using the flashlight app of my phone. It was basically empty, with the exception of a couple of packing cases stuffed with pillows and a length of metal piping laid down on the floor between them. There were also two wooden planks resting on their sides and leaned against the wall. And for no reason that I could guess, at the far end of the attic, there were two moulded orange plastic chairs, of the sort you might expect to find in a primary-school classroom.

Beneath one of them, I noticed a single plug socket in the wall, which was when, for the first time, I glanced back and and saw a bare light bulb hanging from the ceiling.. I found the switch, and the bulb burst into light. It was then, I think, that I became aware that I wasn't alone in the attic. I didn't *see* anything suspicious, not at first. It was a noise that alerted me, the soft sound of someone breathing. Or some*thing*. For it wasn't breathing exactly. It was a sort of gurgling. It was a throaty, liquid sound, like someone in their death throes. No, now that I come to think of it, it was more rhythmical than that. A rhythmical throaty gurgling sound. My imagination went into overdrive. Perhaps it was some creature that had made its home in the attic. A mutant animal, which had been living there for decades. It had gone blind from lurking for so long in the dark. And lost most of its hair. A bald, forked creature, its skin as white and as waxy as parchment, enraged at being disturbed.

I felt a shiver of fear as I stepped from one stanchion to the next, trying to locate the noise. My scalp prickled, and it felt as if droplets of sweat were moving over its surface. The sound, which came at intervals, was like the sound one associates with ghosts draped in sheets, with black circles cut for eye-holes. 'Woo!' it went. 'Woo!'

It seemed to grow louder as I approached the musty window. The glass was so filthy I could barely see through it. But I could make out that, close to the pane of glass on the other side, an eye was staring at me. A single, tiny eye, beady and round. It didn't blink. Then there was an explosion of movement on the other side of the glass. A pigeon flapped away.

My heart rate had scarcely had a chance to return to normal when it was disturbed by another shrill, disturbing sound. This time, it was the doorbell, several floors down.

In a trice I was lowering myself through the trapdoor. I hit the floor, cushioning the impact as I did so with a forward roll (which is known in parkour as a *roulade*). Then I descended to the drawing room. From the bay window, I peeked through a gap in the curtains. It was the delivery guy from Ocado with my package. What service! I opened the front door and received my consignment of cling film.

I rewarded myself with a cup of instant coffee. While I drank it, I watched an episode of the Jeremy Kyle Show. Then I took the cling film and went downstairs to the basement. Clare was right. The smell was definitely getting worse. I rolled back the carpet and with tools from Mr Howard's toolbox prised up the nails from the floorboards.

Bernhardt's body seemed to have been diminished by death. He looked thinner, less substantial, his eyes closed and his cheeks sunken. A few strands of the long hair were stuck to the colourless forehead. I managed to lift him out of the cavity and drag him into the lumber room. I tried not to breathe as I went about my work. Once I had the body safely laid out in the lumber room, I gave the hole in the floor of the basement a good scrub with soap and water. Then I replaced the floorboards and rolled the carpet back over. I unpacked the cling film and commenced to swathe Bernhardt in several layers of what Americans like to call 'plastic wrap'. Once I was satisfied with my handiwork, I began dragging him upstairs. I realised as I did so that it would have been more sensible to have done the dragging first, and applied the cling film later. The stuff kept tearing as I made my way from one landing to the next.

It was hard work. Despite what I said earlier about Bernhardt seeming diminished, he was still pretty heavy. A couple of times, I lost my grip and he went thumping back down the stairs, the cling film ripping as he went. By the time I got him to the top landing, there were wisps hanging off him like shreds of toilet paper. He wasn't naked. I had allowed him to keep his clothes on. In any case, I had had no desire to see his naked body. I have always been rather squeamish about male nudity, particularly in the case of those who are bigger than me.

I don't know how I did it, but with the help of Mr Howard's step-ladder, I managed to lug, thrust and bundle Bernhardt up into the attic. Then I rested awhile, my pulse going like a hammer in my head. It took a long time to regain my breath. Once I had done so, I dragged him to the farthest end of the attic and propped him on one of the orange chairs. Then I nipped down into the basement to fetch the cling film, before again climbing the stairs, in order to patch up the torn wrapping.

* * *

There were things I liked about the attic. I liked the fact that it was so high. I liked the idea that, when I slept at night, I was physically close to Mills, who slept in the room below. One of the worst things about a break-up is the contrast between how close you feel to the other person emotionally, and how far away from them you are physically. One moment you sleep with that person. You wake up with them, make breakfast for them. You keep in touch with them during the day by text and email, and maybe squeeze in a phone call at lunch. If you have evening plans, they're included. If you go to a party, they're on your arm. You arrive together. You walk in together. While you're there, you might circulate separately, but you know at any time, you could always seek them out and they'd be glad to see you.

Do you know what it's like, to go to a party alone, when you haven't done that for years? It feels like you're naked. Do you know how it feels, to sleep alone in a bed for the first time in ages? It's like the bed is huge.

To create a stable base on which to sleep, I laid down two of the planks of wood that I had found leaning against the wall of the attic. I arranged them so they were directly above Mills's bed. I liked the idea that when I slept at night, my body would be mirroring hers. There was a problem, of course, with this new proximity. I had to be more careful than ever. I made my way systematically around the attic, marking with a yellow sticky post-it note every place on every stanchion that creaked if I rested my weight on it. By the time I had finished, the attic was covered with post-it notes. It was as if a swarm of yellow butterflies had flown in through the window and settled over the contours of the room. But I knew that I was safe in the attic, as long as I avoided stepping on a post-it note. There remained the question of how to deaden the sound the trapdoors made when I closed them. I found an old pair of trousers that had belonged to Mr Howard and cut off pieces of material. I used these to soften the points of contact between the trapdoors and their frames.

I also found some spare bolt locks in Mr Howard's tool box, and screwed a pair into place on each of the two trapdoors, so that when I was up there, I could lock myself in. I grabbed the opportunity, while I had the electric drill up and running, to drill a couple of carefully angled holes through the trapdoor above Mills's bed, so I could easily have a look at her, if I wanted, while she slept.

* * *

You only need two things in order to write a good novel: a plot and a voice. Similarly, you only need two things in order to live a good life: a dream and a plan. I had my dream. You know what it was. But how was I going to achieve it? That was the question. And I hadn't completely worked out the answer. I was close. It was coming into focus. I felt as if my future was like some great jigsaw puzzle spread out across a dining table somewhere. About half the pieces were in place, but it still wasn't clear yet what the image was going to look like. I felt as if I only needed a couple more pieces, and I would see it.

One morning, I went into Clare's bedroom and spent an hour browsing through her music collection. Her tastes were pretty retro. She was into Duran Duran. Depeche Mode. She even liked U2. Can you believe it? She had every album U2 had ever made, including the Passengers album. Now if there's one person who really gets my goat, it's Bono. Do you know what I mean? it's the hypocrisy of the man, claiming to be all compassionate and noble, while actually he's stashing all his cash away in off-shore slush funds or whatever. What a prat. And don't even get me started on his music, the twiddly strumming at the start of every song, slowly building to the cymbal-clashing climax. And the lyrics are insane. When you think about it, is it likely you can find, anywhere in the world, a place where the streets literally don't have a name? I shouldn't have thought it was likely. And if, after all this time, Bono still hasn't found what he's looking for, then maybe he should stop looking? You see what I'm saying? He's obviously on a wild goose chase.

Nevertheless, for some reason or another, Clare was a fan. I searched online for a comprehensive discography of U2 songs, crossed off all the ones she had, and then wrote out a list of the few songs she was missing. I then checked on iTunes to see which of these songs had the highest profile. The answer was a rare B-side called *Luminous Times (Hold On To Love)*. I ordered the CD single from Amazon.

* * *

People say you should live in the present but I don't agree. If you took that advice literally, it would mean living like an animal, responding to instinct, without any thought for the future, and learning nothing from the past. The psychologically healthy life, I think, should be one whose energies are divided between the past, the present and the future. Having said that, I suppose I must admit there were times, back then, when I may have dwelt on the past a little too much. There was a game I played, for example, in which I ran through in my head certain experiences I had once shared with Mills, trying to recall every detail. That time, for example, in the restaurant at the top of the National Portrait Gallery, when the strap of her top had slid unnoticed off her shoulder. Then she'd noticed it, looked at me in dismay in case I should disapprove, and once she was sure I didn't, allowed a naughty smile to slide across her face. Or there was that voicemail she had left once, when she was drunk. It hadn't made much sense. She had just kept saying, 'Hi,' and apologising for calling, and somewhere in the midst of all the verbiage, she had said she loved me.

What I'm trying to say is that though it sometimes seemed as if I was haunting her, she haunted me. She was always with me, wherever I was, whatever I was doing. When I woke in the morning, she was literally below me, asleep in her bed, but I could also imagine she was beside me in the attic, watching me. As I went about my business during the day, I would hear her voice, commenting on what I was doing. More strangely, there were times I knew she was out at work, but I would seem to see her, seated in a chair or over by the window. I would walk into a room and she would glance up from a table, where she had been flicking through a magazine.

For a long time, I never heard and saw her at the same time. I would either see her, in which case she wouldn't speak, or I would hear her murmuring in my ear, but on those occasions, she would be invisible. That was the way it was until one afternoon when, without warning, I saw and heard her simultaneously.

It was quite a shock, I can tell you. I should have known, in retrospect, there was something funny going on, because it started with my being able to see Mills in the library, and I had never seen her in the library before. But on this occasion, I walked into the library, and there she was, seated cross-legged on the floor, reading *The End of the Affair*. She didn't look up when I walked in and that was strange too, because she always looked up. This time, she just carried on reading. I had the sense that she was perusing the pencilled notes that Clare had left in the margins.

I went up and selected a Graham Greene book from the shelf. I think it may have been *The Ministry of Fear*. Then I sat down next to her, thinking we could pass a pleasant hour, reading side by side. But as soon as I had sat down, to my surprise, she spoke. She said, 'Come on, then.' She rose and took me by the hand and led me out of the library into the master bedroom. There she raised one of the sash windows and we both climbed out onto the balcony. It didn't feel like a dream.

She adjusted her grip on my hand and effortlessly the two of us rose from the balcony and began to float along Milton Road, about twenty feet above the Tarmac. Then we rose further and we were drifting over the tops of houses, heading south towards Notting Hill Gate. Soon I could see the cars that were moving along Holland Park Road. There was a lumbering bus, with a cyclist pedalling hell-for-leather ahead of it. I could see children playing in Holland Park. A dog bounding after a squirrel. I could see a man relaxing on the grass, his head resting on his girlfriend's stomach.

We rose so high that these figures became tiny beneath us. Then, as we started to descend, I could smell the pollution that was rising from the streets, and we came down underneath the Hammersmith Flyover. We touched down on the pavement with the silent grace of ghosts, and there ahead of me, I could see a boy and a girl. The boy was me. The girl was Mills. Or to be precise, they were younger versions of ourselves. I knew instinctively that it was the two of us on our first ever date.

I checked my phone and saw that it was exactly 13.16. That was the time at which I had suggested we meet, in an attempt to be original. My point was that it was rather arbitrary, the way people always arrange to meet at some regular hour of the day, either at something o'clock, or at half past something. It would make as much sense to meet at 13.16. I had been inspired, I think, by Matt Damon's character in the film *Good Will Hunting*, who explains to Minnie Driver that it's arbitrary to suggest meeting for coffee. They might just as well meet up and eat caramels.

I could see the tentative way that Mills and Jack kissed. For this was their first date in the sense that it was the first time they'd seen each other since spending the night together

130

randomly after an alcohol-fuelled evening (which is known these days as 'getting together'). Because it's tricky, the question of how to greet someone in that situation. If you move to kiss them on the lips, will that seem presumptuous? Or worse still, will it seem needy? But then if you don't, will they feel rejected? Jack moved towards Mills and kissed her on the lips very briefly and rather awkwardly. They both seemed relieved once that was over, and talked freely to each other as they walked, not holding hands, along Queen Caroline Street.

By the time they reached the river, they were holding hands. They were also dressed differently and I realised that a year had gone by. This was Jack and Mills a year into their relationship. They both looked different. Jack was wearing a backpack and looked like he hadn't shaved for a couple of days. He was saying something to Mills, who looked disapppointed, and though I couldn't hear what they were saying, I knew he was explaining to her that he couldn't stay with her that night, because he had too much work to do, and I knew that she was trying not to criticise but was unconvinced.

I glanced at Mills's ghost beside me, and to my surprise, saw her face was pale with anger. 'Okay,' I said to the ghost. 'You've made your point. I was an egotist in those days. I'm different now. I'm more mature.' It was then that I realised the ghost's intention was to show the whole course of my relationship with Mills, how it had gone bad, and how it was all my fault. 'Really?' I said. 'Do you really have to put me through this? I know what I did.'

Despite my protestations, the show continued. Another year had passed and there was Mills, walking along Queen Caroline Street in the rain. She walked so slowly, with such reluctant body language, it was obvious she knew that when she reached her destination, she would face some awful ordeal. She was carrying one of those short umbrellas, which extend when you press a button, and which have a tendency to break. There were already two loose spokes in the umbrella Mills was carrying and it wasn't doing a very good job of protecting her from the rain. When she eventually reached the entrance of the Riverside Studios, she spent a few moments shaking the raindrops off the little umbrella. Then she made a visible effort, as if gathering her resources of courage, and carried on inside.

The ghost gestured to me to follow, but I refused. 'I've been through that once,' I said, 'and it was horrible. I don't want to go through it again.' We argued, then, the ghost and I. It insisted that I should go into the Riverside Studios and re-witness the break-up scene, but I wouldn't be persuaded. I stubbornly stayed on the pavement outside. The funny thing was, of course, that all the time we argued, I knew what was going on inside. I knew what Mills was saying to Jack, and what Jack was saying in return. I knew every word.

Finally, Jack emerged. His face was grey. Angling down from his hand was a traditional long black umbrella. But he didn't bother to open it as he stepped out into the rain. The rain fell on his face, with the result that, in a matter of moments, it wasn't possible to tell whether or not he was crying. But I knew the answer to that.

'Enough, ghost!' I cried out in distress. 'Why are you showing me this?'

But when I turned, I found that I was alone. The ghost had vanished, and I was the only person in the street. It was a disconcerting experience, I have to say. But it just goes to show that L. Ron Hubbard was right. He believed that it is only after you have sorted through the past that you can form a clear vision of the future. And that was the way it went that day. My surroundings slowly disintegrated and I found myself seated again in the library at 69 Milton Road, a copy of *The Ministry of Fear* open in front of me. But that wasn't all that was in front of me. Through the book, which was semi-transparent, I could see the jigsaw puzzle of my future. A couple more pieces had been added to it. In a moment of inspiration, I realised what the whole picture represented. And I saw what I had to do.

VI

AS I SLIDE along the valley of the alley, I pick up a wisp of smoke, and toss it over my shoulder like a scarf. I laugh. Ha ha! My laugh becomes a chuckle. Hee hee! Then I suppress it. It's time to buckle up and knuckle down. To find the beauty in the breakdown, the break-up poetry.

The last time I dropped by, Mills was out and Clare was in. I asked for Mills, but it was Clare I came to see. This time, it's the reverse.

'Hello.' The startled answerer is Mills. 'Are you looking for Clare?'

'Oh, hi,' I reply with a smile. 'This is awkward.'

'Is it?' she counters stubbornly. 'Why?' But then she blushes and red-faced adds, 'You can come in, if you want.'

She has a little scar upon her cheek, souvenir of a fairground ride. It's sickle-shaped, a Persian flaw. When she darkens, it goes pale. And that's what gets me every time. My plan was to stress my empathy with Clare, our symbiotic rapport. Now I'm unmanned. I find myself saying, 'Thanks.'

Armed with alcohol, we face off across the coffee table.

I come right out with it. 'Are you doing anything fun tonight?'

Her eyes sidle down and sideways. Then she looks at me straight.

'Did Clare agree to meet up with you? You don't have to answer that. '

'I think,' I reply, 'it may actually have been her idea.'

'I bet it was!' She takes a sip of her drink. 'Do you fancy her?'

'She says that she wants to talk about my book.'

'I wouldn't have thought that she was your type.'

'I didn't realise I had a type. What's my type?'

'I don't know,' she says. 'But not her.'

'She's clever,' I say. 'She's quick.'

She's a lot like you. But you always told me opposites attract.'

'More and more, with romance, I find myself thinking there's no rhyme or reason.'

What I'm saying is: there was no reason for us. You see? As lovers, we didn't rhyme. I'm hoping that she'll contradict me. But sadly, she just nods.

We fall to small talk. She asks, 'Do you still see much of X?' And I think: *there are only two people I've seen much of recently.* I tell her X is fine. And I ask her about her old friend Y (ie Charlie). She says she's seeing him tonight. Which as a matter of fact, I knew. They're going to the Curzon Mayfair to watch some gory horror film.

When it comes to Camilla Howard, I know everything there is to know. Except, apparently, how to make her glow. There was a time I could have done it. And did, repeatedly. I made her go: oh, oh, oh. But now she can't relax and nor can I. You'd think we might be strangers, to judge from our *quid pro quo*. Hello. Hello. Goodbye. Goodbye. With little in between.

And such a contrast, this, with how it used to be. When we first met, we used to talk for hours on end. Two in the morning would turn to three. And in the street, a blackbird used to sing. Bliss was it in that dawn, and heaven was in that room. It was like we couldn't stop: a kind of talking spree. Picture a horse running rudderless, riderless, ahead of the sprinting pack. His stirrups swinging free. And then, next day, such tiredness, you wouldn't believe. What did we talk about? Anything. Verbal alchemy.

One of us would start a joke, and the other would develop it.

And then we'd continue, creating crazy worlds, with an exuberant cast of characters. So insubstantial, though, it's hard to remember now. It's difficult to recreate. Once, I recall, we came up with an idea for a superhero. He was the worst superhero ever. He had no special powers. In fact, the only advantages he had in his crusade against crime were his alter ego (a mild-mannered pizza delivery guy) and the helmet he wore, which he used for butting villains in the crotch. We christened him Helmetman.

Another time, we composed lyrics for a song called *The Long-Stay Car Park Blues* by a fictitious pop group named Stan Sted and the Ghouls. It was a classic one-hit wonder.

And now? The reverse. Anti-alchemy. Pure politeness. Enquiries after one another's health. I'm serious. She asks me about my back.

Oh, Mills! When did we both become so middle-aged? I want to leave but I can't. I'm mesmerised by our mediocrity. I want to push it to an extreme. Is that possible? Extreme mediocrity? Let's see. I shall only say the most boring things I can think of. I remark on this dispiriting spell of weather, the sodden skies, the endless, mindless rain. I ask if she's seen anything decent on TV. And I almost forgot to inquire. How has her temping been?

Incredibly, this seems to work. It pulls the situation inside out. Its stomach becomes its skin. For Mills goes out to revive our glasses.

And then, when she comes back in…

'Has Clare told you her latest crazy theory? She's convinced there's some old tramp living in our basement.'

'That seems a bit far-fetched.'

'I know, right? I mean, who's to say it's a tramp?'

'Exactly. He might have a home of his own.'

'He might have several.' She hands me my third gin mix.

'He might be a property developer. This is his research.'

'He breaks into people's homes and lives there surreptitiously.'

'Surreptitiously. Exactly.'

She raises her glass. 'Thanks, Douglas.'

'My pleasure, Graham. And who's to say he's old?'

'He could be young. Why assume he's an ageing sexual pervert?'

'I suspect Clare secretly hopes that he's an ageing sexual pervert.'

'She's particularly keen that he should be ageing.'

'Maturing, like a ripe cheese.'

'A camembert.'

'A brie.'

'A stinky gorgonzola.'

'An ageing, sexually perverted property developer with underpants that smell of gorgonzola.'

'Gross.' She wrinkles her tiny nose.

'Don't you like gorgonzola?'

'Not in my underpants, if you please.'

'In some countries, I believe it's de rigeur.'

'It probably brings out the flavour.'

'It gives it a special tang.'

'You know what, Douglas?'

'No, Graham, what?'

'I'm not completely convinced.'

'Okay,' I say. 'Then what?'

'I think he might be an artist.'

'The guy downstairs?'

'The basement man. A musician.'

'Did he work on *The Basement Tapes*?'

'No. Actually…' she tilts her head '…he's a dancer.'

'A Bolshoi ballet dancer? A muscular Russian?"

'Possibly. But with an interest in modern dance.'

'Which is what got him sacked from the Bolshoi.'

'He was too bolshy. It made the others uneasy.'
'Though they recognised his genius. That wasn't in doubt.'
'But it isn't easy, working with a genius.'
'Tell me about it.'
'Oh, I know!'
'Oh, I know!'
'That's why he was given the boot.'
'He was given the Russian boot.'
'He was given das boot.'
'I think that might be German.'
'Okay. He was given the bootov.'
'He was given the kick-off.'
'He had to kick off his pumps.'
'And pick up his pay-cheque.'
'From being a pumped-up poster boy.'
'He found himself a drop-out.'
'A kind of down-and-out.'
'Washed up, at the age of 24.'
'He got a job as a washer-up.'
'In the kitchens at the Ritz.'
'But fell foul of the maitre d'.'
'A sleazy German named Fritz.'
'Who took a fancy to him.'
'Who fancied his Russian ass.'
'And finally Sergei lost it. He went through the roof.'
'Are you sure about the name Sergei? I was leaning towards Ivan.'

Mills is adamant. 'Sergei. Royakovsky. Known as Roy, to his friends.'

'Of which he has none. Except us, obviously. Except you and me.'

'I feel sorry for Roy, to be honest. He must get so lonely.'

We hear the catch of the latch. The glass vase chimes, as it receives its set of keys. And Clare walks in and sees us. She's a little taken aback.

'We've worked out the identity of the man in the basement,' Mills tells her.

'Sergei Royakovsky,' I add. 'An out-of-work Russian ballet dancer.'

'He's been wandering the streets, swigging from a vodka bottle.'

'He must have found the window open.'

'He's friendly. He doesn't mean any harm.'

Clare's hair's tucked behind her ears. Her temple's flecked with rain. It's a strain, it seems, to hang on to your sense of humour, when you arrive home to find the man you thought you were going to have a drink with is hobnobbing with your housemate, who happens also to be his ex. It isn't always easy, when you're tired, to see the funny side of things.

She carries on into the kitchen, and returns with a quick-fix drink. She slicks her lips and smiles. But not convincingly.

'Most of the time,' Mills continues, 'he just stays in his room. But sometimes, when we're out, he slinks upstairs.'

I take over. 'And pushes all the furniture against the wall.'

'And then he just dances. Dances till he drops.'

'He puts on one-man shows for an invisible audience.'

'Reliving the triumphs of his past.'

'His tour-de-forces. His coup-de-graces.'

'Sometimes he's so drunk, he takes a tumble.'

'Other times,' I tell Clare, 'he's better than he's ever been.'

She licks her lips. Then says to Mills, 'I thought you were going out.'

Soon after, that's what she does. Leaving Clare and me.

'What are you doing here?' she asks.

'Who, me? I just dropped by on the off-chance. I hoped it would just be you.'

She shakes her head, forced-smiling. 'Trouble-maker.'

There's a pause then, an unspoken sub-clause.

'I almost forgot. I brought you something.'

I unclip the straps of my backpack and slide out a CD single.

We sit and listen to *Luminous Times (Hold On To Love)*. So simple but so strong. I can tell Clare likes it. But she's determined not to relent. She wants me to repent for making her feel insecure. To punish me, she behaves peremptorily. She says, 'Come on, since you're here. You may as well make yourself useful.' Some women think (I've noticed this before) that this is what men want, no matter what we say. That though we strut and preen, and pretend we want control, we actually prefer to be told what to do. So let it now be noted: we don't.

In this instance, though, to get to where I want to go, I have to submit to it. Especially once I know what's on her mind. We step out into the night. We sally down the alley – which for me is a rewind – until we reach the garden at the back. Then we stand at the top of those stairs, which descend to the lumber room. I place a finger to my lips and smirk, to prove my insouciance. Then tip-toe down the steps. I pause. I suddenly look. There's no one, of course, staring back at me. No hirsute tramp who's reeking of defeat. No property hound priapic. No bisexual ballet dancer, burning for a comeback.

But I pretend there is. I want to give Clare a fright, you see. So I let my eyes go wide. I emit a gasp of surprise. And I croak, *'What do you want?'*

Amazingly, despite my overacting, it seems she was nearly convinced. Because she says crossly, 'Jerk.' And clip-clops down to join me.

We raise the sash. We drop on in. We both hunt round for the key (which is snug inside my pocket). But I pretend that I'm searching too.

Clare, meanwhile, has a second objective. She's looking for

evidence. Some bundled bedding. The remnants of a hasty meal. But needless to say, I wasn't so sloppy. Before I left, I restored the room to its former state, checking with the start-image on my phone. The national costumes hang in the same old places. I left no traces when I went. Or at least, that's what I thought. But then Clare picks up a vase. She takes a sniff and gags.

'Ohmygod!' she yells. 'It stinks of piss!'

Frowning, I take it from her. I have a whiff.

'That's not piss,' I tell her sternly. 'It's urine.'

She dismisses this. And sniffs the vase again. She's right.

It became my lavatory while I was here. When you've got to go, you've got to go. And I had to go quite a lot. In the darkness, then, I'd listen. There's an increase in pitch as the liquid nears the neck. But I never had a spillage. Oh no, not I. I was far too clever. For I had a back-up vase when the first was done. By the time I left for the attic, I only needed that one. These days I barely eat or drink. I'm a self-sustaining organism.

'It's not piss,' I persist. 'When you leave flowers in a vase, they rot. And rotten vegetation smells like piss. It releases a special gas.'

'What freaks me out,' she says, 'is if he's the one with the key, he could be anywhere. You realise there's an attic upstairs. Above my bedroom.'

'Is that a fact?' I say, a little perturbed.

'I'm just saying. You see? He could be there.'

If Clare explores, I'm sunk. She'll find my books, my bedding.

'Are you sure you're not taking this all a bit too seriously?'

She'll find an inanimate Austrian, ready for the fridge.

The next two hours are a nightmare. Partly it's the fact that, step by step, Clare gets resolved on this plan: to burst into the attic. And I'm such a softy I can't dissuade her. But also it's because, in straining to divert her, I show her a YouTube clip. And in return, she shows me one. Then another. Then another. Is there anything worse in life than this?

141

It's like a death in life. Or it gives new life to death. For picture the upper circles of hell: that amphitheatre of agony, where Tantalus endures his repetitive regime. There's Sisyphus, that baffled mountaineer, still steering his ball of rock up the same old hill. And there's me: hunched over the same old laptop, being forced by Clare to watch interminable YouTube clips. And having to laugh! Oh yes! Ho ho! Oh no, but isn't that droll! Would I like to see another? Of course I would! (No choice.) You're on a roll! Oh, god! This is killing me! It's too much! But this is a scream! Oh me! Oh my! Forever drying a mirthless eye.

If there's one thing books have taught us, if there's anything we've learnt from song: it's when you think things can't get any worse… you're wrong.

The next thing I know, I'm shouldering the stepladder, and we're heading upstairs. There's nothing I can do. When I tried, she said that she'd do it alone. She accused me of cowardice. I didn't mind that, though I pretended to. But now my mind runs up the stairs ahead of us. And then it runs down again. Any ideas? No, nothing. It does it again. With the same result. In desperation, I pretend to lose my grip. I let the ladder slip, so it clatters down the stairs.

'Shit,' I say to Clare.

'What's wrong with you?' she asks. 'Give it here.'

'No, I've got it,' I reply. I ascend as slowly as I can, to give myself time to think. What I need is a miracle. Or failing that, an idea.

She watches me, bewildered. But still with patience. She has all the time in the world. On the top landing, I set down the stepladder. I pretend to struggle to open it. 'I think it's broken,' I say at last.

Wordlessly, she unhooks the restraining latch.

'Sorry,' I say. 'I didn't see it.'

I look up at the trapdoor. I position the ladder below it. I look at Clare.

'Okay,' I say. 'Here goes.'

I place my foot on a rung. Then I pause. I shake the structure, just to check it's solid. Playing for time. I glance up again. And then, having no alternative, I start to climb. And as I do, I have a brainwave.

I'll pretend the trapdoor's locked or stuck. I'll say that I can't budge it. But will Clare buy this? She may do, if I act convincingly enough. Come on, Marcel. It's showtime, no? It's time to climb and mime.

At the top, I reach up with my hand and flatten the palm against the trapdoor. I tense my bicep, making the veins stand out on my neck.

'It doesn't seem to want to open.'

I turn and flatten the other palm, so I seem to be pushing with both.

'Nope. It's jammed. Or locked on the other side. Hang on.'

I straighten my legs, so I can seem to put my shoulder to it.

Clare's just staring. 'What on earth are you doing?'

'What do you mean? I'm trying to open this trapdoor!'

'Yes, but why aren't you pushing properly?'

'You're welcome to try, if you think you can do better.'

A mis-step, that. 'Sure. I'll have a go.'

'You won't be able to.'

'I may as well have a try.'

I pause, meeting her eye. But this is the end of the line. There's nothing left. I'm bereft of ingenuity. Everything that has happened has only led to this. So, slowly – oh, so slowly – I start to climb down. I reach the bottom and stand aside, so Clare can climb the ladder in my place. But then, on an impulse, I grab her. She stares at me in astonishment.

I turn her towards me. I hold her by the shoulder. And I kiss her.

It's a clinch. It's 1950s-style. She's leaning back. I support her in my arms. She tries to push me off her and I release. She looks furious.

Then she grabs me and kisses me back. Harder, fiercer by far. Jumping me. Her legs around my waist. I stagger back and lean against the rail.

And that could have been the ending, if we'd both tipped over then, and plummeted to our deaths. I steady us with a hand. Her tongue is in my mouth. Her hands are in my hair. I can feel the grip of her knees. It's weird, what she's doing with her tongue. It's not ideal.

Four floors below, we hear the front door open. And we hear it close again. Clare slides down me, until her feet are back on the ground.

She smiles. And draws me by the hand towards her bedroom.

We close the door quietly. We turn off the light. We lower the blind, to shut out the street-light. Then we sit on the bed and listen as Mills ascends the stairs. She pauses on the landing. We hear her call Clare's name. Neither of us makes a sound. She carries on into her room.

'Okay,' a voice whispers. 'We're going to have to be quiet.'

VII

A PAT OF butter melts. Begins to sizzle and brown. And drown the sound of unromantic drizzle. I crack an egg like a joke. The yolk's intact. The white goes white on impact with the metal. It slides like saliva round the curve of the pan, encasing stripy strips of bacon. Sausages spit and twitch within the oven. Toast pops up like a jack-in-the-box. It's such a smashing sound. It has a ring. Like when you hit the jackpot. It goes *Kerching*.

I retract the tray from the oven. I close the door with a bang. I grab a plate as blatantly as I can. I drum on the kettle with my knife and fork. I pause. I stop to think. I drop the frying pan into the metal sink. I turn the taps on full, so the water will roar and hiss. I do everything like this.

I've lived so long in semi-silence. Noise is luxury to me.

When Mills arrives I'm ready, frozen in a pose. Picture a lost Vermeer. *The Gourmand*. Lips hinting at a sneer, my loaded fork at the ready.

'Good morning,' I declare, and take the tasty mouthful.

But she says nothing. She looks frail and tired, or taut with the effort of suppressing a painful thought. To be honest, she looks fraught.

'Clare had to head off early,' I volunteer. 'She said I could hang around and help myself to whatever was in the fridge. I hope that's okay.'

She flicks on the kettle, which starts to twitch and bubble instantly. And then clicks off again. I raise my mug. Suck in a double-espresso slurp.

'Oh man, that's good. That's just what the doctor ordered.'

She stares at me. Her face is pale. Her little scar is dark.

'There's bacon going spare, if you're interested.'

This silence is starting to grow awkward.

I try another tack. 'Did you sleep alright?'

That's the attack that catches her attention. That ratchets up the tension. It causes a pause, and makes her stare at me in disbelief.

'You know the answer to that.'

'I don't, or I wouldn't have asked.'

I circumcise a sausage.

'Seriously, Jack. How could you?'

'How could I what?'

I dip the tip in Dijon.

'*I could hear everything.*'

'I don't follow you.'

I swallow the mustard-anointed end.

'By the way,' I add, 'there's coffee in the pot.'

And that's the line that does it. Which makes her shake.

'I'm afraid,' she says, 'I think I'd like you to leave.'

That's what she tells me. But what I hear is: *kerching*. It means I'm in. It means I'm getting through to her. I'm getting under her skin.

I lower my cutlery with calm deliberation.

'Can I finish my breakfast first?'

'I'd rather you didn't. I'm sorry.'

My heart is snagged. Her eyes are bleared with tears. I'm almost crying too, but retain sang-froid. I keep my features stern: paternal dignitas.

'You're really asking me to go?'

And wretchedly, she nods.

I raise my eyebrows. I even roll my eyes.

I press the corner of my napkin to the corners of my mouth.

146

Then I fold it slowly. I hold it up, for her inspection. And then I lay it down beside my table setting. I take my last unhurried sip of coffee. And finally I rise.

As I do, I wince. I lean a little. I'm wounded from last night. My skin is raw. I steady myself, a hand upon the table. My pubic bone is bruised.

It doesn't prevent me from delivering a speech that I rehearsed.

'I'm going, because you're asking me to. But just so you know, you don't get to say who I do and don't spend the night with. That's got nothing to do with you. It used to be your call. But after we broke up, you made it clear you wanted nothing to do with me. That was when you lost any say in the matter. I don't know if I'll carry on seeing Clare. I haven't decided. But I'll tell you something. Whatever we do, it isn't up to you. If I do see her again, we might stay at my place, or we might stay at yours, whichever is more convenient. While she's living here, this is her home. And it's my home too, for as long as I'm sleeping with her.'

There's a word for her expression: *unfairness*, it says.

You know what they say about love and war. And this is both.

'I'm sorry,' I say, 'if we kept you awake. We thought you were asleep. But, if you cast your mind back, it wasn't me making most of the noise.'

It's time to depart, or at least to seem to do. But it's hard to resist a parting shot, which I toss over my shoulder like the end of a long scarf.

'I'll be seeing you,' I say.

In the hall, I hesitate. I smile at my reflection in the glass. I move to the front door and open it audibly. But then, without stepping through, I close it again with a bang. I stay where I am in the hall. And I listen.

The house is silent. But isn't it interesting, that silent is an anagram of listen. Listen. Silent. Silent. Listen. Time passes, turning into the past.

I wend my way into the drawing room. I blend into the wall. Spying is an art, like everything else. I do it exceptionally well.

My eyeball moves to the doorway, into the other room. It peeps through the hinge-crack. She's there, seated at the table. Her posture defeated. Her perfect head couched in her perfect hands. Moved, unmoving.

And then, after this pause, she explodes.

Imagine some drums and cymbals, which mark the crescendo, the last blast of a song. They tumble down and crash into a sea of percussion and harmonious falsettos. Consider, for an idea of what I mean, the song *Intro* by M83 (feat. Zola Jesus) at around the three minute twenty mark.

With a fist, she slams the table. Swipes her forearm sideways, sweeping off all the crockery. It splinters as it hits the floor. She's screaming and hammering with her hands, palms turned down, fingers arched against their curve. Hair everywhere. As she detonates the air, she has the arms of a Hindu goddess, a black widow, a witch. Which makes me a warlock. *No more Mr Nice Guy*: that's what I'm trying to say. Time to move in for the kill. And all the windows shatter through the streets of Notting Hill.

The storm is past. The two eyes at its heart becalmed. She picks a way through the debris with a placid pan and brush.

They say a writer should have a splinter of ice in his heart.

In my case, it's the tip of an iceberg.

Not that I don't care. It's because I care I'm pleased. If I can make Mills sad, I can make her happy. You see? Her happiness is everything to me. Whatever it takes to make it, and no matter the sacrifice, that's what I'll do. Well, wouldn't you? I sit on the floor and stick my feet up in the air. Roll back on my arse, and pop my shoes and socks off silently.

She has pulled on her coat. Stepped out into the hall. So I slide through into the dining room, in case she glances over her shoulder. But she's gone, taking with her a bin bag containing the shards of plate, the coffee cups she broke. The door slams like a lid upon the silence. Leaving the house to me.

I'm the floor and the ceiling. I'm the carpet on the stairs. I am this house, do you see, and it is me. I'm Roya-fucking-kovsky.

The smile slides from my face.

Why? I'll tell you.

I've seen something I don't like.

There. Under the kitchen table.

I slough off my clothes like skin.

I'm in. *Équilibre de chat.* Saut de mur?

No. *Saut de table.* And I'm on.

And flatten. I'm the tablecloth.

My fingers grip the rim. For a moment, I don't dare to look. I just stay, stopped on the tabletop, face-down, an inverted Vitruvian man. What did I see, which grazed my gaze? A lump, a tiny shape, a morsel. It looked like a fallen sausage, but it wasn't a sausage, alas. Would that it had been.

I clutch the table like a shield. While I'm here, I won't be able to see what I've come to see. Which my eyes can't bear to look upon, but must.

I edge towards the edge. And I peer.

And catch my breath up. I'm dumb. From either eye, a single tear is forced by the one that follows. The first two detonate.

It's a mouse. And not just any mouse. You know the one I mean.

Matthew. In an unmistakable attitude. On his back, his legs held out. Teeth gritted and bared. Eyes clenched. Unmoving. Moving me to tears.

Oh, Matthew! What have they done to you?

All energy gone, I topple. I tip and drop. I flop to the fucking floor. I'm on my back, spatchcocked, racked, dispatched in grief. Groaning, grizzling, barely able to breathe. Eventually, with infinite care, I reach out a hand and scoop him up in my palm.

When I squeeze, his mouse-mouth opens. As if he's trying to speak.

'What's that, Matthew? Are you trying to tell me something?'

His little mouth opens and closes.

'I'm sorry. I didn't catch that.'

I move him to my ear.

'It was the girls, you say?'

<u>BATH TIME</u>

Written by
Jack Raphael

69 Milton Road
London W11
jack_raphael2015@outlook.com
0044 7985 ******

INT. BATHROOM. NIGHT.

Hot water THUNDERS into a bath, creating steam, which fills the room. Close up on: the big old-fashioned bath tap, on whose surface we can make out the distorted image of a girl. A nude, slight, neat body. It's CLARE. She turns off the tap and climbs into the bath.

                    CLARE
          Sweet Jesus!

She hurriedly climbs out. The bath is far too hot. She adds some cold water and swirls it with her hand. Then, once she's sure the temperature is right, she climbs in again, letting her breath out slowly. It's still pretty hot. Carefully, she reaches for her book, which she left on a chair by the bath.

Something makes her pause. Was it a CREAK she heard in the corridor? She decides that it wasn't.

She starts to read her book, a copy of Aeschylus' Oresteia. When eventually she looks up, she sees JACK standing in the doorway of the bathroom.

                    CLARE (CONT'D)
               (splashing water)
          Oh my god! Oh my god! Oh my god!
               (laughing, embarrassed)
          You gave me— *such* a shock!

                    JACK
          Hello, Clare.

                    CLARE
          How long have you been standing
          there? How did you even get *in*?

                    JACK
Royakovsky let me in.

                    CLARE
No, but seriously.

                    JACK
You left the front door open.

                    CLARE
Did I? That isn't like me. Hey,
don't get me wrong. I'm not
complaining.
        (beat)
I've been thinking about you.

                    JACK
I've been thinking about you.

                    CLARE
Last night was fun.

                    JACK
It was an epiphany.

                    CLARE
Ohmygod. I was so tired at work,
I thought I was gonna die—
        (beat)
Are you okay?

                    JACK
I'm fine.

                    CLARE
You just seem a bit—

                    JACK
I'm okay.

                    CLARE
Why are you looking at me?

                    JACK
Because you're talking.

                    CLARE
Yeah, I know, but why are you
looking at me like *that*?

                    JACK
You're quite a talker.

                    CLARE
I don't think that's anything to
apologise for. I hate people who
sit there and say nothing, who
think just because they're
pretty or beautiful or whatever,
their work is done.

                    JACK
Mills talks occasionally.

                    CLARE
Who said I was talking about
Mills? Okay. You're right. Shall
we make a pact? Let's not talk
about Mills anymore tonight.
Okay?

                    JACK
Okay.

                    MILLS
          Are you getting in?

Jack hesitates. Then he pulls his jumper off over
his head. His T-shirt goes with it, revealing his
slender torso, his articulated stomach. He
undresses until he's standing there naked apart
from a pair of skin-coloured cycling shorts.

                    CLARE
          Are you going to leave those
          on?
              (beat)
          Fine. Leave them on. I don't
          mind that you're weird. I think
          it makes you interesting. Kiss
          please.

                    JACK
          What?

                    CLARE
          Kiss please.

She points at her mouth. He gives her a kiss.

                    JACK
          I'll get in behind.

                    CLARE
              (laughing)
          I can't believe you're keeping
          your cycling shorts on. Why are
          you even wearing those things?

                    JACK
          They make me streamlined.

He climbs into the bath. She leans back against
him. The water level rises, almost spilling over
the sides.

> CLARE
>
> Kiss please.

She points at her ear. For a moment, behind her,
his face contorts into a look of hatred. Then he
leans forwards and kisses her ear.

> CLARE
>
> I'm glad you're here. I get
> spooked sometimes in this big
> empty house.

> JACK
>
> It's never actually empty,
> though, is it, if you think
> about it.

> CLARE
>
> What do you mean?

> JACK
>
> There's always Roy.

> CLARE
>
> (shivers)
> I'm definitely going to explore
> that attic one of these days.

> JACK
>
> I know you are.

> CLARE
>
> If he's there, I'll find him.

> JACK
> I know you will.

Putting his hands on her shoulders, he starts to
massage them gently.

> CLARE (CONT'D)
> Ooh. That's nice. Can you do it
> a little harder?

> JACK
> I see you're reading the
> *Agamemnon*.

> CLARE
> That's right. It's pretty awesome
> actually. I was just thinking—
> *Ooh! That's lovely!*— that if you
> were going to murder someone, the
> bath would be a good place to do
> it. You see my point? If you were
> going to— *Oh, boy!*— chop someone
> into bits—

CUT TO:

INT. LANDING. CONTINUOUS.

We're on the landing outside the bathroom. The
bathroom door is closed, but we can hear voices.

> CLARE (O.S.)
> Because your victim would be off
> their guard. Do you see what I
> mean? When you're taking a bath,
> you're not expecting it. *You
> don't need to do that quite so
> hard.* And crucially too, you'd

be naked. Which would mean you
wouldn't have any weapons. *Jack.*
Not so hard. You're hurting me.

                    JACK (O.S.)
          I'm not Jack.

                    CLARE (O.S.)
          I said— stop it.

                    JACK (O.S.)
          I'm not Jack, Clare. I'm Roy.

                    CLARE (O.S.)
          Isn't funny!

                    JACK (O.S.)
          It's not a joke. I'm Roy. It's me.
          It's always been me.

                    CLARE (O.S.)
          Can't— breathe—

                    JACK (O.S.)
          I'm not Jack. I'm Roy. Do you
          understand? I'm Roya-fucking-
          kovsky. You've done it, Clare.
          You've done what you said you'd
          do. You've found me. I'm Roy,
          I'm Roy, I'm Roy—

While this is being said, we hear the SOUNDS OF A
STRUGGLE. Water being SPLASHED. COUGHING.
SPLUTTERING. LIMBS BANGING AND RUBBING the sides of
the bath. The violence increases. Then gradually it
lessens. At last, there is silence.

A little bit of water seeps out through the gap at
the bottom of the door.

NOTES

* * *

In my previous phases in the house, I had co-existed with Mills. I had listened to her. Watched her. I'd taken an active hand in the proceedings of her life. Now, with Clare gone, for the first time I had Mills to myself. It was like the old days. When she came home from work, I'd be waiting for her. When she watched TV, I'd be in the next-door room. One evening, I even managed to squeeze myself into the marriage chest in the bay of the window. It was pretty uncomfortable but at the same time it gave me a thrill to be so close to her. When she left to go to bed, I waited for a bit. Then I climbed out of the chest and went upstairs and listened outside her door. When I was sure she was asleep, I crept into the room and watched her sleeping for a while.

I won't pretend that the Clare situation didn't make the logistics of my life more complicated. I now had two virtual people to control. Clare, as well as Bernhardt. It required planning. In the first instance, I invented a bout of food poisoning to explain Clare's absence from work. That dealt with the first couple of days. Then I came up with the idea of complications. The infection had spread, and affected her immune system. In the end, her sympathetic employers granted her an indefinite leave of absence until she had recovered.

And what about Mills? How did I explain to her the disappearance of her house-mate? That wasn't difficult. I sent her a text from Clare's phone saying that she'd decided to move out. The final straw, I made Clare say, was all the hassle about whether she was or wasn't allowed to go for a drink with me. The text said that she just couldn't carry on living with someone who tried to dictate her private life.

The first night, by the time Mills got home, Clare was gone. Her room was empty. The books, the framed photograph of her parents, her CDs including the single of *Luminous Times (Hold On To Love)* – all had vanished. There was no trace of her, no sign, even, that she'd ever been there. I waited until the next day to send the text to Mills. Then, when Mills called Clare's phone, I naturally didn't pick up.

My task, in a sense, was like that of a novelist. Clare and Bernhardt were my characters. My job was to make them act and interact like real people. I had to get inside their heads and mimic their voices. When I replied to emails from Clare's friends, I included American expressions such as 'awesome' and 'ohmygod'. She also used to write 'hahahahaha' when she found something funny. This was one of her habits that I had found annoying. But I swallowed my distaste, and began to write 'hahahahaha' in my responses to her friends. I found Clare easier to mimic than Bernhardt because I'd spent more time with her. In Bernhardt's case, I made a study of his previous correspondence. I noticed he had a kind of formality of tone, as if he wasn't only from another country, but also from another century.

Narrative consists of character and plot. I had my characters and I knew how they spoke and wrote. But I needed to invent a plot for them, a story of what was going on in their lives, with developments and chapters, twists and turns. As I think about it now, I suppose you could say that there's something a little creepy about what a novelist does for a living. He spends most of his time inventing stuff. Hanging out with characters who don't really exist. Controlling them. Making them walk and talk and say certain characteristic things.

160

I found myself wondering if this might not, in the end, be the explanation for everything in the universe. We're all characters in some master-novel being written in instalments by the Supreme Being. Imagine *War and Peace* stitched together with *Ulysses* and *A La Recherche du temps perdu*. With a little bit of *American Psycho* thrown in for good measure. And then the whole thing multiplied a million billion times. But how did He keep abreast of all his characters? Did He keep notes, charts, spreadsheets? Did He go for long walks in the afternoon, to allow his more complicated ideas to settle into some kind of coherence? His big themes and hefty leitmotifs. All of which would then pose two crucial questions. The first was: was He writing a comedy or a tragedy? And the second was: who was His readership?

There were times when I felt my actions were being guided by an Unseen Hand. And for a while this held an appeal for me: the theory of the Novelist God, wielding a pen like a thunderbolt. But then it occurred to me: why assume there was only one such god? Wouldn't it make more sense if there was a host, a convocation? A coterie of squabbling, rivalrous pen-pushers, all working on plots of their own. This would explain the contradictions, the repetitions. The untidinesses of life. It made more sense, and was also more pleasant to consider, which is always a key factor when selecting your religion. So the universe, existence, life itself – they were all, as it were, a kind of literary movement.

The question remained, who was the novelist god writing my story? Was it one of the big ones? Was it Graham Greene? The answer was both more mundane and stranger. It was Jack Raphael. It was me. I was the one who made myself do things, who gave myself direction, who outlined and emphasised my major character points. For you see, in addition to Clare and Bernhardt, another character in my cast-list, whom I forgot to

161

mention earlier, was myself. We all do this. We all imagine ourselves giving self-direction, as if we weren't just us, but impersonations of us. Good ones. Sometimes better than the original. But there was more to it, in my case. For you see, by then, I had also begun to write up my memories in these notebooks. As I took certain actions, I would be thinking how I would eventually describe them when I reached that point in my memoirs. I must admit, there were certain things I did purely in order that I could later write about them in a certain way. All of which tended to beg the same questions I asked a moment ago about God. It remained to be seen if I was writing a comedy or a tragedy. And who, for that matter, were my readers?

Ah, Mills, you were becoming one of my characters too. I didn't ask your permission. I'm sorry about that. But it was unavoidable. I had absolute control over the actions of Clare and Bernhardt. I had partial control, most of the time, over myself. And you? That was the challenge. *Hic labor, hoc opus est.* Because by then I had seen what had to happen. I had glimpsed the bigger picture. It was so simple and beautiful, it made me want to weep.

Shall I tell you what I'd seen? Alright, then. It was this. Jack was going to leave the house and Mills was going to leave with him. And Clare and Bernhardt were going to help to bring this about. You see the glory of it? The symmetry. I had entered the house and had made it mine. I had separated Mills from what she thought was her support network, but which had actually been the opposite of that. I had liberated her from the encumbrances that had been holding her back. So now she was free to leave and start a new life. And it was going to have to be abroad. That was obvious. For I knew that, soon, the disappearance of Clare or Bernhardt would be noticed. And then the clock would start ticking.

I had some fun considering where we should go to build our

new life together. Africa? Vietnam? The South Sea Islands? In the end, though, I resisted the temptation to be self-indulgent. The most important thing was that Mills should agree to accompany me. Everything hinged on that. Accordingly it was vital that I selected a country that was likely to appeal to her as a destination, at least at first. And the answer seemed clear. It had to be Italy. Why? Mills was an Italophile. She'd spent a couple of months in Bologna, a few years back, as part of her university course. She still had friends there. And of course, Italy has a lot to recommend it, from any point of view. All I had to do was get her there. Maybe, I thought, I wouldn't even tell her that the move would be permanent. Just persuade her to come on holiday with me, and once we were there, get to work on convincing her to stay.

Before any of this could happen, though, I had to have sex with her. But it was a puzzle, how I was going to persuade her. The last time I'd seen her, she had lost it completely and screamed at me to get out of the house. That hadn't been a particularly promising encounter. But at the same time, it had been promising, in a sense. Pain is so close to pleasure, and hate is so close to love. The death of love, you see, isn't hate. It's indifference.

That was what I told myself. I even managed to persuade myself that it might not be as difficult as I'd feared. My idea was that I would simply call her up and ask her if I might drop round some time, in order to apologise in person for our altercation of the other day. I was about to do this when I was preempted by a text from her. As it turned out – can you believe it? – she was apologising to me. She said that she shouldn't have told me to leave and that I had been right: it was up to me, who I did and didn't spend the night with. She said that if I wanted to carry on seeing Clare, then that was fine by her. Part of her reason for saying this, I presumed, was because Clare no longer lived with

163

her, though she didn't make any explicit reference to this in her text. Nevertheless, I gathered that she felt ashamed of her emotional negativity towards me over breakfast. Her attitude was softening. In a trice, I had my mobile in my hand, and I called her. Alas, she didn't pick up.

I left no voicemail. Never leave voicemails: that's what I say. If you want to control another person, and direct their actions like those of some character in a novel, you have to talk to them. You have to go up against them, voice to voice. If you leave a voicemail, then the ball is in their court. I didn't leave a voicemail, but I waited until her phone had rung about twenty times, and then I ended the call. Mills was frowning at her phone. I knew this because when she didn't pick up after the first ten rings, I went downstairs and spied on her in the drawing room. It was a shame that she hadn't picked up, but I didn't feel too bad about it. While frowning at her phone, she had been blushing too, which suggested a kind of excitement. I sensed that she had felt conflicted. A part of her had wanted to pick up, but that another part of her had been warning her that it might not be a good idea.

I was biding my time in the library later in the day, when Mills called me. It was a weekday. Mills was at home a lot now during the day, because a long temping job she had been doing had come to end, with the result that, for the time being, she was unemployed. I had had to adapt my regime to accommodate this. I'd become still and silent during the day and more active during the night. Even at night, I couldn't stomp around. I had to watch my step. But she was – she had always been – a heavy sleeper. I remember that, when we were going out, I resented this. Why was it, I asked myself, that she was always able to slip into a deep slumber at the drop of a hat, leaving me to toss and turn? Most of the time, during the day, because she was around, I stayed in the attic, hibernating, building up my strength. There was one other room, though, where I could safely be, and that was the library.

I asked her what was up. Not much, she said. She was just returning my call. And oh, that seemed such a triumph! We had again reached the stage, Mills and I, where I could call her and if she failed to answer, she would call me back. Just like normal human beings. Like friends, like lovers. I explained that I had wanted to apologise for my insensitivity of the previous week. She had been completely within her rights to lose her temper. I admitted that I wouldn't have liked it if Mills had spent the night with Bernhardt within my earshot. Then, since the subject of Bernhardt had naturally arisen, I asked her how things were going between the two of them. Had they been seeing much of each other? Or was Bernhardt proving rather elusive? Would she characterise his manner as cold? Had a vibrancy gone out of his tone, when he sent her emails? Would she describe him as lifeless at all?

No, Mills told me. In fact, she had recently had quite a strange message from him. He had told her that he was going to be away for a while, handling a piece of family business in Vienna. Then he'd added that, since he was going to be away, it was probably a good time to confess something he had been thinking about for a while: namely that he didn't want to carry on seeing her. His reason? The truth was, he had begun seeing someone else. It was no one Mills knew, but he thought it best to be honest about these things. Mills's voice cracked with emotion as she told me about this over the phone. And she had to stop, to catch her breath, as she described the crowning insult, which was that Bernhardt had signed off by suggesting that perhaps she should get back in touch with her ex. He explained that when he had met me, that time in the restaurant, I had struck him as a likely-looking fellow. He also suggested that I might still be in love with her. He said he had noticed something in my manner, a

165

hint of unease, a reluctance to smile, and an eagerness to end our conversation, all of which seemed to imply that I might still retain some tender feelings for her.

Naturally, I knew all this before Mills told me, since it was I who had sent her the original email. But I pretended to be surprised, even outraged. I told her that, for the record, I wasn't still in love with her. 'I know you're not,' she replied. 'I mean, I'm fond of you and everything,' I went on in a whisper, 'but that's as far as it goes.' 'I know,' she repeated.

Then she asked, 'Why are you whispering?'

I thought about this for a moment. Then I replied, 'I'm in a library.'

Of course, that wasn't the only reason I was keeping quiet. It was also because I didn't want Mills, who was in the drawing room, to hear me. There was a danger she might leave the drawing room and climb the stairs while talking to me. It was best if we kept the conversation short. So I put it to her straight. I asked her if she fancied meeting up to eat caramels. 'To eat caramels?' she said. 'Or we could go for coffee, if you prefer.' This was all arbitrary, since I had no intention of meeting her outside the house. Why would I, when it could happen here? But the important thing was to get her to agree to meet, and then I could just do my thing of dropping by. The trouble was, she didn't agree. She said that she didn't want to meet up. There was no point, she said. In fact, she went even further than that.

She said there was a very good reason for us not to meet. 'Namely?' I asked. She went silent then, on the other end of the line. But I knew what she was thinking. She was thinking the level of emotion she'd felt, after I'd spent the night with Clare, had been disturbing. She was worried her old feelings might revive. Then she broke the silence. She said, 'Jack, I don't want to go out with you again.' And in the core of my being, I wanted to cry, 'Why not?' But what I said was, calmly, 'Of course not.

166

Who said anything about that? To be honest, that's a very odd thing to say.' 'In any case,' she went on, 'you're going out with Clare. Say hi from me, the next time you see her.' I told her patiently that I wasn't going out with Clare. I had never been going out with her. There had just been that one night, which I regretted, as I had already explained. If I had my time again, I would do things differently.

There was another one of those silences, then. At length, Mills said, 'Okay, well, I think I'd better go now.' And with that, we brought our conversation to a close.

I slid my mobile phone into its accustomed place, just below the waistband of my cycling shorts. They were a little on the small side, and as a consequence, gripped me very tightly around the waist – so tightly that I sometimes worried that they might be cutting off the blood supply. But on the plus side, because of how tightly they gripped me, it was quite easy for me to use them to carry three mobile phones: my own, Clare's, and Bernhardt's. My own, as I say, was held in the centre, pressed to my pubic phone. Clare's I kept on the left, pressed against my thigh, and Bernhardt's, meanwhile, was couched on the right.

I didn't feel downcast after the phone call. On the contrary, I felt excited. Admittedly, I hadn't achieved my objective, which was for her to agree to see me. But apart from that, the vibe had been encouraging. There had been a kind of tension between us, which I could only interpret as positive. When she'd told me to say hi from her to Clare, for instance, it had smacked of jealousy. The word 'jealousy' should only really be used to refer to a possessive attitude towards something you already own. A dragon, for example, guards its treasure jealously. A jealous husband tries to shoot his wife's lover. But jealousy is a valid word for what Mills felt about me. The way I saw it, she did own me. She possessed me. I was hers.

She was mine. *Her soft white flesh was mine. Soft. White. Flesh.*

Was she mine or was I hers? We were each other's. At the outset of the story, there were four main characters. They had now been whittled down to two. The two of us. It was Mills and me. And shortly, I thought, there would be a further whittling. What I mean by this is that when we were reunited, it would be such a fusion, it would be like a marriage service. We would become one flesh.

Sometimes it felt as if that had already been achieved. As if we were man and wife, or (as is less often said) woman and husband. We lived together, for one thing. When she woke up in the morning, I was the first to see her face. We shared the same food (though I partook of smaller portions). Admittedly, we were rarely in the same room, but I kept an eye on her. I performed small domestic chores on her behalf, which I wouldn't have bothered to do for anyone else. For instance, I noticed that the drain had become clogged in the kitchen sink, so when Mills was asleep, I applied a plunger and managed to suck and thrust until the blockage had been shifted. I had also become a regular and committed duster. In the main, I was inhibited by the fact that if I carried out a task that was too noticeable, she might be liable to grow suspicious. Dusting was the perfect compromise. She didn't notice that it was being done, but it raised her general sense of wellbeing. Her cleaner, incidentally, I had long ago given her marching orders. Then I had altered her number in Mills's phone, so Mills wouldn't be able to call her, to ask her why she hadn't bothered showing up for work.

There was so much to do. It wasn't until days later that I realised a mood had settled over me that was so unfamiliar I had forgotten what it was like. It was a mood of peace. The last time I had felt it, I think, had been during that week that Mills and I had spent together in that apartment on the island of Procida in the bay of Naples. Strange, that I should have felt such peace during that week, since it was in the aftermath of her father's death. But I suppose if I can identify a common ingredient to those two periods in my life, it's that in both cases I knew exactly what I had to do each day. In Procida, my duty was to take Mills out of herself: to amuse her, and ease the grieving process, to take the edge off her pain. And now, in the house, my duty was also clear. I had to do whatever I could (without risk of being discovered) to persuade her to change her mind and agree to see me.

I devoted hours to composing fake spam emails and sending them to her yahoo account. Each was designed to set off a train of thought that would ultimately lead to me. For instance, I google-searched for a travel company that offered package holidays to Procida, and then sent her an email, as if from them, advertising a special offer. *'A fortnight in Procida: the undiscovered jewel of Italian islands. More peaceful than Ischia, more real than Capri, Procida is the place Italians go for their holidays. We're offering 14 days in a bijou apartment carved out of the rock of the island's antique Roman port.'* And so on. The email included a link to pictures of an apartment: the very apartment, needless to say, where Mills and I had stayed.

On another occasion, I called her, and then hung up after a couple of rings. Then immediately I texted her: 'Sorry. I think I just pocket-called you by mistake!' Then, half an hour later, I repeated the process: 'Damn! I think I just did it again! Ignore all future calls from me!' She texted a reply: 'Okay!' I wondered if her exclamation mark was intended as mockery. I had thought hard about the exclamation marks in my text messages, and decided that they would convey a desirable casualness. An exclamation mark suggested you were friendly, upbeat, and also that, crucially, you hadn't taken the trouble to think of something to say that was sufficiently interesting on its own, without an exclamation mark.

It was so important, I felt, that I should be light. To be heavy would be disastrous. This was the mistake, I believed, that most rejected lovers made. They became too heavy, too earnest, and thereby confirmed the other person in the feeling that had normally prompted the break-up in the first place: namely that they were not having enough fun in their company. Because that's what it boils down to, as often as not. Are we having fun? This was the crucial message that I had to convey to Mills: that I was fun. I had been fun, I thought, in the old days, when we'd first got together. There had been times when we'd had fun. But somewhere along the way, I had lost the knack. I wasn't sure, in fact, that I had yet regained it, but that didn't necessarily matter. All that mattered was that I should successfully convince Mills that I was fun. It would be a self-fulfilling prophecy. Because if she believed it, then it would come true. Most of the qualities of a beloved are actually self-fulfilling prophecies, I believe. If you think someone is beautiful, you make them beautiful. If you think them intelligent, that's what they become. And if Mills thought I was fun, then fun was what I would be. It's a deeply important insight, this, because it also holds true for negative perceptions. If you think that someone's boring, consider to what extent you are making them boring, by the way that you're treating them. The same goes for jealous, nagging, needy, and all the rest. I really can't stress this enough. You have to start to take some responsibility for the way that other people behave in your company.

VIII

HOW DO YOU know if a girl has fallen for you? You have to read the signs. (It's all about reading. It's all about the signs.) But you have to be careful not to read too much into things. (It comes from too long having to read so much into hardly anything at all.) Eg Mills is sipping a cup of tea. What does it mean? Does it mean she misses me? Not necessarily. While she sips, she watches the video for the song *Firework* by Katy Perry.

My first instinct is to think: that proves that she's in love with me.

Only someone in love, or barking mad, could be a Katy Perry fan.

But then I realise I've got it wrong. For as the singer starts to sing, and as I listen to the words and watch the screen (over Mills's shoulder), my heart swells. My eyes well and I want to weep. Why? Because it's so damn good. The message is simple: each of us has a unique talent and it's our duty to work out what it is and find a way to release it, at which point we will in some sense resemble a firework. The video finds a neat way to get this idea across visually. It presents a series of people who find a way to overcome obstacles, and as they do, sparks and bolts of many-coloured light explode from their chests, while other people look on in wonderment and Katy Perry sings her heart out. There's the fat girl who's initially too shy to join her friends in the swimming pool. Then suddenly she finds the courage and whips off her clothes and charges towards the water. There's the shy homosexual in a club who wants to kiss a handsome stranger.

171

Then suddenly he finds the courage and charges towards him across the room. There's the boy whose parents are always arguing and making him sad. Then suddenly he finds the courage and charges into the kitchen and comes between them. They immediately stop arguing, which is hardly surprising, given that sparks and bolts of many-coloured light are now bursting from their son's chest. It would give anyone cause to pause.

Listening to this song, and watching the video over Mills's shoulder (I'm peering from the doorway in the hall), is a mixed experience for me. Because on the one hand its power is pulsing through me. It makes me feel sparks and bolts of many-coloured light are about to burst from my chest. But on the other hand, I realise the fact Mills has chosen to watch it doesn't prove she loves me. When all's said and done, it's just a fantastic song. It's a real cracker. If I may say so, it's a musical firework.

And then, to my amazement, I see a bolt of light bursting out of me. It's not coming from my chest. It's coming from my cock. My cock's on fire.

No, sorry, my mistake. It's coming from my pubic bone. From where I keep my mobile phone. And when I look at Mills, hers is in her hand.

And so I go.

Back-flip. Half-landing. Up.

Landing on the landing. *Roulade. Franchissement.*

Mine is in mine. I pause. I breathe.

And then I answer.

J: *Millsworth. How's it going?*

M: *Are you in the library again?*

J: *As a matter of fact, I am.*

M: *Sorry. I didn't mean to disturb you.*

J: *You can't disturb me. I'm already disturbed.*

M: *No, it's just I… don't know how to put this.*

J: What do you mean? What's happened?
M: I think I'd like you to come round.
J: You want me to come round?
M: Not if you're too busy.
J: What's happened?
M: I'll tell you when you get here.
J: Okay, fine. I'm coming round now.
M: You're sure you're not too busy?
J: I'll be there in five.

* * *

When she opens the door, her face is pale. Her face. Her face. If you want to know what she looks like, it's the girl in the Bruno Mars video. I'm serious. Check it out on YouTube.

'It's you,' she says, with something like relief. Then lets me in.

'Are you alright?' I say. 'You look as if you've seen a ghost.'

She leads me into the drawing room. Which looks exactly the same as a moment ago. Her laptop's open on the table. Its screen shows the selfsame video. The assegais and the iklwas? They're lined up on the wall.

But I'm finding it hard to concentrate. A mantra keeps repeating in my head. *You can do anything.* These same four words repeat. *You can do anything. You can do anything. You can do anything.* How do I stop it? I have to stop it. Mills is saying something.

'I said, would you like a drink?'

You can do anything.

'What time is it?'

'Half past six.'

'Oh, go on then.'

You can do anything.

I refrain from asking why she asked me here. She'll tell me

173

when she's ready. In any case, I already know. It's because my efforts haven't been in vain, my exertions and excursions on the treadmill of her brain.

And I know what she's going to say. I've always known.

She's going to say: I want you back.

She's going to say: I still love you.

She's going to say: Aw!

She's only human. How could she resist my ministrations? My mild- then-wild manipulations, which mounted to a climax of a cinematic size. Of Imax magnitude. She couldn't. Wouldn't, not if I went over now, and cupped her face in my ecstatic hands.

I could do that, but I don't. I luxuriate in the moment. I recline.

I indicate the image on the screen: so very Perry.

'I fucking love that song,' I say. 'I'm serious.'

Her hand shakes (bless her!) as she hands me my drink.

'Really? I'd have thought you'd have hated it.'

'I love it. I think it's amazing. I particularly like that scene at the end, when all the youth of Budapest converge on Buda Castle, and just start dancing around crazily in the courtyard.'

'I didn't know that that was where it was.'

'Named after the brother of Attila the Hun.'

'Jack?'

'Yes?'

'The reason I asked you here…'

Ah! Here we go. I say, 'I think I know.'

'You do?' She seems taken aback.

'I think so, yes.' *You can do anything.*

'But I don't see how you can.' Poor sweet, she's shy.

'I think I do.' I may as well be round with her. 'You asked me here this afternoon because you think you made a mistake when you broke up with me. You've realised you're still in love with me and you want to get back together. Am I right?' While I talk,

174

I tactfully look away. But now I sneak a look. And find, to my surprise, she seems bewildered.

'No,' she says simply. 'That's not it at all.'

She takes refuge in her G&T. Too long a pause for me.

'What are you talking about? If it wasn't that, what was it?'

And so she tells me. And I couldn't have guessed it. No, not in a million years.

The black facts. Mills had grown suspicious of Bernhardt. Something in a text had vexed her: an offness in his tone. His phone so often off. Or it would come on at night to send an enigmatic bedtime text (which hadn't been his habit). He said he was in the office, when he wasn't. Was he in trouble or off his head? She softened; then hardened again, after she got a message saying that he'd had to go to Vienna. Some family matter.

The problem was this.

His family don't live in Vienna. They live in Zurich. Rotten Swiss.

Pissed off, and only semi-serious, Mills asked Charlie, who works as an aide at Number Ten, to call in a favour from his friends at MI5. Charlie snapped into action. And so did the spooks. They did what's known in the trade as a triangulation. If the target uses his phone, they can pinpoint its geographical location to 200m. That's what they did. Whenever Bernhardt's phone was used, they traced it. It has been used, from time to time.

Bottom line – over the past few days, Bernhardt (or his mobile phone at least) hasn't been more than a stone's throw from Number 69, Milton Road.

'Is that even legal?' I ask, mouth dry.

'I doubt it,' she replies. 'Who knows?'

'Jesus. So what are you saying?'

'I don't know. I'm just scared, that's all.'

'You think he's out there now? In the rain.'

'God, I hope not. But I'm really glad you're here.'

So I let my words go walkabout. I let them off the leash.

'I knew this girl at uni, who told me this story. Her parents got divorced when she was in her teens. It was messy. Not a good break-up. Although, let's be honest, what is? But this was a bad one, apparently. Her dad went a bit nuts. She moved out with her mum, and for some reason they moved into a house whose garden backed on to the garden of the house where her dad was living. I know. Bad decision, right? So after a while, her dad started to know stuff about them that he wasn't meant to know. Like, for instance, he might make some reference to where the two of them had spent the previous evening, even when they hadn't told him where they'd been. It started to freak them out. And one night, they were discussing it, this weird situation, with a friend. It was the girl I knew, her mum, and a female friend of the mum's. So they were there, these three, discussing it in the sitting room. And at a certain point, the friend said, 'I know you'll think I'm paranoid, but maybe he bugged the place.' The others both said this was unlikely. But the friend said, 'Humour me. Have a look behind that curtain in the corner.' So the girl got up, and she went over to the curtain that was in the corner of the room, and she pulled it back. And there he was, her dad, just standing there, his face staring, pressed against the glass.'

Mills has her hands over her ears, her elbows touching.

'Why would you tell me a story like that?'

'I just think we should consider every possibility.'

Slowly we both turn. The curtains of the drawing room are closed.

'You really think it's possible? But why would anyone do that?'

The curtains look back at us. They don't give much away.

'What time was it when you spoke to Charlie?'

'He emailed me. He's in America.'

'And what time was that?'

'I don't know. About an hour ago.'

I nod. I put my palms together at my mouth. I purse and press.

I rise to my feet, and walk to where the curtains meet. Eyes fixed on Mills, I take the parted material in my hands. (She blocks her ears again.) Then, with the vim and thunder of a toreador, I rip those curtains asunder. To reveal: a red-painted Slovakian marriage chest. The panes of rained-on glass. The darkling street.

It's not night yet but it will be. It's getting underway.

'So what do you make of it all? What's your conclusion?'

'I don't know. But I'm scared. Do you think I should call the police?'

'I wouldn't recommend it.' Au contraire.

'Why wouldn't you recommend it?'

'Have you got any cigarettes?'

'I'm running a bit low, in fact.'

'But do you mind if I take one?

'No, of course I don't. Go for it.'

'I thought you were planning to give up.'

'I am planning to give up. But not immediately.'

'Have you noticed how lighters never light the first time?'

'Why don't you think I should call the police, Jack?'

'They always work the second time. You see?'

'But why don't you think that I should call the police?'

'What are you going to tell them? He hasn't done anything yet. I mean, strictly speaking, he hasn't done anything wrong. There's no law against lying to your girlfriend. That's the trouble with cases like this. I had to go into it at one point. For something I was writing. And it turns out that the police can't do anything until the law has been broken. Bernhardt has to threaten you, you know? Or try to kill you or something.'

'In any case, there may be a more normal explanation.'

177

'What possible normal explanation could there be?'

'Maybe he's been tucking into your next-door neighbour. Which is why he's lying about where he is. And why, when the MI5 guys did their thing, he turned out to be within a 200 metre radius of the house.'

'Thank you, Jack, for putting that idea into my head.'

'I'm just saying. There could be another explanation.'

'I don't like to think of Bernhardt with some other girl.'

'It sounds like you were pretty serious about him. Or are.'

She nods. 'We were having so much fun. Where are you going?'

Flight 2a. Flight 2b. Flight 3a. Flight 3b. *Planche*. And into attic.

'What the fuck have you done to her, you fucking Kraut? You sausage-munching squarehead? You sour sauerkraut-sucking fucking Nazi-loving mother-fucker? I'm being serious. She's totally obsessed with you.'

With each of these remarks, I strike a blow. A blow for me, a blow for her. A blow for women everywhere. And Bernhardt takes it, as he must. He was always a bit of a softy, a tad wishy-washy, and he's been getting a lot softer of late. So when my fist finds flesh, it doesn't sting. No, au contraire. The fist goes in. The cling film splits. He's squishy-squashy.

'Are you listening, Fritz? We didn't win two world wars so you could come waltzing in and steal our frauleins. So hands off, Hans. Hans, off.'

His filmic face stares back at me. From slits, something oozes. A nameless liquid, grey as skin. He's been a bit off-colour in recent days. But he still seems kingly. Monarchic. And he's not alone. (Oh no, love, he's not alone.) At his feet sprawls Clare, limbs akimbo, a clingy, gift-wrapped princess. Film flattening her cheeks and hair, giving her a grin.

'And you can wipe that smile off your face,' I growl.

Laché. Atterissage réception. *Forward roll.*

'I've just had an idea. Maybe he's in the house.'

'Jack, please. I'm scared enough already.'

'When was the last time you saw him?'

'I don't remember. It was… Oh god.'

'Maybe he never left. Think about it.'

In fact, he never did. Think about *that.*

'Stop it. I don't want to think about it.'

'You have to. You could be in danger.'

You really should. You really could be, Mills.

'Why are you trying to scare me like this?'

'All I'm saying is, the last time you saw him, he was here. You haven't seen him since. Around that time, Clare thinks she heard someone lurking in the basement. We have to consider every possibility.'

'But why would anyone do a thing like that?'

'They wouldn't. Unless they were completely insane.'

'But he wasn't insane. I mean, he isn't. Bernhardt isn't insane.'

'How do you know? Can I have another cigarette? Thanks. How do you ever really know what someone else is thinking? They can be looking all handsome and well-groomed. Benign, you know? Civilised. But behind the smiling eyes, they're wondering how long you'd keep in the fridge. I know. I'm sorry. I'm just saying he could be nuts. He may not even want to hurt you. More likely he's obsessed. Maybe something happened on the night of the dinner party. It could have been something small, like – Clare said there was some incident. Some wine spilt on his shirt? It might have tipped him over the edge. But he doesn't mean any harm. On the contrary. He's probably watching over you, to make sure you're okay. He probably creeps into your room at night, and kneels at the foot of your bed.'

'I'm about to get really cross with you.'

'We're going to have to search the house.'

'No!' I'm halfway to the door. 'Jack, please…'

'Just to put our minds at rest. It's fine. I don't mind doing it.'

She's clinging to me. I enjoy the feel of her hand. Then I shake her off.

'While I'm gone, you can fix me another G&T. And can you make it a bit stronger this time? Thanks. I'll be two secs. Okay. Maybe three.'

One second later, I return. 'Permission to go into your bedroom?'

Permission granted. Three seconds after that, I burst into the attic.

Hi, Hun, I'm home! (Did you miss me? Did you, huh?)

Start ransacking Clare's things. Looking for that spare pack of fags. She doesn't need them now and Mills only has a couple left. I don't want to have to go out. I want to stay in. TV and pizza with Mills, just like in the old days. The good old days, when we were still in love.

I thought it was in this case. In this case, I was wrong.

I open the second case. Ah, there they are. *They're there.*

I grab the fresh packet and cram it into the fourth pocket of my combat trousers. The other three have phones. 'Thanks, guys,' I say. And I scram.

'I found *this*.' From the cellar, a bottle of Valpolicella.

Mills smokes her final Marlboro Light. The sight is quite instructive. When she inhales, she shuts her eyes. If not, she gets smoke in them. Her hand is still shaking. And if I had to sum up her life in a single emotion, what would it be? The answer's obvious: fear. Not only now, but always. She was always afraid. Afraid of being afraid. Afraid of me.

And what about me, while we're on that topic? What would it be, my signature emotion? The one that defines me. Love? Hate? No, neither. I'd have to say: irritability.

'I think you should send him a text. Tell him to bugger off.'

'Okay.' She kisses the rim of her glass. 'What shall I say?'

'Just tell him to stop being such a fucking stalker.'

'I can't say that. What if it's a coincidence?'

'Tell him you don't want to see him anymore. Tell him you've realised you're still in love with your ex-boyfriend, and you made a mistake when you broke up with him.'

If this is a joke, it goes down rather well.

She smiles her Miley Cyrus smile. Speaks the words as she types.

'*I think I just spotted you in the street. I thought you were in Vienna...* How do you spell Vienna? It doesn't matter. Okay. *Question mark. Send.*'

Almost immediately, something squeaks in my pocket.

She looks at my trousers. 'I think that was you.'

I wave it away. 'It'll be your former housemate.'

'Aren't you even going to read it?'

'She wants to see me before I go.'

'Go?' she asks, as I meant her to. 'Go where?'

And so I tell her my plan: to move to Italy. To travel and write, and live the good life. To roam in Rome, and eat pizza in Pisa. To tour Turin. Then Venice is an option. Florence and Naples. The cultural staples. Italy has an *un imbarazzo di ricchezze*. Or *an embarrassment of richs*, as the Italians say. I might even go Bolognese. Mills has a friend in Bologna.

'What's this wine, Jack? It's really delicious.'

'Valpolicella. *Italian*. You see? It's a sign.'

'I better eat something or I'm going to get drunk.'

And we wouldn't want that, now, would we? 'Cigarette?'

'Yes, please. Thanks. So are you really moving to Italy?'

The lighter doesn't light first time. The second, yes.

'In a couple of weeks. Christ, it's so soon!'

I'm getting a kick, a kinky frisson.

'You're so lucky.'

'Luck has nothing to do with it.'

'I mean, that's really cool.'

'Like I said, you should come with me.'

'Oof. Wowsers. I'm having a massive headrush!'

'It's not as if you're doing anything right now.'

'Sorry. I just need a moment to… Holy-moly!'

'I mean, you don't have a job at the moment. Do you?'

It's not like there's anything important in your life. Is there? She blushes. Then recovers. 'I know. But I can't just leave.'

'Why not? Aisha can keep an eye on things. No, listen. Just think about the Bernhardt situation. We don't know what he's playing at, but I find it disturbing. And no, to tell you the truth, I don't think he's creeping into your room at night, or living undetected in the house. That would be too far-fetched. But his recent behaviour has been peculiar. All this lying, and lurking outside the house. It's weird. If he wants to talk, he can just pick up the phone. At the same time, I have to say: *there is no limit to the weirdness of men.* I've had some experience of this myself. I know, we don't talk about that. What I'm saying is, I've been there. So I can say with some authority that Bernhardt's behaviour is extreme. You shouldn't take any chances. A few weeks in Italy. A trip to Bologna. It could be just what you need.'

'Where would we stay?'

'We'd find a cheap pensione. Like in *A Room with a View.*'

She hiccoughs. 'I love that film.'

'I know you do. And I've always connected you with the heroine, Lucy Honeychurch. You remember that bit in the film when Mr Beebe tells her in his plump, earnest voice that he's about to say something daring? Then he says, *If Miss Honeychurch ever takes to live as she plays, it will be very exciting, both for us and for her.* Remember? Now *I'm* going to say something daring. It's true of you. I feel as if, in your character, there's a bit you never let go. And I don't know, but I feel it's at the heart of you. You've got to let it go, Mills. The bit. Like Lucy Honeychurch. I'm serious. Forster wrote about this a lot. It was one of his favourite themes. He probably never let it go himself, but he knew it. He felt it. And his stories are all about English people who go abroad to get transformed. They get transformed, transfigured. They learn to let go of the bit.'

'You're telling me that I have to let go of the bit?'

'You have to let go of the bit, Mills. We all do.'

'Is this your way of saying I should get hammered?'

'No. It's my way of saying you should come to Italy.'

She hesitates, absent in thought. And this is it. Now. Today. *Le moment de verité*. When all she has to do is say, *I will*. I close my eyes and wish or will it so. I cast a spell from pure desire and let it swell to fill the room. You *do* want to go to Italy with me. You *don't* want to stay in London.

'It's really sweet of you,' she says. 'But I can't.'

'Okay. That's a shame. Why not? '

'First of all, I can't afford it. I'd have to borrow money from someone. And god knows who. I'd probably have to call my mum. So you see, it's not going to work. I'm sorry. Maybe I'll come and visit you in a month or two. Assuming you're still in Bologna, I mean.'

I pause. Then I say, 'Shall we watch *A Room with a View?*'

Not only because it's set in Italy. But also because, like so many other films, its moral can be summed up in a single word. That word is love.

The cinematic mantra. The secret tagline of almost every film. And yet so few of them look at the thing itself. They don't have time. No, they can only scrutinise the prelude. The emotional foreplay. The flirt.

And they confuse love with sex. Consider *A Room With A View*. It's all about sex, isn't it? From start to finish. The contrast between romantic George Emerson, who sweeps Miss

Honeychurch off her feet in a field of cornflowers (at precisely the moment when the word *felicità* climaxes on the soundtrack), and rational Cecil Vyse, whose glasses get in the way. Or are they, in fact, pince-nez? Either way, the point being made is that the former would be dynamite in the sack, while the latter would be a flop.

That's where we stop. The film doesn't even have the courtesy to show us the obvious conclusion: George ramming it into Lucy from behind.

Kisses. Credits. Based on a novel by E.M. Forster, who was gay.

Mills is wearing the strappy top she was wearing in that restaurant at the top of the National Portrait Gallery. Her panoramic top, whose straps seem so weightless, always on the point of sliding. Forever promising to reveal her bared shoulder, and my favourite part of her body: not breasts but where they start. Where the skin is soft under the hem. The swell.

When I arrived, she was clad in a cardigan. Then she took it off. And so I cross my arms at the wrists and I take my jumper in either hand, then, checking that she's watching, lift. So as it comes, my T-shirt rises too. Revealing my ribcage, my slim escutcheon.

And she says, 'Goodness, Jack, but you're thin!'

All the better for setting off your flesh.

'And how pale you have become!'

All the better for setting off your flush.

As Little Miss Mills Red Riding Hood goes for a second bottle, I seize my chance. To raise the temperature. So I send her a text from the Wolf.

I'm going to eat you

But how pale she has become. She shows me her screen.

'Okay,' I say. 'This time he's gone too far. Give me that.'

My thumbs are quick, as if with indignation.

Listen, wolf-man. This is Jack here. I don't know what kind of sick game you're playing but it's got to stop. If not, I'll call the police. Capeesh?

And send. She grabs her phone back.

'What does it mean, *capeesh*?'

'It's gangster speak for "Got that?"'

She screws the corkscrew into the cork. Then hands me the bottle. I grip the T of it. The cork comes out with an obliging pop. A merry note. An O.

The iPhone in my pocket vibrates. I rise and take the ashtray, as if to empty it. From the kitchen, I send a second text to Mills.

I'm going to drink you

Sound, sight, smell, touch, taste. I had them taken from me one by one. I'm going to get them back again. I return into the drawing room. Hold bottle over glass, tensing my bicep.

'Can I chop you up?'

'Can you what?'

'Can I top you up?'

She displays her screen. I look. And then I laugh.

'For Bernhardt, that's actually pretty funny.'

'You think he's joking?'

'He is. He has to be.'

'But I don't get it.'

'You don't send someone a text saying that you're going to *drink* them, not if you're seriously trying to scare them. You see what I mean? And don't forget he's German. He probably finds humour doesn't come naturally.'

'He's Austrian, in fact.'

'The point is that he's twisted.'

185

Question: what did the girl with no arms or legs get for Christmas?

I walk back over to the stereo. I press play. It's play-time.

Answer: cancer.

Mills stops the song. And meets my eye.

'We can't listen to *Perfect Day* again. You're so obsessive.'

What on earth gave you that idea?

I dip my lips to my cup. And pucker for a sip.

'You say obsessive. I'd call it enthusiastic. I've been thinking about this a lot recently. What I call *creative repetition*. Because nothing worthwhile ever got done except by a kind of obsession. That's how someone writes a book or makes a film. The idea comes to them and they disappear into it, and they don't come out again until it's done. It's one of the keys to happiness, this ability to focus completely on what it is you're doing. The ability to choose what it is you want, and commit to that. And it holds true for everything, from the small things to the big. If there's a song you like, listen to it. Play it again and again. Get to know it inside and out. Pay it that compliment. There aren't many things in this world that can be described as truly great. But when you find one, you may as well study it. That's an example of a small thing. But I think the approach is right for big things too. Like love, for example. It may sound cheesy. But when you find the person that's right for you, you commit. You commit completely. You follow them to the gates of hell, and further if necessary. So yes, in a sense, it's like you listen to the song of them. You study the book of that person. You read them. You sing along. This is love, I think. And this is creative repetition.'

Dixi. I place *Perfect Day* into the broken tray. Let's play.

She's being tricksy. The music stops. The tray emerges.

'You're talking rubbish, by the way.'

Her face is flushed, but not with shyness. She looks *slightly annoyed*.

'Either that, or you've changed completely.'

We're standing by the stereo. I look at her floating strap.

'I'm sorry, but it's true. When we were going out, you didn't make any commitment to love. There was no creative repetition. You didn't even think that love existed. Remember? So it's a bit much now to have to stand here and listen to you raving on about it.'

When she smiles, the world stops on its axis. It simply ceases to spin.

'You made it clear, when we were going out, there were lots of things that were more important to you than me. Your writing. That book you were working on. Remember? You wouldn't even stay the night with me on the evenings before your writing days. You said you had to get a good night's sleep. Wednesdays, Fridays and Saturdays. Remember?'

I look at her lips. Her imperfect teeth. The tongue between.

'I'm sorry,' her mouth says. 'I've probably had too much to drink.'

I'm about to kiss her when she turns away. Goes over to the table and tops up her glass with wine. Tries to smile at me across the room.

'So you don't want to listen to *Perfect Day*. I hear you.'

She's on the sofa, shoes kicked off. Bare knees up by chin.

'For the record, though, I have changed. You're right. When I was with you, my writing was the most important thing. It was even more important than you were, Mills. Though I did love you, too, as much as I was able. I hope you realise this. I was never unkind.'

'My god! I can't believe I'm hearing this. You were *so* unkind.'

I pause. I was planning to sit next to her. 'How was I unkind?'

I perch awkwardly on the coffee table. I take the Panama off.

'I want to know. When was I unkind?' I'm actually surprised.

She takes a sip, with her wine-stained lips, from the blushful beaker.

Then hesitates. Then speaks. 'When you broke up with me, it was the worst thing that had ever happened to me. It was even worse than when Dad died. I'm serious. It was worse, because it was done to me deliberately. You see what I mean? And it wasn't just because you dumped me. I'd been dumped before. And sure. It isn't my favourite way to spend a Saturday night. But it was the way you did it. There was no warning. It just came out of the blue. And I'd thought things were okay between you and me. I can't explain. You were the person I trusted most in the world. It was as if my father had turned round and punched me in the face. And the way you told me. God! I feel sick even remembering. You didn't seem to care. It just seemed as if, for you, there was this slightly awkward social situation. How to get through an embarrassing evening, when your ex-girlfriend is crying her eyes out.'

Her eyes. Her eyes. They shine with flashing fires of anger.

She glares. And I actually feel quite scared. Inside I'm thinking:

When she smiles, the world stops on its axis. It simply ceases to spin.

Eventually, I break the silence. 'I think you're being a little harsh.'

It's not ideal, this table, as a seat. I doubt I would be welcome on the sofa. Not now. Not just at present. I slide the Panama back on, as Mills concludes her theme. 'After that, I felt I could never trust you again.'

Revenge. I knew it. When we got back together, I knew it was on her mind. She was going to *pull me back in*. Let me get settled. Then, when I was gulled or lulled into security, she'd act. Let fall the exing axe.

Revenge. It that what I want too, secretly? To fuck or to fuck someone up: is that the question? To do to her what she has done to me? Am I a fucker-upper? As questions go, it's a little academic at present. The way she's looking at me, she wouldn't let me fix her a drink.

I need to think. I have to play it carefully. Come on. Speak.

'You're right. You shouldn't trust me. I'm not trustworthy.'

She's taken aback. I let the notion grow. Then continue quietly.

'If you look at my track record, I mean.' My position's excruciating, so I stand. 'But you were different. I'm serious. You were the best thing that ever happened to me. But did you ever stop to think, did you ever ask yourself why I broke up with you? Just think about it for a second. Think back. You remember when I started waking up at five in the morning? Then at four? Having palpitations. Hyperventilations. Remember the dry-retching? And we put it down to stress at work. But at the same time, I was becoming convinced that I was a genius, that this book I was writing was going to become an instant classic and transform people's attitudes to their most fundamental human relationships. Do you see what I'm saying? It's the only explanation. I was losing it already. Even then, I was losing my mind. You know we always used to think that what happened to me later was caused by you, by your breaking up with me. But don't you see? It was happening already. I'm not presenting this as an excuse. But it is an explanation. Don't you see? I wasn't being unkind. Not deliberately. Not really. I was in the midst of a full-blown, no-holds-barred, copper-bottomed nervous breakdown.'

I, looking down at her. She, looking up at me. Tears in her eyes.

My final line. 'I guess what I'm trying to say is: I'm sorry.'

There's nothing I would change: about this moment if I could.

If I could, I'd end it here. End everything. Press the detonator, and let the room explode. There are times in life that resemble a work of art. This is one. It makes me go, 'Aw!'

189

She glances down to find her strap has slipped. Her shoulder's bare.

And there, revealed under her throat, her collar bone, the paler skin. That swell. She pulls the strap back up and gives an embarrassed look. A sly smile spreads across her face.

'I can't believe, when you came round, you thought...'

'What?' (When she smiles, oh, when she smiles...)

'That I was still in love with you.' She smiles.

'What was I supposed to think?'

'I don't know.' She smiles again. 'I'm sorry.'

'Hey, don't forget. You liked me once.'

'I know! What was I thinking, right?'

Are you trying to get me drunk?' she says. 'It's so naughty of you.'

I shake my head. 'I'm trying to get myself drunk. You just happen to be here.'

'Well, I'm getting drunk, whatever you say. Is it our third bottle of wine?'

'No, it's our second. I like it when you're drunk. You're hilarious.'

'So are you. You remember that time in... where was it?'

'I have no idea what you're talking about.'

'When you went in *there* by mistake.'

She touches her beautiful bottom.

'I think it was Gatwick Airport.'

'The Hilton London Gatwick.'

'I must have been shit-faced.'

'I must have been shit-faced.'

'Yeah, but it didn't last long, did it?'

'No, thank god! It was really painful.'

'Wasn't it there we invented the 96er?'

'At Gatwick Airport. Yes.'

190

'The opposite of a 69er.'

'That was hilarious too.'

'Did we actually do it?'

'We did, I'm afraid to say.'

'I don't think we did.'

'I remember my face in the pillow.'

'With my? I mean, did I really?'

'Yes. On the back of my neck.'

'I always wanted to try the 666er.'

'But we could never find a third party.'

'The Position of the Beast, we used to call it.'

'What happens if you dial 666 on the phone?'

'You get put through to Hell, I suppose.'

'But the number's usually engaged.'

'You can leave a message, though.'

'Leave your name and number.'

'After the howl of agony.'

'After the shriek of despair.'

'And they get right back to you.'

We're both on the golden sofa. So far, so golden.

I've shuffled off my shoes and socks. She's resting her legs on mine. In other words, we're somewhere along that golden line that leads where we want to go. And yet. I've made a decision: I'm not going to make a move. Why? If I failed, it would be catastrophic. So much progress done would be undone. We've both had so much fun. We've addressed some issues. And Camilla has cried three times into that same damp box of tissues. Or that box of hand-ker-chiefs, as her old man (deceased) would have said.

Her dead daddy. He died on her. Her dad defunct. Her *deady*.

'Do you miss your deady?' I adopt a sympathetic look.

She frowns, so I repeat myself. 'I said, do you miss your daddy?'

'Of course I do. Every day. But it's hard, you know, to strike the right balance. At first, I think maybe I missed him too much. That's what Mum used to say, and it made me really cross. I thought she said it because she didn't miss him at all. But now I see she had a point. For whatever reason she said it. Because I did miss him too much. You remember, right? You were there. I used to have that photograph of him by my bed, the one of him jumping off that rock in Spain. And then I used to carry another one in my bag. And another one on my phone. And so wherever I was, at any moment, he was always with me. Except he wasn't. So in a way, although I was proud of doing it, it just kept on reminding me that he was gone.'

'You don't have a picture of him by your bed anymore.'

'I got rid of it last week. But how did you know?'

'How did I know what?'

'How did you know I got rid of it?'

'I was in your bedroom. A couple of hours ago.'

She gazes at me, like something doesn't add up.

'I didn't ditch it totally. I put it in a drawer.' Which I knew. 'And I felt guilty even doing that. Then I deleted his picture from my phone.' Which I knew. 'I've still got it somewhere on my computer. It isn't lost.' Which I also knew. 'I feel bad even telling you this.'

'You mustn't feel bad, Mills. It's normal. It's part of the process.'

'You don't think he's looking down and thinking: you little bitch?'

'If he's looking down at all, I'm sure he understands.'

If he's looking down at all, I'm a monkey's uncle.

'You know what I was saying earlier, about how you have to let go of the bit? I wasn't entirely joking. No, seriously. And I relate it, in fact, to the death of your father. I think this had a big impact on you.'

Does a girl share a sofa with you, if she doesn't want you to pounce?

'Because before, there was this piece of you that was all knotted up and tight. Then, when your father died, the knot just got tighter. And since that time, I think, you've found it kind of hard to trust anyone at all.'

Does a girl rest her legs on your legs, unless what she secretly wants is for you to launch yourself through the air, your arms outstretched?

'Which is why I think you should come to Italy with me.'

'We've been through this. I'm not coming to Italy.'

'But you have to let go of the bit. '

That's once too often. I'm putting too much weight on it. She swivels, removing the weight of her legs from mine, and plants her feet on the ground. Then she reaches for the empty pack of fags. Gives it a shake. It makes no merry sound.

She rises, sighs and says, 'How are you getting home?'

And there it is. Forget sticks and stones. Words kill.

I'm not going anywhere. 'I'm not going anywhere.'

Words can break my bones. Can break my heart. Words will.

'What do you mean? Don't you want to catch the last Tube?'

I shake my head. 'I'm not leaving you here on your own.'

'That's really sweet of you, but I'll be fine. Honestly.'

'I'm staying right here. Where I can keep an eye on you.'

I'm on my feet. Firm of heart, I play my part. But will Mills go for it? It looks, alas, pretty unlikely. To be quite frank with you, she looks furious. She looks seriously fucked off.

But then. (Oh then!) She throws her arms around me in a hug.

Oh, feel that tug on your heart-strings, baby. And listen to those harp-strings weep. They weep for me, they weep for you. And maybe, too, they weep for any man, anyone who's ever been blown away by some silly, pretty girl, and her moments of unimaginable grace.

Her breasts are pressed against my chest. 'It's so nice of you, Jack.'

Then retracts herself, a little self-consciously. But as for me, I'm glad. Why? Because she got the chance to feel, however briefly, the ribbed articulations of my upper body.

'But where are you going to sleep?' she asks doubtfully.

'I'll sleep down here. I don't care where I sleep.'

We both look at the sofa. 'I don't think it's long enough,' she says.

'Then I'll sleep on the floor.' She's looking at me. And this is the moment, now. To squeeze the universe into a ball and roll it towards some everlasting question. But me, I do nothing. Or worse, I turn away. I leave it for another day. I pick up the ashtray, filled with all the butt-ends of my days and ways. And feebly say, 'The important thing is, if you get another text from Bernhardt, you must tell me straightaway.'

She's at the door. 'Are you sure you're going to be okay?'

'Of course.' I pick up the empty bottle. 'I'll be fine.'

I meet her gaze. For another moment, we look at each other. And then she says, 'You can sleep in my room, if you want.'

When Camilla blushes, she blushes. And it can spread. From her face to the sweep of her throat, and from there to that splendour of skin, which is compressed by the hem of her top.

Finally I say, 'On the floor, you mean?'

This puts her at ease. She smiles.

'I think there's room in the bed.' She pauses. 'But if it's okay, I don't think that we should do anything, if you know what I mean.'

'You mean, no funny business?'

'Exactly.' She blushes again. 'No funny business.'

It's as if I've built a house of cards a hundred storeys high. No, not a hundred. Ninety-nine. I'm placing the last card now. Slowly. Oh so slowly. Oh so very slowly.

'No funny business, I assure you.'

I'm glad I have an ashtray in one hand, and in the other a bottle. If my hands were free, I might be tempted to kiss her. Which could be an error.

'It's only because…'

'You don't have to explain. Really.'

'Thanks.' She bites her lower lip. 'Can you give me five minutes? My room's a tip.'

Which I happen to know is true. 'Take as long as you like. I'll do some tidying up.'

'Don't worry about that. We can do it in the morning.'

'It's fine. It won't take long. I can make a start, at least.'

'Okay,' she says. And with one last summer smile, she's gone.

Leaving me with a bursting heart. And it's not only my heart that's full. I'm also full down there. I feel with my hand. Brimful. Ready. Steady. Go! No, *let her wait.* I've waited so long, she can wait a little. For this date, everything must be perfect. Like her face, which is a perfect ten. She asked for five. I'll give her a perfect ten.

I carry the ashtray and the empty wine bottle into the kitchen.

I drop the bottle into the bin. I empty the ashtray. I turn on the tap.

I can see my reflection in the rain-flecked pane of the window. I am the night. I'm as black as the ace of spades. I let the ribbon of water twirl over the ashtray, sluicing dirt off the naked curves. My finger does the rest.

I dry it. I place it on the drying rack. I consult my phone.

Four minutes have passed. That ought to be enough.

X

FLIGHT 2A. FLIGHT 2b. I make no sound. My feet don't touch the floor. Flight 3a. Flight 3b. *Forward roll.* I'm at her door.

I push it open gently. And I'm in.

She's already in bed, her hair upon the pillow wild. Her eyes closed. But she's only pretending to be asleep.

'You should get in. It's so lovely.'

She always loved to be in bed. She loved to sleep. If you asked her favourite pastime, she would probably say sleeping. Though that would be a lie. It was her second favourite thing. Convenient, I always thought, that her two favourite things should occur in the same room.

'Do you mind if I use your toothbrush?'

'Will you bring up a glass of water?'

The old routine.

As I place it on the bedside table, it spills. I glance at Mills.

She smiles. Her room is almost tidy. Clothes are draped over chairs.

My T-shirt's downstairs. I'm only semi-clothed. Panama and combats.

I doff my hat. *I doff my hat to you, my dear.* I take it off. Then toss it away from me. I bend. Attend to my multi-pocketed trousers.

I take them off. Then clutch them close, as if in bashfulness. I'm play-acting. And watching me, she laughs. I thrust them away, extravagantly. They bang as they hit the floor.

They clump with the weight of hidden mobile phones.

'What on earth are those?' she asks.

For a moment, I think she means the phones. But she's staring at my cycling shorts.

'What, these old things?'

I leave space for her to speak. She doesn't. So I explain.

'End of the week. You know how it is.'

'Can you turn the light out please?'

In the dark, I reach. I find the edge of the duvet. Raise it. And I'm in. In bed with Mills. I reach and find her hip. It's bare. The curve of her. Her thighs, her waist. Unclothed. Unclad.

'Hi,' she whispers, naked.

'Hi,' I reply. Like kids in a den.

All seems well. But. B.U.T. (Or, equally, then again.)

She doesn't reciprocate. Which is discouraging. On the other hand, she's naked. In the four minutes while I was downstairs, she was up here, pulling off her top and skirt, so by the time I arrived, she was ready for me. And what can this be, if not a kind of sign? Having said that, she always sleeps in the nude. So if she'd worn pyjamas, *that* would have been a sign: a sign to me not to try, to retract my hand. But the fact that she's naked means nothing.

'I thought we agreed that we weren't going to do anything.'

'I'm not doing anything. This is me not doing anything.'

My hand is on her bare shoulder. It's on her breast. And still she doesn't react. My heart contracts, compact as a fist. My fist is open. My palm is almost flat. My fingers glow. They know her warmth. They seem to give it back. I move down, hardly touching, to the skin between stomach and hip. She still does nothing. Then finally, she speaks:

'Please, Jack,' she says. 'Please.'

Rewind. Two and a half years. We're at the start.

When Mills and I got together, it was on the back of fifteen hours of drinking, and I remember thinking that it was almost sacrilege to take a girl so beautiful to bed. She was made to be admired from afar. And she would be shocked, no doubt, to be fucked, she wouldn't be used to such crude behaviour. But when it came to the point, she begged.

'Please, Jack. Please. Please.'

Same bed. Same beg. Same pleas. Same please.

I do my best to tease her. But they're strange, these urgent pleases. Because why are they needed? Why, precisely, is she saying Please?

'Please. Please. Please, Jack. Please. Oh please.'

What makes her think it might not be going to happen?

And so now, for the first time, a seed of doubt is sown. I become aware of *un petit problème*. I'm going to spell it out.

I'm not hard. Down *there*. Not yet. You have to give it time.

But it's strange, because with Clare, there was no such problem. Despite the fact she wasn't a patch on Mills. I hardly fancied her. Yet when we hit the sack, I was hard as nails.

Yet the same thing couldn't be said now. *Au contraire.*

She tugs at my skin-coloured cycling shorts.

'Please, Jack. Please.'

Maybe it's because it's hot. I throw the duvet back. Mills takes this as her cue to climb aboard. Which wasn't what I meant. She straddles my stomach. Reaches back to remove my shorts. Does so. And yet alas, the problem persists. Down there. That. *There.*

Camilla stoops to kiss me. Her nipples are in my chest-hair. Then she reaches back. I intercept and grab her wrist. Push her off me. Then climb on top and kiss her.

At least, while I'm kissing her, she can't say *please.*

At least, while I'm holding her wrists, she's trapped.

But I can't keep kissing her forever. I need to breathe.

And when I gasp, I hear her say, 'Let's go to Italy.'

I catch my breath up. And I ask her what she said.

'I want to come to Italy with you. If you'll let me.'

And reaching with her mouth, she kisses me.

This is my moment of triumph. We'll go on the run, Mills and me. Like Bonnie and Clyde, except Bonnie won't know about Clyde's kills, or his special skills. We'll be Bonnie and Mr Hyde. We can either roam or stray. We can go our own way. Strolling and stone-rolling from Tuscany down to Rome, and then to who knows where or who should care, and no one will ever catch up with us, no one, ever, or know where we are or even give a damn. We'll be too clever. We'll live together for ever and ever. And no one will ever find us, ever.

She pushes me off again. And climbs on top. I can't be sure, but I think she's smiling. She kisses my lips. Her tongue-tip's slippy. It slips against mine. I can't smile. Why? Because she's reaching. And again I intercept. 'Please,' she says. She thinks I'm teasing her. But I'm so damn hot. Shall I go down and adjust the dial? Reduce the temperature a notch?

'Please, Jack,' she says. 'Please fuck me.'

But there's nothing there. Oh, no, no, no, there's not.

It's like a sickness, this lack of thickness, this weakness at my core. And a third time, she reaches. And this time, she succeeds. There's a moment's hesitation. But she decides to have a go, to give it a whirl. Jiggles or juggles a bit. Jangles it like a bell.

And I know what's going through her head. Or I can guess. She's thinking: the trouble is that he's not turned on. I must redouble my efforts. Which is the opposite of what I need. I need a rest. To breathe. Or probably the best thing might be to take a break, just for an hour or two. And I'm about to suggest this, when something catches my eye.

Above her head, a trapdoor. The trapdoor into the attic.

It's too dark to see the peep-holes, but I can picture them. And I know of another pair over there in the corner, in the door of the cupboard. She's kissing my chest. Licking around my nipple, which someone once must have told her was sexy. Bernhardt, I suppose. And what, I wonder, must *he* be doing now? Could he not – would he not, if he could – have oozed his way across the floor, sad incubus, and glued his sockets to those evil black holes? And what about Clare? That boozed-up floozy. She must be in the cupboard. Crouched or hunched. Mad succubus. Her mouth pressed to one of those holes. Sucking. Extracting my spirit.

Mills is rubbing herself, for some reason, against my knee.

So they're to blame. Of course they are. It all makes sense.

Steady, my soul. Don't lose yourself so close to your goal. Give it one more try. And concentrate. How? Focus all your love and hate, and pride and will, and send it down to that overriding point. Then let it grow. Go on. Do it now.

But what was that? *What was what?* I thought I heard a sound.

M's apparently oblivious. She's trying to fellate my ear. But there was clearly a creak. Upstairs in the attic. I heard it. Didn't you? There! And there! It's Bernhardt. Shifting his position. Getting a better view.

And there! A clump. A clumsy thump. You must have heard that.

It's Clare. In the corner cupboard. Knocking against the wooden door. Is there anybody there? Is there anybody out there? Does anybody care?

This is the final straw. I shove Mills off me and reach for the light.

Click. The room explodes into life. But it loses sound.

The noises have stopped. And I'm losing ground.

I put my feet on the ground. I stand on my own two feet.

I stare down at Mills. Who stares up at me. 'What's the matter?'

You're not fooling anyone. I turn. I glare at the cupboard. Clare could never have hidden in there without Mills knowing. They're clearly in cahoots. In the minutes before I came up, she must have called to her. She must have said: quick, before he gets here. Well, I won't stand for it. It's time I made a stand. Against this rough injustice. This one-against-three.

Muttering, 'What can the matter be?' I cross the floor, as naked as I am. And no one's as naked as I am when someone's been annoying me. When someone's been toying with me. Which is what has been happening here.

Because I must admit: at this moment, I feel *slightly annoyed*.

The toy cupboard. Emblem of Mills's youth. If I stretch, I can get my arms around it. And it must look, from where she's sitting, like I'm trying to make love to it. I'm not, I swear. I want to give it a shake. Show Clare I'll take no shit. I get a grip. I shudder. My body judders.

And I shout, 'Come out, come out, wherever you are!'

'Have you gone insane?' This is Mills to me.

I release the cupboard. I say, 'Don't give me that.'

'What?' Doing her hurt-innocence look.

I point at my floppy cock. 'This.'

'What are you talking about?'

'This, Mills. This is this.'

'I know, but I don't see –'

'How do you explain *this*?'

'Please. Just come back to bed.'

I grab the handle of the cupboard door.

'Where's the key? I need the key.'

'What key?' This comes out as supplication. Almost as a moan.

She's not fooling me. What key, indeed.

That just proves her guilt. When a man rattles a cupboard door and asks for the key, and the woman says, *what key*, you know there's something funny going on. Can you smell? There's something in the air. And it isn't love. No, *au contraire*. It smells fishy. It smells foul. I put my eye to one of the peep-holes, expecting to see some eye staring back at me.

An eyeball in the darkness. The glare of the abyss. That's not what I see. I see something, but not that. Can you guess what I see? I'll tell you. It's a nipple. I'm serious. It's a nipple. Clare has thrust one into the peep hole, in order to mock me. In order to say, fuck you.

'Stop it, Jack, please. You're scaring me.' *Well, fuck you too.*

I'm not going to stay another minute to be insulted in this way. I hunt for my pale-pink cycling shorts. As I thought, they're wedged where they always end, at the end of the bed. Mills tried to hide them. She can't hide things from me. That's my game. I'm the hider.

But now I find she knew I was there. She must have done. She knew what I've done to Bernhardt and to Clare. Or how else could she have recruited them? So I stoop. I scoop up my trousers. I tug them on. And Mills, meanwhile, is doing her innocence routine.

'Jack, please stop it. You're really freaking me out.'

She always tries to turn things on their head. But she's the one in bed, her sweet body swathed in feather-soft duvet. While I'm the one shivering like a racehorse, stripped to the waist, present-tensing my abs, shimmering with silver, sylvan sweat.

She always acts like she's the injured party. Well, that can be arranged.

If she wants to be injured, I'll happily oblige. I'll smack her in the face. I'll twist her arm back until it breaks. I'll kick her in the fucking womb.

I think it's time. To leave this place. The time has come to go. I look up. I flick a violent V-sign at the trapdoor in the ceiling. And then (feeling slightly annoyed) I go. I leave the room.

Downstairs in the hall, I lean. I try to breathe. I open my eyes.

Jesus H. Christ. Want to know what my life's like? It has all the hassle and the hangover of drugs, but without the kick and pleasure of the ride.

202

I look at my reflection in the mirror on the wall.

To my dismay, it meets my stare. What are you looking at, you bastard? Peace, perturbed spirit! It's merely the stress of your unrestful mind.

Pull yourself together, man. And as I gaze, my eye falls on my corporal architecture. My abdominal columns. The entablature of my pecs. The pediment of my collar bone. So taut, so tight. This torso-temple soothes me. Gleaming in the midnight, moonlit night.

My brain begins to clarify. And I realise: I just had a moment.

I behaved like a screaming maniac. A certified, axe-wielding loon.

As I remember my behaviour, I giggle. *Sometimes I'm so nuts!*

Yet here's a niggle. It's not that funny. Now I must try to limit the damage. Two questions, quickly. What did I do and why? Answer to 1: I rattled Mills's cupboard. I put my eye to the lock. I pointed at my cock. I effed and blinded. Answer to 2: I overcomplicated things.

Solution to 1. Tell her that I dreamed it. Tell her I fell asleep in the sack and dreamed her boyfriend was in her cupboard. Which is why I grabbed and grappled with the thing. It could be true. She can't prove otherwise. We often dream of the matter in hand. What's more, I'll apologise. And if that doesn't seal it, it's no matter. She'll still let me back into bed. We'll go to sleep in silence, back to back. And then, in an hour or two, I'll wake up with a monumental stiffy, and screw her into tearful submission.

Solution to 2. Simplify. Simplify. Simplify. Why? Because it's all so simple.

I can do the minimum and still achieve my goal. Then why am I so fearful? It's crucial that we have sex before dawn. The hard work's done. The art work has been drawn. We've had fun. We got drunk. I showed heart and brawn when I searched her house and insisted on staying, to protect her from the night. But none of this is needed now. There's no more need for mugging. Or for texts from Bernhardt's iPhone.

Let alone from Clare. I'll turn them both off, and go upstairs. Not off. Airplane mode. There. That's hers done. Now where's his?

The relevant pocket's empty. Clare's is clearly Clare's. It has her photo on the front. I put it there myself. Mine's the same. (A head-and-heavy-chest shot.) But that's just two. There used to be a trio of phones. So where's the third, goddamit? Where's Bernhardt's iPhone?

Not panicking, I descend to the basement. The last place I recall I saw it. It might be on the cistern. My snigger dies. It's not.

I climb the stairs. Enter the drawing room. I know where it must be. Or where it ought to be. On the sofa. Where I sat with my knees up, having a knees-up with Mills. It must have slipped, as we sipped, from my thigh.

Pulse quickening, I dismember the sofa. I fling its limbs to the four winds. And what do I find? Some crumbs. A solitary five-pence piece.

Frantic, I whip out my phone. Bring up Bernhardt's number and call it. I need to regain control. If Mills gets her hands on his handset, I don't know what I'll do. But she hasn't yet. It's ringing. I hold it away from my ear, to hear where it's coming from. Yet I can't hear a thing except that ring, which is coming from my earpiece.

Then I hear something that freezes my blood. That stirs my scalp. That smears my throat with drought, sends saliva sliding down my spine. A silverine spit river. A silver sliver.

A sound I never thought I'd hate to hear. Mills's voice.

'Hello? Jack? Jack? Hello, is that you?'

I hang up. I stare at the iklwas on the wall. I give a shiver.

For a second, I pretend it isn't true. Then I pull myself together. 2a. 2b. 3a. 3b. Forward roll.

I lean. I lounge in her doorway.

My breathing: neat as a guillotine.

She has her back to me. Pulling on a jumper.

'Going somewhere?' I say. She jumps, as if I'd thumped her.

I apologise, as I said I would. 'Sorry. I didn't mean to startle you.'

I look at her hand, which is holding a phone. She moves it behind her back. Then she brings it out again. Shows me the incriminating screen.

A photo of Bernhardt. I sigh. 'I thought I'd give it a call. But yours was the last voice I expected to hear. Where on earth did you find it?'

She doesn't reply. She hasn't said a word since I appeared.

'Talk to me, Mills. Why are you squinting like that?'

'It was on the floor. It was under the chair.'

'And how do you think it got there?'

'It was where you left your clothes.'

'Is that a fact?' I take a step forward.

She takes a step back. She backs away from me.

'He must have put it there,' I tell her. 'He must be here.'

I pick up the Panama from the floor. I position it on my head.

Mills is staring at me, as a toddler stares at a stranger. Openly. Mouth open in an O. (You see? I've done it. I've made her go, 'Oh!')

Finally, she speaks. 'It fell out of your pocket.'

'Are you crazy? What are you talking about?'

'It must have done. There's no other explanation.'

'What would I be doing with Bernhardt's iPhone?'

'That's what I want to know.'

'I don't have it, Mills. You do. Look. It's in your hand.'

'But why did you have it before? I don't understand.'

205

You don't. But you will. I'll make you understand.

I take another step towards her. She takes another step back. It's a kind of dance. Except this time, she stumbles. The back of her ankle knocks against the bed. And she sits down suddenly. His phone is in her hand.

'I was hoping to avoid telling you this.'

'Why have you got Bernhardt's phone?'

'It wasn't me. It was Clare. She had it.'

I hold my palms as if quelling applause.

There's a pause. So I'm forced to go on.

'Clare was jealous of you. You knew that.'

'But what's she got to do with anything?'

'I'm trying to explain, but you must listen.'

I'm calming the sea. Rebellious to command.

'Just tell me why you have Bernhardt's phone.'

She glances past me. I step into her line of sight.

'I'm telling you. I'm trying to explain. It was Clare.'

'Don't give me that. Please, Jack. Just tell me the truth.'

She tries to rise. I suppress her shoulders. 'Sit down, Mills.'

'Get off me.' She tries again. Pushing at my hands. Almost succeeds.

So I shout, 'I SAID SIT DOWN!' I thrust her back. She falls. She sprawls across the bed, nearly hitting her head. And I say, 'You see? Look what you made me do.' I stoop and pick up the Panama. 'You made me drop the hat.' It's a bit dented. So I push it out from the inside with my hand. I restore its regular shape. 'It's fine,' I say. 'There's no harm done.'

She's hunched against the headboard, hugging the phone to her chest.

Panama askance, I reach a hand. 'I think you'd better give me that.'

She's turned away, not looking at me. 'Why have you got his phone?'

This comes out as a whisper. I whisper back. 'Give it to me, Mills.'

She shakes her head. I grab her wrists and wrench them apart. Twist the phone from her palm. 'The phone is mine!' My pocket gapes. It swallows with a sigh. 'How can you listen if you're fiddling with a phone? That's not very polite, is it? You should be listening to me.'

She shrinks away. I may have shouted quite loudly in her ear. But I had to, to make her hear. She re-repeats (and not for the first time), 'Why have you got his phone?'

Lord, but this is testing. I swear, if she asks me one more time, I might have to lose it completely. I might have to give her a piece of my mind.

'There's no point in talking if you won't listen. Will you listen?'

She peers down, bleary-eyed. Her cheeks are tear-smeared.

'Blub, blub,' I observe. 'But are you really going to hear?'

Her silence is acquiescent. And actually, it's her essence. The essence of Mills, her inner scent. She likes to be touched. She doesn't like to feel.

'I'm innocent, I swear. It was Clare. At the dinner party.' She's touchy but not feely. 'She was jealous of you. But no, that's not right. She wasn't jealous. She was envious. She envied you. It was me she wanted for herself.' I sit down on the bed beside her. 'But she knew that could never be. Because I'm yours. Do you see? I'm yours. I always will be. It made her crazy. It killed her, literally and metaphorically. So while you had your party upstairs, she went down and murdered Bernhardt. Your poor boyfriend, who never hurt a fly. She cut his throat in the church. You have to believe me. She gave him a second smile.'

Mills looks strange. Wearing next to nothing but a big woolly jumper. Yet I can see from the way she's sitting (knees up by chin) she has her knickers on. It's a pair I like. Cream-coloured, with a strawberry motif. I'm something of an expert on Mills's underwear. If you're looking for a tour of her knicker drawer, look no further. I'm your man.

And normally, this pair placates me. Many has been the time, when Mills was out at work, or buying milk, I've gazed on them serenely. I even squeezed into them on occasion, or draped them over my face. I'll be frank. When it comes to these knickers, I'm a fan.

Yet today, by contrast, the sight of them infuriates me. When I left, she was completely naked. Who told her that she could put her clothes back on?

'She loved you, Mills. She loved you and she hated you. Because there are things about you that are worthy of love, that couldn't fail to move the hardest heart. And there are other things that are more worthy of hate. I'm not saying Clare was right to hate you. I just want you to try to see things from her point of view. You're beautiful. But you're also a narcissist. You don't see anything further than the end of your own nose. And it's so tiny, your nose. You build a bubble around you and decorate it like a boudoir, like the good witch Glinda in *The Wizard of Oz*. All pink and sugary like fairy cakes. But as a result, you don't see the pain you cause. It's because you don't look. I realise that. But you need to understand that you cause a lot of pain. I know it's distressing, and I'm sorry. But I have to make you see. You have to look at it, Mills. You have to look at what you did.'

I reach into the back pocket of my combats and bring out the body of Matthew, which has seen better days. But then again, it's never especially fetching, the posthumous look. We'll none of us look our best, *post mortem*. Not even Mills, though she looks good now. Her eyes brim prettily with tears, as she gazes at what's in my hand.

A misshapen lump. Covered in fine white mould. It's hard to

tell he was ever a mouse. He could be an antique Mini Mars Bar. Or else a petrified turd.

I move him close, so she can really see him. I hold him under her nose.

'Smell it, Mills. Smell the mouse.' She sort of shakes her head, her eyes tight-shut. 'Look at it. I swear to god, Mills, if you don't open your eyes, I'll open them for you.' She opens them. She's crying, but I'm not fooled. 'Now look at it.' She looks. Her cheeks are glazed with tears. I use Matthew's squishy body to dry them. I must be cruel, only to be kind.

'You want to know what this is, Mills? It's my heart. That's right. My heart. I know it looks like a mouse, but it's really my heart. You killed it. You laid down trays of poison and you killed it. You contaminated my heart. I'm only saying this so you understand. Because you think you're so sweet and innocent and you just kind of skip or tiptoe through life like a lovely little bunny rabbit, but I want you to know that that's bullshit. Bullshit. Bullshit. Look at me! Look at what you've done to me!'

I'm crying now. And my face is all contorted. But it's good I'm crying, because she's crying too, and I wouldn't want her to be the only one with a wet face. And it's good that my face is all distorted and burning, gurning like a gargoyle. I want her to see me. I want to make her understand.

'This is what your beauty does. This. This. This. Your kiss kills. Your smile eviscerates. Your touch, it rips the skin from every limb. Oh, before I met you, I was fine. I did my things. No, everything was good. Or better than. I was a good man. I was clever. Strong. I had ambition. My mission: to turn literature into song. To write like a piano man. And maybe it was crazy. Baby, maybe it was. But it got me out of bed in the morning. And then you came along. You, with no mission or ambition but to have fun. Or to *have a nice time*, as you once told me. And I almost spilled my fucking drink. I almost threw it in your face. But even then it was fine, it was fine. I didn't even realise the peril I was in. Truth to tell, it was only when you left – no, it wasn't even then. It was a few days later. It was afterwards. I woke and knew I'd tasted heaven. And everything now would be hell.'

I point at the thing in my hand. 'This, Mills. This. This. This.'

Between sobs, she says, 'Jack, you need help.'

But your honour, I'm not done. I've barely begun. 'You haven't been listening. If you had, you'd understand. You cut out my motive. You cauterised my meaning. You amputated my morality. Don't you see? By showing me something perfect. You. Something perfect. You.'

'Please stop this. Please, Jack. Please.'

'Stop what? Stop this?' I thrust it at her. 'You think, like a stopwatch, it can be stopped? You think you can go back in time and undo what you've done? Look at what you've done! Look! Do you see what's in my hand? But you won't ever know or understand. You have eyes without pupils. A nose without nostrils. A mouth without a tongue. And you like to be touched, but do you ever think to reach out a hand? You block! You stone! You cannot know, no, you can't begin to understand, what it's like to be someone other than you.'

My face is close to hers. She's covering hers with her hands.

'No, Mills. You have to look. It's your turn. I've been looking and listening for so long. Hearing. Seeing. Do you hear me? Do you start to see? I'm drowning without you. I'm in the sea. You are the sea. You're drowning me. I'm trapped in a nightmare. A horror film. Some shit teen movie. A slasher flick. And do you want to know what it is, the horror, the monster? The freak that looms from the shadows, swinging its scythe? It's not me. It's the Absence of You. It's everywhere. The Absence of You. When I wake up in the morning or walk down the street, you're not there. In a shop. On a bus. In bed at night. You're not there. It makes my nose bleed and my head ache. I carry it in my hand. Do you begin to understand?'

'Oh god. Oh god.' She's gone religious. 'Oh god. Oh god.'

'Look at it, Mills. See what's in my hand. The Absence of You. Eat it. I want you to eat it. Eat it, Mills. Only then will you understand. Eat the Absence of You, as I have done.'

I push it at her mouth, the rotting mouse. The mouse that was in her house, her house in Notting Hill. She has to eat it. She will.

I smear it against her lips, forcing it between them. And then.

With sudden violence, she ducks beneath my grasp. Leaps off the bed and sprints for the door. Before I can do anything to stop her. But it's not her lucky day. She slips in her socks on the wooden floor. Slides and smacks, full, into the wall. She falls. Then lies still.

I'm amazed. It simply hadn't occurred to me that she might try to run.

In all the talk and tangle, my hat has slipped again. I put it back on. I tip it to the requisite angle. And I rise. Mills lies where she fell. Unmoving but still moving. Come closer now. See the rise and fall of her chest. Not dead but yet not conscious. She's unaware. I kneel at her side. I slide a hand under her jumper. And softly I fondle one of her breasts.

PART FOUR

XI

I AM. BUT what am I? A man. An animal, in a manner of speaking.

Sleeping, eating, and the other three. And what's left? Love.

It epitomises me. It epitomises man. The man in love, you see, is twice a man. A man most fully human. Apart from the lover, is there another?

The suicide! How human is he! How sapient! To see the tears in things. To sense the hopelessness inside, when every other option has been tried. And then to have the strength to stand and say: *enough, no more! It is not so sweet now as it was before.* Believe me, I cried. I tried each and every highway. I walked upon the water. I turned water into wine. I told anyone who would listen I was the Son of Man. Why didn't they crucify me?

I open my bag. I extract three packets of ZALEPLON. In these brave capsules lies a cure for all life's ills. And by a cure to say we end the heartache – not just for me, but for Mills. She could not guess, she never knew. My death will give her back her ease. It must be done.

I have a favourite photograph of Mills. I took it of her while she slept. I prop it on the TV set and drag an armchair close. And sit, legs spread before it, naked but for my shorts. I force the pills out of their plastic pods. They twitch and jostle in my palm. I scooch forward an inch. My crotch bulges in the TV screen. I look up. I fix my eyes on the picture.

I'm about to fill my mouth, when my iPhone screen goes blank.

Damn it! I grab it and go into my Settings. General. Auto-Lock. It's fixed on 1 Minute. The other options are 2, 3, 4, 5, and Never. I select Never. It's fitting, I decree. I'll die, but Mills's face will never fade.

I prop the iPhone where it was. I concentrate. I focus on the photo.

It's a hell of a shot. It reminds me somewhat of that painting by Courbet. The one of two nudes entwined at midday. Entitled, I think, *Le Sommeil*. He wasn't fooling anyone. They're asleep, yes, but *why*?

An image of perfection, this. The final thing I'll see before I die.

I raise the sleeping pills. But as I do, my iPhone slips. It flops. *Zut alors!* It hits the floor. I pick it up again. Okay. Sure. I'll hold it in my hand. One hand has pills, the other has my phone. I must stare at the former and swallow the latter. By mistake, I get it the wrong way round. I eye the pills and take a bite out of my phone. *Fool! Have some respect.*

You're following the Roman fashion. Suicide. It's a Roman word. Self-slaughter. Most noble and antique tradition. I think of Seneca, who slit his wrists, but owing to his Stoic veins, bled slowly. So he got in a hot bath, which is said to impede clotting. Dictated one or two epigrams to nodding secretaries, and waited. It still eluded him, so he took poison. But his lack of blood blocked its progress. He must have been *slightly annoyed*. In the end, he suffocated in the steam, which filled the attentive air.

The time for hesitation's past. It's dinner time. My final feast. *Bon appetit.* (Or as the French prefer to say, *have a good appetite.*) I raise the pills. Murmur *Gezuar* to Mills. And stuff them in.

I press my lips together. I stare at the image in my hand. Then feel two drops of water sting my cheeks. My vision blurs. I open my mouth and dry-retch. And catch my reflection, contorted in the television screen. Pills bristle on my tongue like little quills.

My eyes are wet and my mouth is dry. When I pick them off, each pill takes with it a tiny piece of skin.

I get to my feet. What would Seneca do? I know what he did, and I can do it too. I go upstairs and run a bath. Steam billows through the room. It will rise through the house and on up into the attic. Seeping through holes and cracks, caught by the light of that single bulb. And Mills will wonder: why is he having a bath at midday? Little will she know.

Knock, knock. *Time to go.* I climb in. I'm Seneca!

Hang on. I've forgotten something. I still haven't cut my skin.

I climb out again, dripping. Hunt for a razor. I think Mr Howard has a cut-throat kind, which I shall now rechristen: a cut-wrist razor. But now I come to think of it, old Seneca (though in fact he was the Younger) slit more than his wrists. He also carved his knees and Stoic legs. Or so says Tacitus. So that makes it a cut-leg blade. A cut-knee blade. Let's just call it a cut-me razor. But at the moment it's academic.

All I can find is a packet of Bic safety razors.

I guess they'll have to do. I select one and slide back into the bath. My phone's propped on the shelf above the sink. Because of the steam, I can't really see it. I don't care. I mustn't let excuses hold me back. The crucial thing is that when I'm found, motionless and rather pale (think *The Death of Marat*), the steam will have cleared. They'll see what I was looking at.

Goodbye, cruel world. *Tetelestai.* We owe a cock to Asclepius. Etc.

But wait! What's this? (If this is dying, I don't think much of it.)

This razor's designed to make it impossible. However I try, scratching it across my wrist, swiping it under my knees, slapping it against my ankles, the bloody thing won't oblige. Maybe that's why it's known as a safety razor. I feel, as you might imagine, *slightly annoyed.*

217

I demand the right to die! What's more, the water's getting cold. This bath is dying, leaving me alive. I'm Seneca, denied my end by practicalities.

But what if I go further back? Not Seneca. Diogenes. Go Greek.

You remember the guy. Lived in a barrel. Insulted Alexander the Great. The stories are well-known. Less so, his method of death. He committed suicide, at the age of 89, by refusing to breathe. I'm serious. Just held his breath until he died. So fired up by the injustice of some law, he closed his mouth and cleared his throat, and croaked most eloquently.

An example to be followed, so follow it I shall. I rise from the bath like a kraken. I dry myself and slip into a kimono (which was her dad's). But I leave the sash untied. So then, when I stride into the master bedroom, my gown wafts wide, revealing my toned physique.

I mount the bed. I lie back, prone. I'm so alone. But which of us isn't, these days?

The master bedroom. The room of mastery. What is this act but mastery of death, the defining human deed? I spread my legs. I point my toe-tips at the farther posts, my fingers clasping those behind my head. No. Hang on. I fish my phone from my pocket and place it face-down on my chest.

So now, when I'm found, her image will be in the midst of me. I hope they find me before the battery dies. Everything's ready. I stretch out like *Vitruvian Man.* (My penis is lolling to the left.) I take a deep breath. I hold it. This is it. The pressure builds. I close my eyes.

I call on the spirit of Diogenes. Is he with me? I feel a little dizzy. My cheeks expand. The pressure's building in my head and chest. Ah Christ, the pain! How long have I done now? 20 seconds? 25? I'm still alive. What gives? Death must come soon.

My face is like a child's balloon. I can't hold it much longer.

I explode, weeping. An old man wailing for his demon lover. I can't. I tried. You saw. You watched what happened.

I gave it my best shot. So now what? Kill Mills? Kill Camilla? I don't want to kill her. But do I have to, now? What, right away?

Of course I don't. First consider.

I've spent so many months in hiding. Sliding behind doors. Flattening against walls. Fattening in the dark before full term. Now I want to stretch out. Step out from behind my screen and make some noise. Let out a luxurious scream. Just consider for a moment, that haunting painting by Munch. What makes it so daunting? It's the silence. The mouth is open, but no sound comes out. Why? Because it's a painting, not a TV screen. And the screamer realises. That's why he's screaming. He's screaming because he knows he's in *The Scream*.

I, by contrast, feel as if I used to be in a Munch painting, but now I'm let off the leash. So I dash round, knocking into things. I slam doors and rearrange furniture. Insert a film in the player and turn the volume up full. Which do I choose? *Scream*, of course. That way, if anyone in the street hears screaming, they'll assume I'm watching another in a series of slasher flicks. Or better, torture porn. There's a tautology for you. But that's just the audio-visual aspect of the entertainment system. There's also pure audio. The stereo. Which I uproot and carry, cords trailing like intestines, up to Mills's room. Arrange it on the bed, with speakers pointed at the ceiling. Then play *Perfect Day* at full blast, on repeat. I know it's a song she likes. And it communicates my mood far better than I could. I sing along with the chorus – then listen, to see if she joins. She doesn't, but I presume she can see me.

You see, I told her about the peepholes. We're peephole people, she and I.

I wait until it's night, then go down to the basement, where I throw the mains electricity switch. Climbing the stairs in the dark isn't hard for me. For I know this house like I know myself. And I know myself very well. I rise like a ghost, materialise in the bedroom and light two long candles. So this white candle-light is rising through those peep-holes, sliding two sabres of light, which invade and zing in the dearthy darkness of the attic.

It isn't completely dark. But then nothing is, is it, in the end.

There's a window with rusty bars, which permits a little light. It can be opened, but you can't climb out. You can hide, but you can't run. And many's the time I gazed at the London sky at night, that red-orange glow, which makes the city seem on fire. I found in it an image of my soul.

If I want to drink, I can. I can pour cans of lager into the sink and drink them through a straw, before watching a film for the fifth or fifteenth time. If I want to eat, I eat. I take what I want from the fridge. If I feel like dancing, I can do. I can do the can-can. (If not, not.) I can do a do-do. Can go-go to the loo-loo whenever I want to-to. In or out of the can. In the library, I can tear a page from any book, and wipe my arse with it. I can.

But a voice in my head says: *nothing's as much fun on your own.*

I can spend the whole day naked if I want. I want to all the time. (The reason I wore shorts was to stop myself flapping.) I can spend the day clothed. I can mess about in a kimono or don Albanian dress. I can search her father's wardrobe for his swellest suit. Tie a tie. Apply a Trilby. A felt hat. A fedora. I can go up to her room and beat a tattoo upon the ceiling. I think she might be amused. I can do his walk. I can even do his talk. I can. His entitled, old-world drawl.

I can crawl downstairs head-first. The hat topples as I go. Then, if I'm in the mood, I can unzip and really let fly. I can piss on my reflection in the glass. I can face my face, and trace the lineaments of defeat. The veins of disaster. Its lines. I can headbutt my reflection with a cry, so the mirror cracks from side to side. I can tear the veil of my temple, so I bleed. I don't care. I can do whatever I need to. And I do. I really do. I'm doing it now.

But a voice in my head says: *nothing's as much fun on your own.*

There are three stages to any relationship.

Stage 1. PRE. After you meet, before you get together.

Stage 2. INTER. The relationship itself, while you're going out.

Stage 3. POST. Everything that happens after you break up.

The first two have had all the attention in literature and film. Especially the *pre* (as I've already mentioned). The emotional foreplay. But even the act itself, the *inter*, the heart-fuck, that's had homage. But the third of the three – the *post*, the emotional after-love – this has been neglected. Yet with Mills and me, that's what it's all about.

What happens after two people break up is often as interesting and (for one of them at least) emotionally extreme as anything in the *inter*. And it's strange because the *post* is a kind of shadow life, defined by things that don't happen. An honest post in a *post*-diary might begin: 'I didn't wake up with X. I didn't have breakfast with X. I didn't walk with X to the tube station and kiss X on the mouth, before I went to work.' It's about the things you don't do. You don't see them or speak to them. Now and then, your lives intersect, but glancingly. You might meet someone who knows them, or hear a word of news. After a year, you bump into them in the street. You don't talk long. One of you has an appointment. But that's not to say there are no events in the *post*. Because at any minute, something can make you think of them. Some street. The look of a passer-by. You can be drinking an espresso or just reading a book, when the feeling breaks over you like a wave. It wakes you and you drown.

I'm starting to think that maybe this can last. Maybe her mother won't come back from India. She'll settle there with an indigent fakir, who flogs wristlets to listless travellers. Maybe the fuzz won't bother to investigate a foreigner's disappearance. What's a missing Austrian between friends? Or a single girl, if it comes to that? It sounds unlikely, but have you noticed? Their phones have gone very quiet. It's days since either buzzed or rang.

Maybe the world has come to an end. Maybe Mills and I are the only people left alive. For isn't this what it feels like to be in love: like you're the only people left alive? So it's hardly a surprise if I'm then tempted to this conclusion. And in this case there's concrete evidence, too. Or rather, I'm influenced by the lack of contrary evidence. The reason why Clare's and Bernhardt's families have been slow to get in touch is because they've been wiped out by a nuclear holocaust. Ditto for the entire West London constabulary. Gone. Annihilated in one throw. Some Middle Eastern country (which I didn't even realise had weapons of mass destruction) has gone and reached for the red button. That's why the curtains glow.

I'm serious. This could be the apocalypse. It could be happening now. I know I haven't devoted much time recently to the analysis of international affairs. But when I first arrived in the house, the world was on the brink of war. North Africa was ablaze. Egypt had burnt. Libya smouldered. Yemen was starting to sweat. With forest fire. With furnace fear. And I remember I read a scare piece about something called a photon bomb. There was no explosion. That was what made it so lethal. Like me, it didn't announce its presence. It hung around, unseen. But contact with these photon waves was deadly. And get this: they wouldn't penetrate bricks. So Mills and I, by chance, could be the only people in London who haven't gone outside over the past few days. Which is why we're the only ones left alive.

Listen. No cars pass. No bell tolls. No workmen rattle scaffolding.

Wouldn't it be wonderful, if true? It seems like the only solution for me. I know I won't be able to persuade Mills to come to Italy: not now she knows. And I don't want to kill her. And I can't kill me. Should I go, then, alone? To Italy or further? Turkey. Tahiti. Timbuktu?

I'd rather die than live a life alone. But if I stay, the police will get me. It's tricky. As Freddy Mercury put it, *This is a tricky situation. I've only got myself to blame.* But if (on the other hand) the population of the world has been wiped out by an unforeseeable catastrophe, leaving only Mills and me, well, I must say, that would be exceedingly convenient.

Listen. No dog barks. No voice rises. No postman thrusts mail through the front door's metal flap. No letters drop, going thump upon the mat.

I approach the glowing curtains. They pulse and thrum. I hesitate. What sight may scald my eyes when I part these drapes? With trembling hands, I divide them.

And see (ah, what do I see?) a scene that amazes me.

The street is deserted. Stunned and silent. The only thing to move is a plastic bag, looking unduly optimistic. But even the rain seems to fall more gently. With reverence. As though acknowledging this miracle: a depopulated city. Pavements not walked-upon. Avenues not driven-on. Highways and high-rises left high and dry, rising in a kind of humanless, humourless, post-apocalyptic world.

My moment of triumph! Praise be! At the eleventh hour –

Ding-dong-ding-dong. Ding-dong-ding-dong.

What's that? What's this?

Ding-dong-ding-dong. Ding-dong-ding-dong.

A churchbell. The clocks still strike. As you'd expect them to.

Dong. And then a car drives past, from left to right. *Dong.* I didn't see a driver. Was there one? *Dong.* Did I imagine it? Am I going mad? *Dong.* I ought to close the curtains, see no more.

Dong. But here's another, going the other way. *Dong.* And now pedestrians. A smug young couple. *Dong.* She with a pushchair that contains their younger. *Dong.* He with the older, a foot at either shoulder. *Dong.* Now here comes some dog, dragging its owner. *Dong.* They reach our gate. It lifts its leg and starts to piss.

Dong. The eleventh knell. Dragging me from heaven into hell.

Buzz, buzz. Two iPhones (neither mine) vibrate with texts.

11am on a Sunday morning. It's the morning after the night before.

And something flutters before my eyes. It descends, a yellow butterfly. Did it really happen? Am I losing it? No, here's another one. But it's not a butterfly. It's paper. A yellow post-it note. I open the window and manage to catch the next. Then read the message blotched on it in biro.

My name is Camilla Howard. I'm being held prisoner in 69 Milton Road.

I crumple it in my hand.

Then crumple it again.

And then I crumple it again.

But then again, I'm rather proud of her. That took initiative. Unpeeling post-it notes from the rafters and writing on them rescue pleas. Some girls in her position would have given up the ghost. Then posting them through the bars of the attic window. The window's at the side, not the front of the house. She must be waiting until the breeze is right. It can't be easy.

On the other hand, this signals the end. I know what I must do.

And so do you. It's the morning before the night to come.

Right? Right. *Right.* (Right.) Right.

Do you know what I need you to do? I need you to look away. Go on. Avert your gaze. The things I have in mind aren't fit for human sight.

I have no choice. And I know it's a crime against reason, and

224

a treason against love. But there's a mercy in it, too. You must see that. Now I have to concentrate. Tonight is going to be a high-definition performance.

But why was I in the kitchen? Let's see. Try to remember. I was in the drawing room. I stared out at a scene of desolation – which turned out to be a standard Sunday morning. The couple that walked. The dog that pissed. The yellow post-it notes.

Camilla. Camilla? Camilla. *Camilla.*

She must be pretty hungry by now. We don't want her getting thinner. *Au contraire.* We want to feed her up, not feed upon her. Prepare her for the fight to come. I open a cupboard and find a packet of Twiglets.

I do a little dance. I have a sing-song.

I run out into the corridor and cartwheel up the stairs. I reach her room. Remove the packet of Twiglets from my teeth, so I can speak. Then I chant up at the ceiling, 'Dinner time!' There's no reply. No, nothing. Not even a creak.

She's wary. She knows she shouldn't snack. But this is a meal.

I tear open the pack. I balance on a chair. I reach for a peep-hole, and then I – oh yes, I do – push a single Twiglet through.

GRAND GUIGNOL

Written by
Jack Raphael

69 Milton Road
London W11
jack_raphael2015@outlook.com
0044 7985 ******

INT. ATTIC. NIGHT

CLOSE UP: a corpse wrapped in cling film.

We hear the CRUNCH OF SOMEONE EATING A SNACK.
Outside, the PATTER OF RAIN. The corpse is
identifiable, with some difficulty, as CLARE. Pan
back to reveal the larger corpse of BERNHARDT,
which is similarly swathed in cling film.

We hear the RUSTLING OF SOMEONE TURNING A PAGE.

The attic is tent-shaped, divided by wooden rafters
above and below. The ones below are marked with
countless yellow post-it notes. At a certain point,
suitcases are piled, together with an assortment of
objects, including a large garden spade wrapped in
cling film. Opposite, there's a window, crossed by
iron bars.

Rain flecks the glass, and as we watch, the London
sky flickers with lightning. There is a rumble of
thunder. Again, we can hear the CRUNCH of someone
eating, and the RUSTLE as they turn a page.

MILLS is seated on the floor of the attic, clad in
an outsize jumper. She is reading a notebook,
pausing occasionally to nibble Twiglets, of which
there's a pile in her lap. She's reading a series
of notes that have been written in a small, precise
hand.

                    What happened with Bernhardt
                    wasn't planned. I thought he was
                    an idiot, but I didn't hate him.

Another RUMBLE OF THUNDER. Rising to her feet, she
moves to the end of the attic and kneels beside a

trapdoor. We hear faintly the sound of someone
CHUCKLING. There are two holes in the trapdoor and
she puts her eye to one of them.

MILLS'S POV. We can see JACK in the room below. His
head is freshly shaved and he is naked apart from a
pair of skin-coloured cycling shorts. He's
reclining on the bed, his head propped on pillows,
a laptop against his thighs.

Because he's wearing earphones we can't hear the
dialogue of the film he's watching. We can hear his
LAUGHTER though, which starts out sounding
reasonable but at length becomes deranged. The film
he's watching is *Scream 2*. The murderer, who is
running amok amid a crowd of implausibly attractive
teenagers, sports a mask resembling the face in the
Munch painting *The Scream*. Jack's laugh becomes a
HAMMER HORROR LAUGH. He puts his hands to his face,
pressing his palms against his cheeks, and opens
his mouth and eyes wide into three gaping circles
of horror. Keeping his hands held like this, still
framing his face, he tilts his head back until he
is looking straight up at the camera. At us.

JACK'S POV. There is a trapdoor in the ceiling,
with two holes in it. Zooming in on one, we can see
there's someone on the other side. We can see their
eye, which blinks.

                    JACK (O.S)
          Whatever doesn't kill you—
              (beat)
          simply makes you—
              (double beat)
          stranger—

A SERIES OF RAPID-FIRE CUTS.

THE MASTER BEDROOM: trashed.

                                              CUT TO:

THE LIBRARY: trashed.

                                              CUT TO:

THE FRONT HALL: trashed

                                              CUT TO:

THE KITCHEN: trashed.

                                              CUT TO:

THE DINING ROOM: trashed.

                                              CUT TO:

INT. DRAWING ROOM. CONTINUOUS.

The drawing room has been trashed, like all the
other rooms. The floor is littered with books and
cushions, and spears that have been plucked from
their brackets on the wall. On the space that was
occupied by the spears, the words 'NOTHING'S REAL
BUT LOVE' have been scrawled in what looks like
blood. The film SCREAM 2 PLAYS on the TV.

THE SCREEN SPLITS into six (3x2). Each section
holds a shot of one of the aforementioned rooms,
with the resolution of CCTV footage. From the
section showing the drawing room, we can hear the
SOUNDS OF SCREAM 2. In the film, a character called
Randy is explaining the rules of movie sequels.

>   RANDY (O.S.)
> There are certain rules one must
> abide by in order to create a
> successful sequel. Number one,
> the body count is always bigger.
> Number two, the death scenes are
> always much more elaborate. More
> blood. More gore. *Carnage candy*.
> And number three, never, under
> any circumstances, assume the
> killer is dead.

While this is said, we see Jack walk through the
front hall. He emerges in the drawing room. He
stands there a moment, listening to Randy
pontificating. Then goes through the dining room
and on into the kitchen. He approaches a knife
rack. The CCTV-style footage zooms in on his hand,
which moves along the line of knives, taking its
time. In the end he selects the largest knife: a
butcher's cleaver.

We see him cross the floor of the dining room. We
catch a glimpse of him in the front hall. Then he
continues up the stairs. Now we can't see him in
any of the six visible sections. *Scream 2* continues
to play in the drawing room.

THE SCREEN RE-SPLITS into four: master bedroom,
library, kitchen and drawing room. There is no sign
of Jack.

THE SCREEN RE-SPLITS into two: the master bedroom
and the library. There is still no sign of Jack.

INT. LIBRARY. CONTINUOUS

Many of the books have been pulled from the shelves
and scattered on the floor. Pages have been ripped
out and torn to shreds. Some have been burnt,
others used as loo paper. One bookshelf has been
pulled away from the wall and lies collapsed on the
floor. Pan back and retreat from the room. On the
landing, turn and start to climb the stairs. Jack
is on the top landing. He is lying on his back,
looking up at the trapdoor in the ceiling.

His face is expressionless, devoid of feeling. Then it
contorts into a mask of misery and remorse. Then,
after an effort, it becomes expressionless again.

> JACK
> If I could just go back—
>> (beat)
> If I could rub everything out—
>> (double beat)
> Starting with myself—

He has the cleaver in his hand. He moves it to his
mouth, gripping it in his teeth. Then he gets to
his feet and climbs on to the banister. Reaching up
with his hands, he unbolts the trapdoor from below.
The bolt makes a BANG as it slides back. He pauses.
There's no sound from above.

> JACK (CONT'D)
>> (calling up)
> Sequels have had a pretty bad press
> over the years, Mills. But this is
> just the kind of thing people say.
> It's the fashionable opinion. In
> practice, sequels are frequently
> superior to the originals.

He pushes the trapdoor open, so it THUDS down on

the other side. He listens. The house is silent.
Smoothly, with a practised air, he raises himself
into the attic.

INT. ATTIC. CONTINUOUS

The light is on, but otherwise there's no sign of
Mills. Jack turns, the cleaver raised in his hand,
as if he might be attacked from any angle. She's
nowhere to be seen.

On the floor, there's a bundle of bedding. A few
Twiglets lie scattered here and there. He closes
the trapdoor.

> JACK (CONT'D)
> (softly)
> Come out, come out, wherever you
> are!

Cleaver in hand, he starts to search the attic.

> JACK (CONT'D)
> Strictly speaking, *Cape Fear*
> isn't a sequel. It's a remake.
> But the point still holds. Work
> has already been done, which
> allows the film-maker to focus
> all his energies on style.

The way the space of the attic is divided by rafters,
there are places at intervals where Mills might have
concealed herself. Equally she could be behind the
pile of suitcases, which are stacked beside the wall.
The alert viewer may remember that a few minutes
earlier, a large spade, wrapped in cling film, leaned
against them. This spade has now disappeared. Jack
moves slowly, still speaking aloud.

                    JACK (CONT' D)
          And style, in the end, is what
          it' s all about, when it comes to
          making movies. It' s all about—

Raising the cleaver, he takes the last step,
revealing the space behind the pile of suitcases.
Mills isn' t there.

                    JACK (CONT' D)
          —style.

He looks down the rest of the length of the attic,
to the end of it, where the corpses of Clare and
Bernhardt sit, swathed in cling film. He starts to
move forward again.

                    JACK (CONT' D)
          Money too, now that I come to
          think about it. Because sequels
          invariably rake in a lot more than
          the original at the box office. So
          when it comes to movies, it' s
          about style. Of course it is. But
          it' s also about—

He takes another step, revealing the space behind
one of the rafters. Again, she isn' t there.

                    JACK (CONT' D)
          —money.

He is approaching the end of the attic. There are
now only three rafters left. As he moves, the
corpses of Clare and Bernhardt seem to watch and
listen, like an audience.

                    JACK (CONT'D)
          Sequels, which are all about style
          and money, represent the essence
          of Hollywood. You could even argue
          that Hollywood itself is a sequel.
          Since all stories are essentially
          the same, when you strip them down
          to their component parts.

There are now only two rafters left.

                    JACK (CONT'D)
          So the history of story-telling
          has been a trilogy. The first
          instalment was poetry.

He takes another step, to see that she isn't
concealed behind the second last in the line of
rafters. There's now only one rafter left: only one
place remaining, in other words, where Mills could
be hiding.

                    JACK (CONT'D)
          The second was the novel.

As he watches, Mills steps out from behind the last
rafter. She is holding the heavy garden spade in
both hands. The light flickers, and there is a
RUMBLE OF THUNDER.

                    JACK (CONT'D)
          The third is Hollywood.

Her face is white. She tightens her grip on the
spade and raises it. Jack holds up his cleaver,
showing it to her. Then stooping, he places it on
the ground. This is when Mills hits him. She brings
down the flat of the spade across the side of his

face. It knocks him sideways and he drops to his
knees, reaching out with a hand to support himself.
She raises the spade again and brings it down as
hard as she can on the top of his head. Jack falls
forward onto his hands. His arms support him for a
moment. Then he collapses. She drops the spade,
which CLATTERS on the floor. Then she starts to run
the length of the attic.

Stumbling and tripping, Mills makes it to the far end
of the attic, where she tries to lift one of the
trapdoors. Unfortunately for her, she picks the wrong
one. The one she tries is the one that's still locked
from below. It won't budge. Eventually, sobbing in
desperation, she moves to the other one. It opens.
She lowers herself through it.

A SERIES OF RAPID-FIRE CUTS.

MILLS: drops onto the landing at the top of the
stairs.

                                              CUT TO:

JACK: motionless in the attic.

                                              CUT TO:

MILLS: running down the first half-flight of stairs

                                              CUT TO:

JACK: motionless in the attic.

                                              CUT TO:

MILLS: running down the second half-flight of
stairs.

CUT TO:

JACK: motionless in the at230tic.

CUT TO:

INT. ATTIC. CONTINUOUS
Jack lies sprawled on the floor of the attic,
motionless. The spade lies there beside him.

His eyes open.

XII

I'M DISAPPOINTED TO find myself still alive. But I'm up. I'm here.

I'm outa here. Bang. Reach the trapdoor.

Franchissement.

Atterissage réception.

3b.

3a.

2b.

2a.

1b.

1a.

Laché into the hall.

Roulade. Roulade. And reach.

And grab her by her baggy jumper, just as she reaches the door.

I wrench Mills backwards. Her arm swings and she misses the handle.

She shrieks. *I'm sorry baby but I just can't let you leave.* For one thing, I haven't finished telling her my theory about movie sequels. But that's a blind. I don't give a damn about films. I just think I'll sound more scary if I say I do. And it seems to be working. She looks completely terrified.

She's standing with her back against the wall. I have my arms on either side of her. For a special effect, I put my face close to hers, and roar like a grizzly bear. She screams most gratifyingly. Ducks out from under me.

Hot-foots it to the stairs. And I go after her, as I must. But at the foot, I pause. I catch sight of myself in the mirror's shattered face. I have to say, I'm looking pretty hot. I touch one hand to the top of my head. *Hot damn, that hurt!* But it didn't do the job. (It did not.) The job I'd planned for it. I'd hoped she would deal me a better blow. A better kind of blow job.

As Dr Faustus might say, *Her lips suck forth my soul!*

I examine my hand. It's cut. It's bleeding. But a pretty colour, no?

I must have cut it on some smithereen. I dab a finger in the blood and smear it on my tender lips. That looks nice. I add a bit of rouge. I paint red circles on my chest, one around each slender itty-bitty nipple.

For this, you see, is my plan. To intimidate her into killing me.

There couldn't be a better one, not in a hundred million years.

I know she won't do it just because I ask her. Hence all that palaver in the attic, pretending I was after her. All that laughter in the farther room. (Was it too much?) And hence this chase. The only way she'll do it is if she's convinced I'm going to do it to her.

Speaking of which, where is she? Ah, she went upstairs.

I follow her. And find her talking on the phone.

'Milton Road. No. *Milton*. Please…'

I enter the master bedroom. Where can she be?

'Just get here as quickly as you can… Oh, god!'

Behind the bed. A landline pressed to her ear.

I take the phone from her. I replace it on the hook.

'Oh dear.' I shake my head. 'Oh dear, oh dear, oh dear.'

'Please. I don't know what you think I've done to you…'

She breaks off. My hand is raised. As if about to hit her.

'It's not what I think you've done. It's *what you did!*'

My hand is high. It's trembling in the air. (Am I overdoing

it?) Little does she know, my Millicent, how far I am from hitting her. From ever doing so. It would be like hitting myself. The reason I pretend is just to frighten her, to scare the holy innocent into retaliation.

But on that note, wouldn't it scare her more if I did? If I gave her a light slap? A little split lip? Of course it would. Which means that I should.

She cowers beneath me. The end will justify the means.

Sorry, my doll. This will hurt me more than it hurts you.

And I do it. I really do. I give her a proper slap. I hit her. I do.

I strike her across the face. A fraction harder, I confess, than I meant to. I went in open-palmed. *Strike one.* Lending her an artificial blush.

And then I do it again, this time a backhand. *Strike two.*

I think, that time, it may have hurt her more than it hurt me.

But I had to. And I hope you understand. Because Mills is incapable of killing *me*. Which only leaves one option. I must become *someone else*, to persuade her to take that fatal step. I have to behave like someone other than me, some messed-up psychopath. You see?

She tries to hit me back. I catch her wrist. She tries with the other hand. I catch that too. And this time, I twist it firmly behind her back.

'Do you want to know the greatest sequel of them all? I'll tell you. It's *The New Testament*. The Bible, Part II. The Word of God, Reloaded. It's essentially a retread of themes that were explored in the original.'

I'm saying whatever enters my head. Things designed to scare her.

'Please, Jack,' she pleads. 'Don't hurt me. I won't tell them anything.'

'Do you want to know what it is, the central theme? It's sacrifice. The most moving theme in literature. The one that always chokes us up. That gets us every time. There's Jesus. Captain Oates. *A Tale of Two Cities.* Remember? *It is a far, far better thing that I do than I have ever done. It is a far, far better rest that I go to than I have ever known.'*

As I declaim this quote, I pretend to be overcome. I let my grip slacken, so she can slip away. She struggles to her feet and starts to run.

I count three seconds in my head. *One. Two. Three.*

I give her one more for good measure. *Four.* Then I go after her.

I overtake her in the hall. So this time, when she reaches the door, I'm already there. I say, 'Think not that I am come to send peace on earth.'

She yells and backs away. Makes for the stairs again. But this time she descends. When I catch up with her, she has locked herself in the loo.

I say through the frosted glass, 'I came not to send peace, but a sword.'

Then I smash the glass with my fist. 'Listen to that language, Mills. It's beautiful. I *came not to send peace, but a sword.* So simple, so strong.'

I reach through with my arm and unbolt the door. She, meanwhile, is wrestling with the latch of the lavatory window. Which is absurd, since it's far too small for anyone to climb through. I pause. I dawdle a bit.

I've scuffed the skin of my knuckles. I've also cut my feet.

I select a jagged shard of glass from what's left in the door. I pick it out of the frame. I offer it to her with one hand. My other I rotate, presenting her with the underbelly of my wrist. Vain tendons. Tender veins.

'Go on, Mills. Take it. Finish what you started, damn you.'

She takes the sliver of glass. And I think: at last. It's going to happen. I thank you, god. Into your hands I commend my spirit. She presses it to the flesh. Her lips are pressed together. I can see

241

that tightness, the meanness around the mouth, which I've seen before, and which I'm now relying on for salvation. For this is the side of Camilla that can kill me. She's holding the point of the glass against my wrist. I press my wrist against it.

But it's all pretence. She just wants to scare me. *She scare me?* That's a laugh. But I'm not laughing and nor is she. She's crying again.

Oh, for crying out loud, woman! What now?

She drops the shard. She dithers. She needs direction.

I'll give it her, literally. I pick her up in my arms ('You're coming with me'), and half-carry, half-drag her out of the loo, wailing like a baby – up the stairs, and on into the dying room. Sorry: I meant the dining room. It's not here killing must occur. It's in the kitchen. *The skullery. The bonery.* Where bones are broken, and blood is spilt. Where the knives are kept.

I left mine upstairs. No matter. There's others more to the purpose. *Go.* I thrust Mills from me in the direction of the rack. She takes the bait. She grabs the largest, the heftiest knife (which sticks out at the end) and points it at me with quavering hands. Then makes odd, darting gestures at me with the point. Little does she know. This is what I want.

Maybe this time. Maybe now. But I must give her impetus.

So I kneel. (*On your knees, boy.*) I present my chest. I sneer.

'You don't have the fucking guts! Go on, then. Show me mine.'

For this is my deepest secret wish. Disembowelment. *Yes, please!*

How fitting it will be. She broke my balls. So now (if she'd be so kind) I'd like her to extract my bowels. My guts. My twitching intestines. And perhaps (why not?) my spleen.

She's hesitant. She needs a hand. I grasp her blade. (Pay no heed to my bleeding palm.) I pull the knife towards my chest, positioning the point.

242

Now all she has to do is push. But all she does is sob and blub. Then says (in a croak): 'Oh, Jack. How did we ever get to this?'

It's a good point, now that she raises it. But I don't have time for philosophical speculations. Was there a moment when I might have said no? Have said *enough, no more, it is not so sweet now*? Perhaps there was. But it's too late now. How late it is, how late. I've been too far out all my life, waving among the waves. And I'm just so terribly tired.

I take her point. I take it between finger and thumb, and transfer it from the foothills of my chest to the valley of my throat. One thrust from her, and I'll croak. I'll choke no more.

I snarl, 'ONE OF US MUST DIE!'

She chokes. Her hand seems to stick in the air. The knife clatters to the floor. And tottering, doddering, sputtering, she drifts towards the door.

For the first time, I consider the possibility of failure. By which I mean *not* being killed by Mills (*consummatio consummationis*) but wielding the knife myself. Killing the thing I love. And not with a kiss but a sword.

Never. No, never. But I cannot let her leave. I'd rather die than hurt her. Than touch a hair on her head. *I'll make her kill me.* But if she won't, I swear, I'll kill her. I'll fucking murder her. *Quick! She's getting away.*

She has reached the hall. I materialise like a phantom between her and the door. My arms raised, my hands waggling. Drooling over her. And as she goes *wah-wah!* and flees, I swipe a hand (it's slo-mo style) and miss.

She's back towards the stairs. I'm at her heels, a frightful fiend.

'I'm going to cut you into little pieces! I'm going to strip your skin!'

She hooks a right, back into the dining room. I follow her.

'I'm going to rip your ears off! I'll suck out both your eyes!'

243

She's on the other side of the table. She hesitates. Her hair's awry. Her sweater's on the large side. Its sleeves flap. She's sweating, the sweet, but I have to say: she still looks lovely. The exercise has given her a glow. She's breathing hard. I'm barely out of breath.

'I'm going to make a necklace from your teeth!'

She takes a step to her right. I move left.

We both step back to the centre, almost smiling.

She takes a step to her left. I move right.

We both step back to the centre, almost smiling.

I execute a bow.

She takes a step to her right –

– and then, unsmiling, bolts. She makes a dash for the drawing room.

I'm after her in a second. I block her path to the hall. I grab the back of her trailing jumper and drag her back, so she bangs into the back of the sofa, tips over it, and lands on pizza boxes and abandoned crusts. I still have hold of her jumper, straining the wool. She wriggles out of it with energy. To reveal that beneath she has nothing on but bra and knickers.

So now we're even. We're each of us clad in our underwear.

I hold her discarded sweater before my face and stare at it disgustedly. Then fling it away and clamber over the sofa. She cowers in the corner, which is just where I want her. By the spears. The assegais and iklwas. To which she turns. *That's right. Take a long one.* She selects a spear.

You don't have any choice. She really doesn't. Because I take my stand right there in front of her, and glare and growl at her, and grind my words from the bottom of my soul, and the dingiest corners of my mind.

'He that is not with me is against me!'

There's a footstool before her, up onto which I step, so that I may tower over her all the more, and present a more obvious target. For what?

'And you're not with me. Sometimes I wonder if you ever were.'

To be speared, as Christ was speared (albeit after his death) in his side, between the smooth white articulations of his honed and well-toned torso. Out of that wound came forth blood and water, and water and blood shall also come from me, when I'm speared by her with her thrusting assegai.

'You never understood me. Sometimes I wonder if you even tried.'

Which she holds. Draws back and flings at me. But in her haste, throws wide. It misses and falls to the ground. She grabs another and throws that too. Uselessly again. It hits but sideways on. She tries a third time. And a third time, too, she misses. Despite the fact I'm right in front of her.

'Why, Mills, why? Why hast thou forsaken me?'

I raise my arms on either side, and let my head hang loose.

For this is when I know I've failed. In all the unpopulated rooms. In the sick, sticky months when I walked alone. In the bedrooms of my grief and the basement of my soul. In the weeks when I stalked by myself, and was beside myself. In the days when I lay hidden in the leaden-lidded attic. In all this nightmare, I never tasted, ever, such complete and utter misery.

So I fall. I topple forward toward her. And she, she moves aside.

Before I hit the ground, I grab at the weapons on the wall, all orderly in their rack. I pull them down on top of me. They come away with ease.

While Mills, she's running for the door. Instinctively, without thought, I find an iklwa in my hand and I fling it. Send it spinning after her. Then I collapse on the floor. Spent. My heart rent. Betrayed. By the one I trusted most. Oh, Mills. You let me down in everything. Even this, even now.

'Go on then. Tell them what they need to know.'

My eyes are closed. I'm lying in a heap, covered in weaponry.

'Tell them what they want to hear. That I'm a beast. A bastard.'

I'm sobbing, choking on my words. Listening for the slam of a door.

'But don't tell them the truth, whatever you do. They wouldn't understand. They couldn't. That everything I did, I did for love of you.'

Still no slam. I suppose when she left, she must have left the door open. Leaving me alone. And just as I'm having that thought, I hear a groan. A Mills-ish moan. A boon unlooked-for. Passionate-sounding. As if she might have hesitated in the doorway and listened to my speech. And heard the sincerity in my voice, and been moved to love once more.

Aw.

Remember that she loved me once. She groans again.

I open my eyes. 'Mills? Is it you?'

Aw.

I'm on my back, staring at a chandelier.

I push the spear-rack off me and sit up. She's lying on the floor over by the coffee table. An iklwa sticks up out of her back. She goes *Aw*.

In seconds I'm at her side. *Oh god. What have I done?*

'Mills, speak to me. Tell me that you're okay.'

She says nothing. I can only see one of her eyes. Which watches me. In it, there's no rebuke. She always hated pain. But I never meant to do it.

She was my god. *And is and ever shall be.* And is she dying? Is this the death of god I'm witnessing? The blade is wedged beside her spine.

I've done it. I did it. I made her go, Aw!

So I take hold of the handle, wrapped in ancient string.

Her one eye closes. 'I'm sorry, Mills. I'm sorry, darling.'

And with that, I try to pull it out. But all I extract is a scream. The bloody thing's stuck fast. 'Oh god. I'm sorry. I really am.'

Her eye is open again. I look at it. I meet her gaze. Then I say the only thing I can in the circumstances, which I ought to have said long ago.

'It was because I loved you. Everything. All of it. Because I loved you. Do you see? Despite all your faults, and notwithstanding my complaints, I loved you. And I do. I love Mills. I love Camilla Howard. Jack loves Jill. He does. He always will. I love you. Do you begin to understand? I love you, Mills. I completely love you. I love you. I love you. I love you.'

<u>CAVALRY</u>

Written by
Jack Raphael

69 Milton Road
London W11
jack_raphael2015@outlook.com
0044 7985 ******

EXT. A STREET. NIGHT

CCTV footage of an empty street. The rain is
falling hard. A plastic bag has snagged amid the
branches of a tree. It flaps optimistically in the
wind. Then everything lightens with the arrival of
a police van. Its lights flash. Its wipers are
working hard. It pulls up, the doors open and four
police officers climb out: three men and a woman.

One of the men carries a taser gun. They walk
towards the house. As they open the gate, they hear
THE SOUND OF A WOMAN SCREAMING, which actually
comes from a horror film, which is playing on a TV.
But they don't know this. They exchange looks and
quicken their steps up into the porch. POLICE
OFFICER 1 leans across and peers into the front
window through a gap in the curtains.

She sees a scene of mayhem. Among the debris, a
semi-naked girl lies on the floor. A semi-naked man
is astride her. His hands are on a dagger, which
sticks out of her back.

                    POLICE OFFICER 1
          Jesus.

                    POLICE OFFICER 2
                 (into radio)
          Bravo Sierra. Active message.
          We're going to need an ambulance
          as soon as possible.

                    POLICE OFFICER 1
          The door. *Quick!*

> POLICE OFFICER 2
> (into radio)
> A girl's been stabbed. We don't
> know how serious it is.

POLICE OFFICER 3 gives a kick to the front door, which opens to reveal a hall, the floor littered with shards of glass. On the wall, someone has scrawled in blood the words 'DIPLOMATIC IMMUNITY'. POLICE OFFICER 4 readies his taser gun. Police Officer 3 reaches back with his hand and opens a leather holster, which contains a can of CS Spray.

INT. HOUSE. CONTINUOUS

When they enter the house, all they find is the girl, MILLS, lying motionless on the floor of the drawing room. The man has disappeared. Police Officer 1 kneels at Mills's side, while the others fan out to search the house.

> POLICE OFFICER 1
> Alright, love. We're here now.
> There's an ambulance on its way.

TRACK IN ON: MILLS'S EYE, which is open. It blinks, and the blink triggers A SERIES OF RAPID-FIRE CUTS.

POLICE OFFICER 2 approaches the dining room.

> CUT TO:

POLICE OFFICER 3 descends the steps to the basement.

> CUT TO:

POLICE OFFICER 4 heads upstairs.

For a moment we join Police Officer 2, who pauses at the entrance to the dining room. We can hear the

sounds of Scream 2 playing in the background. He
enters the dining room, and takes fright at the
sight of the grizzly bear, which has been dressed
in ethnic robes.

We join Police Officer 3, descending the stairs.
Arriving in the basement, he turns the light on. He
tries the door into the store-room, which is
locked. He cautiously opens the door into the
lavatory. There's no one there.

INT. FIRST-FLOOR LANDING. CONTINUOUS

Police Officer 4 raises his taser gun with his left
hand, and with his right pushes open the door into
the library.

                    POLICE OFFICER 4
          Christ.

There are crumpled pages, which have been torn out
of books, and smeared with excrement. He gags and
coughs. Otherwise the library's empty. He retreats
and enters the master bedroom. The bed has been
slept in. Cupboard doors stand open and the floor
is littered with clothes. His attention is caught
by a sound coming from the bathroom. RUNNING WATER.
He approaches, holding his taser in both hands.
Reaches the door. Hesitates. Then enters the
bathroom. It's empty. The bath is overflowing.

INT. DRAWING ROOM. CONTINUOUS

Police Officer 1 is crouched over Mills, speaking
to her in a gentle voice. She is watched by Police
Officer 2, who is talking into his personal radio,
asking when the ambulance is going to arrive. The
TV has been switched off.

> POLICE OFFICER 1
> Can you tell me his name, darling?

We can't hear Mills's reply, but we can see her
lips move. Police Officer 1 lowers her head, so she
can hear better.

> POLICE OFFICER 1 (CONT'D)
> His name is Jack?
> (beat)
> And this Jack— you know him, do
> you?

TRACK IN ON: MILLS'S FACE. We're seeing her in
profile, so we can only see one eye. The eye blinks.

INT. FRONT HALL. LATER

TRACK IN ON: THE GRAFFITI ON THE WALL.
TRACK IN ON: THE SHARDS OF MIRROR ON THE FLOOR.

Police Officer 3 and Police Officer 4 descend the
stairs. Police Officer 2 leans into the hall. The
others shake their heads.

> POLICE OFFICER 2
> Attic?

> POLICE OFFICER 3
> What?

> POLICE OFFICER 2
> Is there an attic? Or a cellar?

> POLICE OFFICER 3
> (rubbing his forehead)
> We didn't think to look. Right.
> You go up. I'll go down.

Police Officer 4 nods and starts to climb the
stairs, while Police Officer 3 again begins to
descend.

> POLICE OFFICER 2
> Wait. We'll ask the girl.

> POLICE OFFICER 1 (O.S.)
> What's that?

> POLICE OFFICER 2
> Ask her if there's a cellar.

> POLICE OFFICER 3
> If there is, we'll find it.

He glanced down the stairs. And as he does so, a
semi-naked figure appears, as if by magic,
sprinting up towards him.

BULLET TIME: in hyper-slow-motion, JACK
gymnastically twists and ducks under the clutching
arm of Police Officer 3, before leaping and placing
one of his bare feet on the turn of the banister.

NORMAL TIME: he continues towards Police Officer 4,
who aims his taser gun.

BULLET TIME: the gun is fired. The Taser darts
detach, but Jack miraculously avoids them, raising
his arms above his head and swerving his lithe pale
body so the darts miss. In the same movement, he
springs upward, reaching a ledge with his
fingertips, and pulling himself up.

NORMAL TIME: we see his legs and feet disappear.

There is a moment, then, while the Police Officers

just stare at each other. The probes from the taser
are imbedded in the wall of the staircase. The
wires that lead to them crackle with electricity.

                    POLICE OFFICER 2
               What the fuck was that?

His words seem to spur the other two to action, and
they both start to run up the stairs. Police
Officer 4 drops his taser gun as he goes. When they
reach the top landing, there's no one there. They
look up and see an open trapdoor in the ceiling.
Through it they can hear BANGING.

With the help of Police Officer 4, Police Officer 3
climbs onto the banister and reaches up for the
trapdoor. He almost misses it, pressing the ceiling
with his other hand. Then he grabs it. He grabs it
with his other hand too. Hangs for a moment. Tries
to lift himself up into the attic. Fails. The
BANGING continues.

He tries again, and this time, helped by Police
Officer 4, who supports him by the legs, succeeds
in raising his head and shoulders into the attic
space above.

Jack has the spade in his hands, gripped at either
end of the handle. He pauses, muscles tensed,
statuelike. Then continues striking at the bars of
the window with the spade. He drops it and pulls
away what remains of the rust-rotten bars. The
pieces come away in his hands.

Police Officer 3 climbs up into the attic, but too
late to prevent Jack from climbing through the
window.

He goes after him, and we see behind him Police
Officer 4 emerging through the trapdoor. With
difficulty Police Officer 3 climbs out of the
window onto the tiled roof of the house. It is
slanted and slippery. The rain falls hard. The wind
is loud. The sky goes white with lightning.

Jack is standing at the far end of the roof. He is
looking at the gap between the house and the one
next-door, gauging it. The gap is pretty wide. He
moves sideways a pace, and looks down over the
edge. He takes in the size of the drop.

> POLICE OFFICER 3
> (reaching out a hand)
> Don't do it, mate. It's not worth
> it.

There's a pause.

> JACK
> I'm not going anywhere.

He stretches out his arms, like someone on a high-
diving tower. Then he dives. Police Officer 3 puts
a hand over his mouth. Then he looks away. Police
Officer 4 has appeared at the window.

We rise up, away from the roof of 69 Milton Road,
retreating upwards into the night. We can see, very
small below us, an ambulance arriving in the
street.

FADE OUT.

PART FIVE

XIII

Precipitous and scarcely touching
The ocean skim a thousand birds.
I take what I can take: nothing.
I give what I can give: words.

MAKE A SURVEY of the skies. See the moon that rises pale as ice. Head south towards the islands in the mist. Hear the owls and the cicadas. See the fireflies flashing in the dark. Amid the sleeping trees, the shadows shift. The seas of Greece are restless. Antarctica. Sargasso. Skim the foam. Go slow, then silently and fast. Feel the wind beneath you as you soar. The mountains of Morocco capped with snow. Return to the heart of this concrete capital, and alight in a secluded square, as lightly as a ghost. In Kildare Gardens, say.

How long have you been gone? A year.

And what have you learnt from song?

You reach a point, you too will reach a point, where the past is more real than the present, and the only future you have is the hope of getting her back. Is this it? This is it. The secret that gets shouted. That keeps getting outed. That's written through the planet like a stick of Brighton Rock. So how is it a secret? I'll tell you. The secret is: it's true.

Despite the fact that everyone says it. Even though it's the moral of every tale. The politicos believe it. So do the ad execs. The spiritual gurus and self-help freaks? They believe it too. Yet despite all this, it's true.

259

You see that old woman on that bench, the one with the plastic bags? She knows it's true. The pigeons pecking at nothing among the grass? Them too. And how about you, in the shadows there? Come closer. Don't be scared. Push open that metal gate, then let it close behind you with a bang. Can you feel the moisture in the air, how it gathers among your hair? Refreshing, isn't it. But now let's stroll along Milton Road until we're at number 69. There. It looks like any other house. You wouldn't know, you couldn't guess, the things that it has seen. So stand a moment beside this false acacia tree. And watch what happens. Look.

The front door opens. A pretty girl comes out, fumbling with a pink umbrella. She calls over her shoulder, 'I'll see you tonight.' Then sets off down the street. You wouldn't suppose she'd been through anything out of the ordinary. If it weren't for the way that she walks. She has a little limp. A slightly halting gait. See? There. *There.* And then she's gone.

Listen up. Focus in. Above the porch is a balcony, which fronts the house, cupping the windows of the master bedroom. And is it your fancy, or do those curtains twitch?

In the front hall, Mrs Howard is doing the hoovering. A miracle perhaps, but she does the domestic chores herself. One has to be so careful these days. And something else. There are bars over the windows in the basement. A burglar alarm's in place, which gets switched on at night. But still there are times when Mrs Howard gets the jitters, if she's in the house alone. Like now, for instance. She could have sworn she heard something upstairs. A footfall. A telltale tread. Her hoover off, she listens. Then she shakes her head.

Upstairs, in the library, I lick my finger. Turn another page.

I'm pale but interested. A focused mind. Re-re-reading *The End of the Affair*. And Christ, it's good. Oh, brother. You reach a point in prose (you too will reach a point) where the words take on a life of their own. Past, present and future slip away. The writer disappears.

I close the book and stand. I wrap an arm around the nape of my neck. I slowly raise a heel until it touches a shoulder blade.

And then I snap into an *équilibre de chat*.

Passe muraille. I'm halfway up a bookshelf on the wall. *Laché*. And leap and grab the ceiling light. *Atterissage réception*. I land with barely a sound. *Roulade* towards the door and there rebound, followed by a *saut de bras*. Leaving me hanging from a curtain rail. *Atterissage réception*. *Passement* over a Chesterfield, and *planche*. Onto a table and freeze.

But only for a moment. I cartwheel across the floor. *Franchissement*. I dive between two armchairs, fists clenched, and then flatten them as I hit the floor. And forward roll. And bang into a book shelf…

On the highest level, a novella teeters. Then it falls. I catch it just before it hits the floor. And turn and look at the door.

In the hall below, the sound of the hoover stops. Mrs Howard is staring up at the ceiling. She looks dismayed.

I execute a *passe muraille*.

She starts to hurry up the stairs.

I segue into an arabesque.

She reaches the first half-landing.

I perform a pirouette.

She carries on up the second flight.

Grand jeté. Pas de chat. Tours en l'air.

She grabs the handle of the library door. She opens it.

I'm not there.

ACKNOWLEDGEMENTS

Alastair Gourlay, without whom nothing would have happened. Then my publisher Humfrey Hunter and agent Charlie Campbell. My wife Anya Yermakova, who startled me after reading the book by announcing it was very similar to her own recent experience. The list of others who helped or inspired me in one way or another includes Thomas Fink, Judith Murray, Ciorsdan Glass, Charlotte Price, Thomas Leveritt, Dominic Hodgkinson, Kerry Glencorse, Bret Easton Ellis, Ki-duk Kim, Nicholas Hodgkinson, and of course my parents.

Made in the USA
Charleston, SC
15 May 2016